A Nightmare You Can'

Joshua Stevens-S

While every precaution has been taken in the preparation of this book, the publisher assumes no responsibility for errors or omissions, or for damages resulting from the use of the information contained herein.

A NIGHTMARE YOU CAN'T SCREAM AWAY

First edition. July 21, 2021.

Copyright © 2021 Joshua Stevens-Shachar.

Written by Joshua Stevens-Shachar.

CONTENTS

1. A Normal Day in Echoway

Blood smells like metal. It leaves a strong sour taste in the back of your throat and forces you to feel like you're choking on metal.

In your dreams, you can only experience what you have known in the real world. A blind man will never be able to imagine colour, a child who has never tried cream soda can't magically taste it in their dreams. They may taste what they think it's like, but never the real thing.

James had just woken from a peaceless sleep. He was drenched in sweat, his blanket sticking to him, as he gasped for air. You see, James had just endured such a nightmare. Where he relived a memory so vivid, he started to choke on the smell of blood.

In this dream, a body was sprawled on the shiny yet worn wooden flooring. Screams filling the open area. The closer James came to the person, the bloodier the area became, the pungent red liquid soaking into the person's clothing, a gradually growing pool of it seeping onto the floor. Walking turned into running but it never made a difference. James wouldn't ever be able to reach the body before waking.

But the smell would always stay with him. Until the moment he awoke all he could do was focus on the blood. Burning his throat with each harsh breath he took, haunting him till he screamed himself conscious.

It was a perfectly ordinary Wednesday morning in Echoway. The bright blissful sun emerged on the horizon and lit up the small town as it always did. Sweeping through every field, street, and window bringing light to the eyes of everyone.

James had just started to drink his water from the same cup as always placing it back down on his dented bedside table. He took a couple of seconds to try and get comfortable in his bed, after flipping the sheets that had become damp with sweat.

Lying down he hoped more than anything that there would be more time to rest. Last night had been a long one and it was only until his phone died, that he realized the birds had started to scream. Prompting him to get a couple hours of sleep, after plugging in his phone preparing for the dreadful day ahead.

Staying up all night felt like the better option. He wouldn't have had to endure the nightmare again. James had tried on multiple occasions to simply stay awake, but it would always end up with him passing out at some point during the day, only to have the same nightmare anyway.

His phone which so rarely gave him good news showed that the time was 6.58am. Damn. The extra hours of rest and sleep that his body craved were not going to be satisfied, the wicked phone would, in under two minutes, be going off with the same monotonous alarm James had been using for the past three years. The same melody that he had grown to hate so dearly would, as usual, force him to leave his comfortable bed and his safe predictable house into a world where nothing could be controlled, and nothing was safe.

James couldn't help but feel angry, he had just wasted almost half the time remaining of his rest by getting worried and anxious about how his day was going to go. This was something that happened far too often for someone who was 'just a kid'.

James would disagree with people whenever they said this to him. He would argue that being sixteen years old meant that he wasn't a 'kid' and had a lot of things to worry about, bullying, exams, and the pressures of doing well in life, were just a few. Along with the fact that his life had contained more trauma in the last year than most people would have in a lifetime. This argument would, of course, take place in his head and nowhere else.

Bzzzz Bzz Bzzzz Bzz.

There it went. That sickly tune laughing at him for wasting those precious moments of rest. Laughing like he knew everyone else did.

By now the sunlight had broken through the gaps in James's bedroom curtains and scaled most of the wall. Telling everyone that the day had started and that it was time to rise just like it had done so elegantly. To get ready and head out into the world.

Out into the world is an overstatement, as almost everyone who lived in Echoway town would be born there, raised there, and eventually buried there. Very few worked far from the town and even fewer left.

It wasn't a perfect place, but it was reasonably safe, and everyone knew everyone. Whether you went to the same butchers, or your sister used to babysit their niece, or you were part of their book club. One way or another walking through the streets would result in seeing only familiar faces. Not always friendly or law-abiding, but familiar.

Most commonly you would know of someone from the school they, or their child went to, considering there were only two high schools in the town.

The first, Echoway East or EE, was a superb school. All the rich families would send their children there. It had a prestigious history filled with the most talented people the town had ever seen. Most of the students at the school would go off to some high-end university like Yale and would usually be the only people to leave the town in search of any kind of interesting life. This meant that EE received major funding from those rich families, giving the school all the expensive equipment and the best tools for education. Unlike Ramwall.

Ramwall was still a decent school, but it was slightly worse than EE in every possible way. The teachers were less experienced, working at a slightly lower salary, which made them less inclined to care about their job. Meaning that the students at EE would be better educated, often making them smarter than those at Ramwall. Their football field slightly greener, and the equipment slightly better. Which meant that all the athletes at Echoway East would, on average, be stronger and better trained. Because of this, Ramwall had never won a single football match against them.

With all of this put together and the fact that the majority of the students at EE were snobby rich kids in the first place, they held the common belief that they were simply better than those at Ramwall.

Recently, all activities between the two schools had been cancelled. Due to a fight that happened at their last football match. It looked as though Ramwall, for the first time since its doors opened, had a chance of winning the game. All thanks to Andy. Andy was the best athlete the school had ever produced. Even better than those at EE. Someone who with a bit of luck could turn pro.

With only five minutes left on the timer, Ramwall was in the lead. The crowd was electric with excitement. Cheering louder and harder than the lightning ripping down from the heavens, as the rain fell on that cold night. All of the town had come to watch the match, from the nerds to the goths, the farmers to the scouters.

Everyone watched Andy as he weaved past player after player, like the wind blowing so heavily in the dark grey sky, unstoppable. It was a sight to see, something magical. As Andy scored yet another touchdown the crowd all cheered his name. Thousands of people adoring him.

Then, as bitter as the freezing air, just when Ramwall had some hope of success, a group of players from the EE team brutally tackled Andy to the ground. Fracturing his leg in the process.

It was so blatantly done on purpose that Andy's teammates went after those that injured their star. Punching and grappling one another in the mud. The referee kept on blasting his whistle, but it made no difference. Like a snowball rolling down a hill the fighting grew in size, becoming more violent as students from either side sprinted onto the pitch.

Furious by what had happened, it didn't take long for all of Ramwall to start brawling all of EE. The entire town watched as their children battled with rage and anger, unlike anything they had seen before.

After the fight had finally been broken up with the help of the police, both headmasters decided to cancel all further events until things cooled down between the two schools. Not that the schools had ever been friendly with each other.

Those from EE would never hang out, date, or so much as talk to someone from Ramwall and vice versa. There was such a strong hatred between them that the majority of minor crimes within the town, in the form of public fights, vandalism, and theft would almost always be spawned from the bitter rivalry.

Whether it was some EE kids egging the house of a Ramwall student, or a fight in the park after someone was caught wearing their school uniform out in public, there was always something going on to fuel the hatred between students.

James didn't come from an exceptionally rich family or one with ties to EE. So, he had to go to Ramwall, which wasn't all too bad except for the lack of security measures, and other normal school problems.

As the morning progressed James started to complete his daily routine. On his way to the bathroom going across the landing, he heard his sister Kara throwing up in her on-suite toilet. Caused by drinking too much at the party she wasn't allowed to go to, because it was a school night. The party that James hadn't been invited to.

This was another common thing in James's life, even though he and his sister were in the same year, she always seemed to be going to parties whilst he was left by the side to stay at home. Not like he wanted to go to the parties anyway. He would have no idea what to do or say and the repercussions as his sister was so eloquently demonstrating didn't seem worth it.

James continued to think about how unfair and uninteresting his life was until he noticed someone was speaking to him.

'... by yourself, as your sister is ill.'

He searched around the breakfast table and noticed it was his mother droning on at him.

'Ok.' James replied not having heard the full monologue, but just enough for him to work out that Kara would be getting the classic favouritism treatment by being allowed to stay home.

Now that James had been rudely interrupted from his thinking, he noticed that he was already having breakfast. Which was odd because it felt like he had just been getting into the shower. Although considering he had been doing the same routine for most of his life, he knew that he had just done everything else on autopilot without noticing, like a baby pissing itself without noticing as it's too busy contemplating about the vastness of the universe.

One of the nice things about living in a small town was that everything was close to him. By the time James had gotten ready the time was 7.45, he left the house by himself and knew that in less than fifteen minutes he would be at his destination.

A silver lining for Kara getting to stay home was that now he was able to walk in peace listening to music and, of course, thinking about how his day would go. On the normal repetitive day, his sister would refuse to let him walk in peace. Always trying to talk to him about uninteresting unimportant things like who she was dating or that her friends did something that nobody will ever care about or, recently, on the rare occasion, would talk about how she missed their dad.

Stupid conversations. Stupid conversations that could achieve absolutely nothing by having them and should therefore be left unsaid.

James jammed his headphones in his ears and blasted music at the highest volume. Not having to listen to anyone or think about the things going on inside his head was a very rare treat. By the time he had arrived at school, James was in a significantly better mood. But he knew that his day was bound to get worse, it wasn't like it could get any better.

As he walked through the glass entrance doors onto the old shiny wooden floor, he noticed that people were smiling at him when they walked past. James was aware that this was meant to be a nice thing. That anyone else would have loved for people to smile whenever they saw them, but he knew the truth. He knew exactly why everyone had started smiling at him, over the past few months, and he would rather they didn't look at him at all.

James started to fill his bag with books from his locker when a loud noise made him jump.

'Have you done Heman's homework?' demanded Tom, slamming into the lockers next to James. 'The math homework?' He explained after James was not able to respond a half-second after the question was asked.

'Yeah, it's in my- I think it's in my bag.' James replied, still startled.

He noticed the few seconds he took to reply were complete torture for Tom, who couldn't seem to stay still for more than a second and was consistently running his hand through his sandy blonde hair, a habit he would do when anxious.

He swiped James's bag up from the floor, found the homework at a truly impressive speed, and had already started copying the work, using a locker to write against, before James had been able to so much as take a breath.

Over the last month or so, it had become increasingly annoying to be around Tom. It wasn't because he was always copying James's homework, that had been happening for years. It wasn't even Tom as a person that made it such a challenge to be around him. The problem was that they used to be inseparable, doing everything together. Just them.

But recently, Tom had been going to parties where he would make new irritable friends to spend time with. Which James took as a direct insult. As though he wasn't doing a good enough job as Tom's friend. As though he has to be replaced by crappier, less interesting people.

Tom wore casual outfits, blending in amongst the sea of students that dressed the same way, and because he was rather short, it made it near impossible to find him in a crowd. People always wanted to chat with him on the way to class, leaving James to hover behind, not wanting to speak to anyone. He had never been a fan of talking to people, even before everything happened. Nobody ever had anything good to say.

'Aaaand done!' proclaimed Tom as he put extra emphasis on the last turn of his pen.

Typically, he was able to get away with not doing the homework, coming up with elaborate stories that kept him out of trouble, but Mr Hemans was different. Everybody handed in their work to him without fail because they were completely terrified of him. Mr Hemans had some very obvious anger issues. So, when you entered his class, you wouldn't speak unless spoken to and you wouldn't set a foot out of line out of fear of being screamed at till you cried in your seat. This had happened on multiple occasions throughout his two-year residence at Ramwall.

It felt like he was one bad day away from throwing someone out a window. People would make sure to stay out of his path when he walked down the corridor, both students and teachers alike. All in all, he was someone that didn't make James any more excited about going to school.

Unfortunately, Wednesday mornings started off having double maths. Which would without fail be one of the best ways to make any student question their happiness. With very little enthusiasm Tom and James started walking to Mr Heman's classroom.

Tom started to talk about the most recent party he had been to, involving someone being pushed down a hill in a shopping cart. It was becoming more common for Tom to tell these kinds of stories. Stories about his new friends. How they would cause far too much trouble and do things that could never be fun. After he finished his tale, Tom asked if James wanted to come with him to a party next Saturday.

'Sorry I can't make it. I have to help out with the family.' James said, in a way that resembled a voicemail as he had used that excuse so often in the past few months when someone, usually Tom, invited him somewhere.

Nobody really wanted him at the party. Tom was just trying to drag him along so that he didn't seem like a bad person. But there wasn't a chance he would go to a party where he would be left to the side having a panic attack. No. It would be far more enjoyable and comfortable getting his entertainment from the television and video games. By this point, Tom knew better than to argue with the response and accepted that he would be going to the party without James.

The pair had now arrived outside the classroom where the majority of the class was already lined up silently waiting to go in. The other students were still freely talking to one another, leaning against their lockers, and merrily walking down the corridor, because the bell hadn't rung yet. When it came to Mr Hemans the class was aware that it was best for their wellbeing, to arrive well before the bell had rung and to wait in complete silence. James and Tom received a nod and smile from their classmates as they waited in line.

This was a small minuscule positive of having maths with Mr Hemans. Nobody would try and talk to James, a nice break from the usual where people constantly asked how he was doing. He was very aware, they didn't really care and just wanted to act like a decent person in front of everyone else. James was convinced that most people in the town pretended like they were good people, but he was certain that behind closed doors, they were evil.

The bell must have gone without James noticing, as everyone had started to head off towards their lessons. His classmates marched into the room with a significant absence of a smile.

They loaded themselves into their seats, at their clean undamaged desks, taking out their books and pens in an orderly fashion. James and Tom had seats next to each other, not in the hope of talking, but simply for emotional support during the training.

Mr Hemans was positioned in his chair at the front of the class, with a rigid posture. He stared at the students as they prepared for the lesson, making sure none of them stepped out of line. James had noticed that his teacher seemed to blink less than normal people. He wasn't sure if this was because he had trained his body to need less maintenance, or if he was just insane.

Their classroom was colder than any other part of Ramwall. It didn't have any posters, motivational or educational, nor extra accessories. All that survived in the room were: perfectly distanced rows of desks, the teacher's table with a computer, a pristine whiteboard, four bare brick walls, and a door to trap them inside. Making it feel like they had been transported into a kind of soldier's quarters.

'Page 142, Exercises 1, 2, 3, 4, and 5! When you are done come to the front of the class and I will check your work!' Mr Hemans barked in a way that sold the idea that the students had accidentally joined the army.

This was routinely how the lessons would go. Each student would work as if their lives depended on getting enough questions correct to satisfy the monster. How many questions you could get wrong depended on his mood, but usually, 95-percent was the requirement to not get ripped to pieces. So, in near silence, the class turned their exercise books to the correct page.

Straight away, James could tell something was wrong. The poor soul behind James was taking far too much time to retrieve his exercise book from his bag. The student started to take quick and harsh breaths. James didn't dare turn his head to see exactly what was unfolding, but it wasn't hard to work out. The book wasn't in his bag.

The student behind him was called Freddie, but at that moment it didn't matter. Freddie was as good as dead. The dead man sitting decided there was no point making more noise searching in his bag. The book wasn't there, and he would just make it worse by stalling. Slowly, he raised a trembling hand into the air.

'S-sir, I'm s-so very sorry, but I, I, erm I think I left my exercise book at home when I was, when I was doing your homework.'

The class stopped writing. Everything lay silent.

James could hear the class next to them talking away. It felt like they were at a party celebrating someone winning the lottery, and on his side of the wall, James was left in no man's land. Completely silent in that moment, but he knew in a few seconds the guns would be going off, and the grenades, and the defining tanks, and he was stuck in the middle of it all.

Mr Hemans rose from his chair putting his hands on his desks for support, like a cannon being strapped down so it wouldn't fly away after firing. He was massive. You could see his muscles gasping for breath as they pushed desperately against his suit. He didn't say a word for almost a minute, he just stared at the terrified kid, veins bulging from his head. The death row inmate shook at his desk, failing to hold any kind of composure.

After the minute of silence that must have felt like an eternity to the pupil with no future, the teacher spoke.

'What did you say?' Mr Hemans asked in a very calm and collected voice.

'I-was-doing-your-homework-and-left-it-on-my-desk-I-am-so-so-sorry,' Freddie said in one breath so quickly that James wasn't sure if Mr Hemans heard it all.

'So, you are saying it is my fault that you are unequipped for my lesson?'

His tone rose in anger and fury.

'No-no-no-no-no of course not sir, it was all my fault completely mine sir.' replied Freddie in a way that suggested he was close to tears.

The teacher slammed his hands onto the desk making everyone jump.

'THEN GET OUT OF MY CLASSROOM! IF YOU CANNOT COME EQUIPPED FOR MY LESSON THEN YOU DO NOT DESERVE TO BE HERE! GET OUT NOW!' Mr Hemans roared at full volume, so loud it felt like a bomb had exploded in the room.

Freddie shoved all his things into his bag and didn't waste time zipping it up. As he stumbled past his peers, James noticed that tears were now coming in full flow from his eyes, dropping onto his dark blue wool sweater.

'WHY DO I NOT HEAR YOU ALL DOING YOUR WORK, PAGE 142 EXERCISE 1, 2, 3, 4, AND 5!'

Almost the entire double period had passed after the outburst, and nobody had said a word. All of the students had gone to the front and given in their work by this point, received more the moment Mr Hemans had checked it. Nobody showed any sign of annoyance when greeted with more work out of fear that they too would be verbally shot at.

James had been anxious about giving in his first piece of work, Mr Hemans was not in a good mood and so the pass boundary would only allow for one or two slip-ups. When he finally gained enough courage to hand in the work, James was grateful to be given the next piece.

Even though the classes were pure hell, it wasn't possible to argue about its effectiveness. All the students he taught obtained the highest grades which meant that the school couldn't afford to let him go.

The headmaster, Mr Glass, hated Mr Hemans. Everyone did. He made people unhappy and caused more students to cry than all other teachers combined. However, the board of directors wouldn't allow him to be removed due to the grades his teaching methods produced.

There wasn't so much as a trumped-up charge that the headmaster could use to fire him. Mr Hemans was smart. He made sure to never say anything he couldn't or do anything that was against the rules. Which meant that James was likely to go through the rest of his years at school alongside the devil's left-hand man.

James was coming to the end of his second piece of work when the speaker came on and asked for a small list of students including himself, to head to Mr Glass's office. He would be able to miss out on the rest of the lesson. James didn't care what the reason was. Anything was better than this. Making sure to be careful how he went about phrasing his sentence, James politely and clearly asked if he could be excused due to the summoning. Mr Hemans nodded his head, confirming his divine escape.

On the way out, he risked a glance back at Tom, who was glaring at him through slits in his eyes and a pursed lip.

2. A New Program

As James strolled down the halls to Mr Glass's office, he thought with glee about how lucky he was to miss some of his lesson. He then realised that, in reality, he wasn't lucky as he still had to deal with Mr Hemans in the first place.

In no time at all James had arrived. A nice thing about Ramwall was that it was a small school, which meant there weren't many students. EE had even fewer because it was meant to be a harder school to get into, even though the building was the size of a medieval castle.

With so few people at the school, gossip would spread like wildfire. For instance, there was a situation where someone in the year above James shat themselves at a McDonalds. It took less than two days for the entire school to know. One morning the already embarrassed student opened his locker to find it stuffed with adult diapers. Nobody was caught, but the whole school knew it was Sarah Lee, she was always the one responsible for those cruel kind of things.

Without realising it James was sitting down in front of Harvey Glass the headmaster of Ramwall. Once again James must have gone in and sat down, without even realising he was doing it. Being completely in his own world. Mr Glass was wearing his ordinary blue suit and a tie covered in black flowers. The headmaster wore a different tie every day. Presumably to add a little flavour to his otherwise bland job.

It appeared as though he was waiting for an answer, and as the two people who had apparated next to him were also glaring at him, James deduced that they were waiting for him to say something.

'Yes.' James said hesitantly.

What else could he say? He had no idea what had been asked of him, and there wasn't a chance he would ask to hear it again, it would be far too embarrassing. He had responded with yes, because the most common question people asked him was, 'Are you doing well?'

Despite what James thought was a smart deduction, he quickly realised he was mistaken.

'Very well,' the headmaster replied in a disapproving tone, 'I shall have to deal with that later.' He continued staring directly at James with a frown.

James hated himself for saying the wrong thing; he knew that at some point in the near future his response would come back to hurt him. What made everything worse was that James respected Mr Glass, because of how he had dealt with James's and Kara's situation with their father.

The tall, bald, decent man had an incredible British accent, as he was born there and spent a great deal of his life somewhere in London. For some reason, he decided to move with his family to Echoway town. Doing this didn't seem like the best idea to have a happy life considering how much of a let-down the place was. All the same, his English accent made James feel like he wasn't the same cardboard copy as everyone else and had some kind of uniqueness to him.

As the four of them continued to wait, James turned to the left so that he could properly see who was next to him, in an attempt to forget about the awkward situation. James was surprised to see Sarah Lee to his left, the girl who had almost definitely filled the locker with diapers.

In James's opinion and a lot of other people's opinion, Sarah was a very attractive girl. She had long straight black hair, bright blue ocean eyes, and a pearly smile. She had only been at the school for a year, getting expelled from EE after drugs were discovered in her locker. Nobody would be friends with her out of fear that she would drag them down to her level, a negative stigma coming from so much as talking to her.

Sarah stood out easily amongst the crowd because she would only ever wear black, black lipstick, black skirts, and black jumpers with the hood up. She presumably only wore that kind of outfit to try and hide into the background, but it achieved the complete opposite. People stared at her as she walked down the halls, sometimes out of hatred or anger, but then she also had her large share of secret admirers.

James noticed that she was smiling at him. It wasn't a flirty kind of smile, more of a suppressed laugh. Evidently, his response and the awkwardness that followed was amusing to her. James wasn't sure if he should be happy or annoyed by this, but he was very aware it didn't matter. Nothing would ever happen between them.

Wanting to get away from things that never would be, James turned his head to the right and saw Andy Miller, the star athlete and school celebrity who sparked the brawl on the muddy field over a month ago. His cast was gone by now, but he still couldn't train or play in any practice matches, having to sit on the bench and watch.

Being the most popular person in the school meant that his entire cast had been filled with people's writing, signatures, and funny graffiti. There were a few weeks at school where James had to wear a cast on his arm, after falling out of a tree. Due to it being before the incident, nobody had cared to sign it except Tom and Kara. James couldn't help but resent Andy whenever he would look and see his cast without a single dot of white on it.

In the halls or in class, Andy was the centre of attention, a crowd around him no matter what. People were desperate to be his friend so that if he made it pro, they could leech off of him. However, it never seemed like he cared about that, basking in all the attention and living for the fame. Talking to anyone he saw, high-fiving people in the halls, and photobombing selfies. No matter what he did, people loved Andy.

Some hardcore fans of his had started to call him Hercules, because he was their hero and saviour. Andy kept it going, posting it on all of his social media posts. Now it had reached the point where people chanted the name Hercules at football games and in the school halls.

Even the outfits he wore screamed athlete. He would always wear the black and yellow school varsity jacket over some kind of fitness shirt, and flexible trousers that could allow him to do a workout whenever he wanted, or to simply mess around with people.

Kara said that whenever Hercules came to a party everyone went wild, as if they had been given the gift of partying with a god. James could only imagine the things he did at those parties in the form of drugs and too much alcohol, things that would ruin any athletic career. Then again, he could only imagine as James was never invited to those events. For all he knew, Andy could be spending hours on end leading Bible studies converting everyone to have a holier life.

Sitting next to these two people, James could not work out why they had been called to the office. If you somehow found yourself in Sarah's company, it would be due to a detention, and if it was with Andy, it would be for football training or some kind of award. James had never received a detention, nor did he participate in any kind of sports activities.

After waiting for a few more minutes, the receptionist walked into the room to inform the headmaster that Michael Luxon was ill and would be sent an email about what was happening. She then left the room closing the door behind her.

Mr Glass explained that they had been randomly selected as a small control group for a new program, one that partnered students from Echoway East and Ramwall together to help improve communication skills across schools. Each student from Ramwall would be paired up with someone from EE and would work together in different sessions to try and reduce the hostility that the students had towards one another.

The headmaster continued to say that the program would be very valuable on CVs and university applications, then looked towards Sarah, saying that it might even help them get on a better track.

James knew for a fact that Mr Glass wanted to say that the school was desperately trying to connect with EE, and this was their pathetic effort to try and get the fighting to stop. It now became more obvious as to why Andy was 'randomly' selected. If they could get him and presumably another athlete from EE to somehow become friends, they would be able to resume the football matches without any fighting.

What James didn't quite understand was why he had been selected along with Sarah who was sure to be a terrible choice, considering she was expelled from EE.

'... with Grayson Millet, and James you're going to be partnered with Ella Davis. You will be meeting the students on Friday. At 1:00 p.m. you will leave school early and head over to Echoway East for your first day with them.'

Luckily, James managed to focus back on the conversation at the right time, so he didn't miss anything too important.

The headmaster turned to directly speak with Sarah.

'To make sure you arrive at your destination by 1:20 p.m. and don't use this as an opportunity to do what you want. Mr Kennedy will act as your group leader for that day, and all other days that this program takes place.'

EE was only a fifteen-minute walk from Ramwall, so it was common for students to walk to and from each school for competitions, both athletic and academic. Generally, people would go to EE as they had better equipment and larger rooms. Although, at the end of the day, it didn't matter where the competition was held, EE would almost always win.

There had been those few life-peaking moments where Ramwall had managed to snatch a chess tournament win, and a few other smaller wins, that took away a spotless win record from

EE. But nothing to be too proud about, considering EE would then make sure to win the next twenty tournaments in that field to prove a point.

The program itself felt like it could only fail. Not only were the two schools barely a month out of their largest brawl to date, but it was also a stupid idea that anyone would want to do childish activities with some random person. It was even more stupid that the school had chosen him for a program that consisted of communication and building relations when James had only one friend.

Then again, James and Kara were often picked for new things the school was offering, as a kind of service to the family after what their father did. This infuriated James who didn't want to gain anything from what his father had done or get any kind of special treatment because of it.

Even though James hated the idea of doing this program, he knew better than to try and get out of doing it. His mother would always say that it would 'do him good', and force him to attend whatever it would be. On the positive side, this program got him out of school for a couple of hours on Friday and then presumably on a couple other days, which was always a welcome experience.

The bell rang its hideous noise as James made his way back to Mr Hemans's classroom. They now had a fifteen-minute break to cry about how terrible school was. As Tom was relatively small it was often hard to find him amongst the crowds. Even in the small school, it could take a good while to find him if he wandered from the class too far. However, on this occasion, he was directly outside their maths classroom, leaning against some lockers, talking to Jodie, running his hand through his hair.

As of late, Tom was talking to a lot of girls and would often invite them over to their table at lunch. This was becoming exceedingly stressful for James, who struggled in large crowds.

It used to just be the pair of them having lunch together, but now there was a whole parade of people at their table chatting away, making James's anxiety rocket through the roof.

Tom had started going to parties almost every weekend now, which was odd because he never seemed to be interested in them before. He invited James to most of them as a plus one, but it was obvious that nobody else wanted him there. If they did, they would have invited him themselves. So, he would use the old reliable excuse of having to help out with the family, leaving Tom to go with Jodie.

Jodie was exactly what a generic popular rich girl looked like. Long dark brown hair that had been done by a professional salon in an obvious way, shiny expensive-looking ear piercings, and a designer handbag instead of a school bag to carry her books. Plus, she wore the highest-end clothing available as if she was some kind of celebrity.

Jodie was one of the first girls to invade James's table at lunch and was probably the least interesting person in the world, but for some reason, Tom, who had a lot of lessons with her, seemed to think that she was one of the most incredible people on earth.

Unfortunately, at the start of the year when Tom and James scanned through their new timetables, they discovered that they only had maths together, unlike the last two years where they had identical classes. This led James to spend his time in class, doing the work without saying a word, then dropping his head onto the desk and leaving as soon as the bell went.

You might think that with all that time being able to focus on his work James would be doing well at school. That was far from reality. Refusing to ask people for advice, or the teacher for help when stuck, or even focusing on the work at all, turned out to be the worst way of learning. The majority of his grades were fails with very few satisfactory grades in any subject other than maths.

Tom and Jodie were still chatting away. Not wanting to interrupt what was sure to be an interesting and important conversation that would stick with them for the rest of their lives, James decided to get some water from the fountain close by.

As James bent down at an awkward angle so that he could drink the almost-cold water from the drinking fountain, he noticed that Kieran was holding some poor kid by the collar of his dark blue wool sweater, claiming the person's lunch money for himself.

It used to be James on the receiving end of his cruel bullying, but Kieran had stopped hassling him ever since the incident. Presumably out of respect, like every other good thing that had happened to James. Respect. There was nothing that should be respected about the incident, as his father had done the wrong thing. He should still be alive.

He longed for the good old days where nobody would smile at him. When Kieran would take his lunch money every day and make him so scared that he would only feel safe at home with his family. When he had a whole happy family.

By this point, water was hitting his cheek instead of going into his mouth, and James only noticed what he was doing when the bell above him started to ring with the same trivial tone every student had heard for years on end, almost as many times as they had their dreams decimated.

Tom hadn't noticed that James was waiting for him and had left without saying anything, leaving James to walk alone to science. As this class wasn't maths, or more specifically wasn't with Mr Hemans, people felt inclined to talk to him and ask how he was doing. Meaning that as he entered the classroom he was in a terrible mood, being forced to speak to people he didn't like.

Unlike the normal classrooms which would have a desk for each student, the science rooms all had special rows of tables that were 'safer' for mixing chemicals and doing basic uninteresting experiments. Such as mixing water with salt. It would be fair to think that talking would be down to a whisper as everyone was much closer together. But that was the thinking of a sane person, which had very little merit in a classroom.

Normally, the lesson would start with students whispering as expected, but soon everyone would be whispering, making it harder to understand the person you were talking to. Then one person would raise their voice slightly so that they could be heard, then everyone else would raise their voice so that they could be heard. Until it reached the point where everyone was shouting and the teacher couldn't scream to be heard.

It seemed possible that today's lesson might differ from the norm as a lot of people were missing. James's sister Kara was ill, Michael Luxon, as the receptionist told the headmaster, was also ill, along with Daphne Miller who had presumably been at the same party as Kara. This meant that the already small class of nineteen had only sixteen students in it.

James was hopeful the teacher would be able to control a class of only sixteen. Then again that was a job for an Echoway East teacher. For some reason, Jodie had decided to sit next to James, which was odd considering she rarely spoke to him when Tom was with them, let alone without him. Even though Daphne was sick, Jodie still had plenty of friends in the class, like Andy, who already had a group of people trying desperately to sit next to him now that his girlfriend was sick.

Jodie carefully placed her expensive bag under the table so that nobody would trip on it. It was a rule to place bags by the cabinet next to the door when you entered so that nothing would be spilled on them, and as it was a tripping hazard. This was something that stopped happening almost immediately, because people couldn't be bothered to continuously go back and forth to their bags. It wasn't like Mrs Dinkley was capable of enforcing any rules anyway.

James could smell some kind of overpowering perfume which Jodie would wear and was probably worth a couple hundred dollars. She placed a new stick of gum in her mouth and started chewing loudly and obnoxiously.

The lesson got underway and the teacher stood at the front of the class, explaining that she had finally managed to mark the tests they had completed almost five weeks ago. Mrs Dinkley also decided that as there weren't many people in the class today, there wasn't much point starting the new unit. Instead, they would spend the lesson going through the exam as very few people did well.

James was confident in thinking that Emma Rodgers and Michael Luxon were the only people that did decently in the test. Nobody else cared about science, not because it was particularly boring, but because there weren't any jobs in the town that required being good at science, unless someone wanted to be a doctor, which James very much didn't. They did far too much work and had far too much responsibility.

Before the tests were handed back out, she explained that the highest in the class, Emma or Michael, managed to get 92 percent. The lowest, probably James, had received 8 percent. Science was an especially challenging subject for him, none of the information ever seemed to stick with him. Also, all topics involving blood and the human body made him feel weak and light-headed, as he could only think about that moment where the smell of blood was so strong it made him choke.

It was with great surprise that when Mrs Dinkley gave James his lazily marked test, he had received 16 percent. Naturally, that was abysmal and considering there was no point in comparing himself to other people, he really should be disappointed in himself. However, he couldn't help but feel some pride that he hadn't done the worst for once.

Searching around for the class dunce, it wasn't hard to work out who got the lowest. When the teacher reached Freddie, she gave him the test face down on the table without speaking to him. Normally, a teacher would place the test in the hand of the student with words of improvement and encouragement. Making it a dead giveaway that Freddie, who was already having a bad day, had done the worst.

James noticed that he hadn't bothered to flip the paper, Freddie knew what mark he had received. Proceeding to drop his head on the desk where it would probably stay for the rest of the lesson. His stretched sweater making him look like a very large misshapen blueberry.

It was a sorry sight but at least it wasn't James in that position. To be fair, it was almost always James putting his head on the table for the lesson. He was almost excited to see what the class was like now.

Whilst James was analysing Freddie, Jodie had taken the opportunity to sneak a peek at his results. When he noticed what she was doing he instinctively turned the paper face down. Jodie didn't seem to care that she had been caught or that she had annoyed James, giving a strange smug kind of smile.

'I'm thinking of getting a nose piercing, Tom doesn't think I should. What do you think?' Jodie said, chewing her gum with an open mouth.

James had no idea what to say, nobody ever cared about his opinion. Then again, the only reason she was asking him was because Tom disagreed with her presumably along with everyone else. She was just trying to find someone to justify her decision.

Jodie must have asked everyone else she knew before going to him. It was like when a child asks for chocolate and their mom says no, and so then asks their dad who also says no. Then the child searches for anyone that will give them what they want. In this analogy, James thought he was somewhere in the realm of step-cousin's lost dog.

'I don't know, I guess I would go with what Tom said.'

Mrs Dinkley was now speaking with Emma about the few questions she managed to get incorrect. She'd given up discussing the test with the entire class, as nobody else was paying attention to her.

This time before Jodie spoke, she made a point of moving all of her high-quality brown hair to one side so that she could see James properly and look him in the eye.

'Look, I know you and Tom are friends and I need you to come along to a party I'm having. It's the only thing that will make him shut up about you.' She said all this with a smile that didn't seem even close to sincere.

James had no idea what to say. Jodie was having the party and had invited him, whilst also insulting his friend. He couldn't go. It would be a party, filled with people drinking and doing drugs. It was too scary; he couldn't do it. There was a lump in his throat, he had been backed into a corner and he didn't like it.

'I'm sorry, I don't want to go. Please just leave me alone.'

'Fine, you know what, fine. Do what you want. I was just trying to help your friend be less annoying, screw you.'

Jodie said this all in a way that showed she was offended, but there was something in the way she spoke that made James feel like she had somehow got exactly what she wanted. Picking up her bag a little more forcefully than needed, she went to sit with her normal crowd, where Hercules was telling some hilarious anecdote.

James hadn't meant to be rude or offend her, she was sort of trying to be kind to his friend. Hating himself more than usual, he dropped his head onto the desk where he let it lay for the rest of the lesson.

3. The End of an Era

Science went by slowly as James thought about his conversation with Jodie. Thinking about things he should have said differently. How he could have avoided the conversation entirely. After what felt like days the skull-rattling bell started to ring again.

James was thinking about what it would be like to bunk the lesson and just go home. He couldn't be bothered to go through another fifty-five minutes of the same boredom that made his life so uninteresting. However, what James thought to do and what he did were two very different things. Before he was able to imagine watching shows at home with his feet up on the couch, he found himself standing lined up for his fourth class of the day, English.

James saw very little point in this lesson, considering he already spoke the language. It didn't matter much as the teacher never stopped James from resting his head on the table and ignoring the entire lesson. Not having to do a single line of work. Most teachers would let James get away with that kind of stuff, they didn't want to be mean to the student who had 'been through so much'.

Another long hour later, the lesson finished and it was time for lunch. Spending time on the same table as Jodie was the last thing he wanted to do. What with her being angry at him and the fact that he never wanted to sit next to her in the first place. James thought about asking Tom to simply spend lunch alone with him, just the two of them.

But when James finally found Tom by a water fountain, his eyes and face were red with anger. Tom stormed over and came far too close into James's personal space.

'What the fuck is wrong with you!' Flecks of spit were coming from Tom's mouth, hitting James in the face. 'Jodie tells me she tried to be kind to your miserable soul, but you were so rude to her, she almost broke down in tears! I don't know why I put up with you, I try inviting you out and you give me the same crap excuse every time.'

This felt excessive. For Jodie to say she was almost in tears because he told her to leave him alone, for not wanting to be ripped out of his comfort zone. The day was already going terribly and this was making it so much worse. James had the idea that Jodie was overexaggerating what happened.

'All I told her was that I didn't want to go to her party. I don't want to go to parties and I don't understand why you keep on inviting me. I don't understand why you go to them in the first place. Why can't you just stick with me and stop bringing all these people into our lives?'

'I did stick by your side James I did my best, but I got bored! You never spoke to me and you ignored everything I would say! I found people who care about my life, and I'm not going to let you bring them down as well!'

People had started to gather in the corridor to watch the argument. Tom noticed and it made him cool down.

'I invited you to those parties so that I didn't have to go alone. I was nervous, really nervous. But you let me down. All you ever say is that you have to help with your family, which we both know is a lie. You never help your family, not now and not when your dad was alive.'

It was always a sensitive topic for James and as soon as Tom mentioned it, he knew he had gone too far. He switched his tone to a calmer one.

'I know you're hurting and I tried to be there for you, but you just keep on letting me down. Ever since he died you've given up on everything. It's time for you to move on with your life and do something with it.'

James was angrier than he had been in a long time, Tom wasn't shouting anymore but that wasn't going to stop him. 'No,' he yelled. 'I'm not going to move on! My life should be getting worse, not better! When someone dies, your life should fall apart! Nothing good should ever come from it!'

James had never spoken about his father so openly, about how he hated that he was gaining things from his death. Popularity, opportunities, respect, and everything else were corrupted with people's gratitude for his father's death. He had finally said what had always been on his mind but never dared to say, and it had taken Tom by surprise.

'What are you talking about? Your dad saved the school. If he hadn't taken those bullets, so many kids would be dead before they could experience their life. Your dad was an exceptionally good man. Just because he died doesn't mean the world stops, and it doesn't mean that everything should be shit. For you or anyone else. The entire damned town has helped your family, it's not something that you should be angry for. Your misery and hate will be the death of you James.'

James felt a desperate need to respond but he didn't know what to say. Nothing like this had ever been said to him. He remained silent and so Tom continued, wanting to get everything out into the open.

'You have been living your life refusing to do anything, you won't take any risks because you're too afraid of failing. I love that I have failed at things. I get up, I fail harder than before, I fail better than before, it makes me a better person. I've been your friend for a long time now and before everything happened, you were awesome. Now I don't know what to think. I tried helping, but I give up. You need to work through everything by yourself now.'

Tom walked away leaving James behind.

James stood still, unable to move. In shock. For the first time, he had nobody to call a friend.

Nobody cared about him anymore, so from now on, he would stay at home all day, playing games and watching T.V. Those were the only things that made him happy. But did they? James couldn't remember the last time that he had genuinely smiled or laughed so hard he couldn't breathe or even see something that he thought had nothing wrong with it. There was always a way to see the negatives in things.

For the remainder of lunch, James replayed the argument in his head. He had thought of multiple comebacks that would have been perfect responses at the time but now had no value whatsoever.

In what felt like no time at all, that sickening noise was being played again. The one that made James feel like he was in a mental institute and the inmates were banging their heads against barred windows. He couldn't remember what lesson he had now and didn't have the willpower to search in his bag and find his timetable. Instead, he roamed around the school until he found the classroom he needed to be in.

The rest of the day dragged on, James continued to think about his fight with Tom, their long-lasting friendship broken into pieces. He decided that it was all Jodie's fault because if it wasn't, it was his.

After his day at school finally finished, and he was allowed to head home, James used his reliable way of drowning out his thoughts by blasting music into his ears. He had started the day with what he thought would be a normal bad day, only to leave school feeling the worst he had in a long time.

James thought, even through the blasting music, about how much better his day would have gone if he hadn't left his house at all. He wanted the day to be over already. To get home and sleep until he died. However, as he had spent all of his lunch moping, he hadn't eaten anything.

With the addition of having barely any breakfast, James knew he couldn't go to bed on such an empty stomach.

If he was Kara, with her favouritism, James might have been able to eat an early dinner, but he was the lesser of the two children. He was going to have to wait several hours until his mum decided to make dinner.

James climbed the stairs and entered his room, slamming the door behind him without a word. Gazing around the comfortable bedroom, he launched his school bag onto the floor, his shoulders aching from lugging around the heavy bag all day.

James had the best moments of his life within these four walls, and the exceptionally terrible moments of his life always happening outside the safe haven. This gave him the idea to stay locked in his room for the rest of his life, like some ogre under a bridge.

His walls were covered in posters from his favourite bands and movies. There was a great deal of colour coordination that went into this collage. Making sure that the colours on the posters close to each other were always the same or complementary, such as reds with blues, or yellows with purples.

At this very moment, Tom would be running his hand through his stupid hair, talking to Jodie who had finally managed to get what she wanted. Maybe they would become a happy couple tonight. If they did, James doubted it would last long. Or perhaps it would. Both of them were cruel, toxic people, a perfect match for one another.

Sitting down on his bed James crossed his arms over his bent knees, his head curled up between, like he was some kind of ball. As he waited for the computer to load up a decision was made there and then, he would take tomorrow off and relax.

Most students that got to ten sick days in a term would start getting into trouble for missing out on too much school. Ellis Bowler, one of the few likeable people at the school, had taken nine days off and had a full investigation into his sick days. It was as if he had killed someone the way the school went about seeing if he was truly ill. However, because of James's special circumstance, he was now up to thirty-two missed days.

Mr Glass had personally told James and Kara that it was important for them to come to school as much as possible, for their education and future, but explained that at the end of the day their wellbeing was more important. Giving them permission to take as many sick days as needed to help recover. This was one of the reasons why people liked the headmaster at Ramwall. He was someone who always put the student above everything else, and it showed through his actions that he genuinely cared.

Due to this respect towards Mr Glass, James would only take sick days when he truly needed them. He wouldn't think about milking his ability to skip school. He didn't want Mr Glass to be disappointed in him. On the other hand, today was a rough one, and after weighing the positives and negatives, he decided to take Thursday off, and then go back on Friday, as he was only doing half a day due to the new program.

For the next couple of hours, James sat happily on his bed playing games with the knowledge that when his classmates would be learning maths and English, he would be doing the same thing he was doing now, something that gave him some small morsel of happiness.

At around 8:00 p.m. he was called from his den into the dining room. James wasn't the best at observing people, but it was clear that Kara wasn't faking her illness. She was as white as some of the drugs she had presumably been doing at parties, and when Kara reached over to grab her bottle of water, he noticed she was shaking. As James sat down opposite the jittery ghost his mum brought in a large bowl of spaghetti and cut up sausages, Kara's favourite.

Dinner was often a boring part of the day as Kara wouldn't stop talking about absolute rubbish, but today she must have thrown up her tongue as she didn't say a single word throughout the entire meal. The silence at the table was like music to his ears, as he ate spaghetti in peace.

As James fell back onto his bed, there was a small slice of joy in him. There would be no school in the morning, so he could sleep in to his heart's desire. Presumably, Kara would also take the day off, but he wasn't worried about her telling their mum that he skipped another day. No matter what Kara would never snitch on James and he always returned the favour. At least Kara knew what it meant to be a sister, unlike Tom, who couldn't work out how to be a decent friend.

There was a part of James that was getting worried about his older sister. She had taken more days off than he had and she was starting to look worse and worse. Perhaps he should say something to her? Ask if everything was all right? She was, after all, going through the same thing as him.

Then again, Kara never asked how he was doing. Well, that was a lie she asked a lot, but she never wanted a proper response, she was just doing maintenance on their relationship. Although, James knew she wasn't the kind of person who would do something like that. When she asked you something, which was often, she wanted a real answer because she cared.

James only needed to go over to her room, knock on her door, and ask how she was doing. Kara would most likely tell him she was fine and tell him to leave. There was little risk of a hard conversation and James could clear his conscience about being a good brother. On the other hand, she was probably sleeping and he had no intention of waking her. That never turned out well.

All the same, he made a mental note to make sure that the next time it was just the two of them, he would ask how she was feeling and if he could help. It wasn't what he would normally do, but now that he had no friends, he had might as well try and talk to his sister. Before he somehow loses her too.

He spent the rest of the night playing video games without another thought about school, his family, or anything other than the person he was killing online. James was playing worse than normal, which was a shame because he was so close to ranking up in the competitive mode from platinum rank to diamond. It didn't matter. He would be able to continue working towards his goal once he had a full night of rest. After his mother went to bed, James decided it was best to stop playing on his computer. That way, his mum could believe he at least intended on going to school the following day.

James wrestled into a comfortable position under his blankets and put some headphones on, watching T.V shows on his phone until he very slowly closed his eyes and fell into what he hoped would be a calm relaxing sleep.

At first, his dream started off as the normal nightmare. His father on the floor of the school's main reception area, blood leaking out of his many bullet holes. Students screaming as they watched James running towards the body, trying as best as he could to help. But there was no point, his dad was already dead. That wretched smell of blood overwhelmed James once more, but this time instead of waking up he found that the nightmare had changed.

He was his normal self. Standing in a field that was covered with black flowers stretching all the way to the wonderfully red horizon. There was a strange tingling in his legs, and he knew that for some reason it meant he could fly. Pushing off hard against the ground, James took a massive leap through the black field, reaching the clouds, and then landing softly on the ground.

Keen to explore this new power, he took off once more, this time not landing back on the ground but staying suspended in the sky. James enjoyed gliding through what was now an empty desert with his headphones in, listening to his music. Nothing could stop him. It was just him the silky sand and the bright blazing sun, shining down on him. The spectacle, the magnificent, the incredible human that could fly.

However, just like Icarus, James couldn't help but start flying too close to the sun. He was flying high and he didn't want to stop. James had passed the tallest buildings and the highest mountains, going until the sky around him turned black.

He was now face to face with the sun, and was mesmerized by the big ball of light. For some reason, it was melting like a scoop of ice cream turning to liquid on a hot day. James wondered what could possibly melt the sun, the massive fireball suspended in space, the thing that was able to keep entire planets warm and blind people for looking at it too long? He then wondered that if the sun was blinding, why could he see it so clearly?

James had been staring at the sun for a long time now and yet he was fine, he didn't even feel hot, just a cold emptiness. Then he realised what was happening. He was the reason the beacon of light was falling apart, just like he burned and destroyed everything that came close to him. James was doing the very same thing to the sun, the thing that people needed to survive. Now the world would be put into eternal darkness due to him, the plants would die, and the doors to heaven would freeze shut, all because of him.

Beneath him was earth which he took in one last time before falling back down. He was soon going to be the only living thing in existence, the devil that melted the sun because his hatred was too strong, nothing could bear witness to it. Maybe this was how it was meant to be, him against the world. Him against the entire universe. And James coming out on top, nobody getting in his way. The life of a lonely monster.

He was falling fast now, much faster than when he could fly, he didn't try to stop it. Why fly now? There was nothing left to enjoy; he had destroyed it all. Falling and falling until ... BANG.

James had fallen out of his bed and dropped to the floor. His alarm hadn't gone off yet but the sun was already shining on him. He rubbed his elbow, the first thing to hit the floor, which was sending shooting pains down his arm.

It took a few moments for James to realise that he had been dreaming. And had, thankfully, not destroyed the sun. Although, it was reassuring when he opened his blinds to see the glowing ball hanging above.

There was no real need to do most of his normal routine, he would have all day to complete it. For his plan to work, James made sure that his mum saw him leave for school whilst she had her morning coffee. He then did a lap of their neighbourhood and made sure the car was gone from their driveway before he came back. He let himself in and jumped back into bed for a few more hours of rest. The dream of melting the sun still looming at the back of his mind.

A few months ago, to get out of school James would have explained that he wasn't feeling good enough, and it would be enough. But his mum no longer allowed that as a reason to stay home, because of how much Kara and James's grades were plummeting.

Their parents had always been exceptionally smart, especially their father. Sadly, neither Kara nor James had inherited that intellect or any other natural talent their parents had. Kara received the majority of their dad's features, the blue eyes, the black hair, and that incredible wide smile. While James, as his mum would say, 'looked a lot like her pops.' Her pops was tall, with similar green eyes and dark brown hair.

For most of their childhood, James and Kara would play with each other, as their parents were always busy with work. The only thing James did with his dad was fishing. Which would happen about once every month. Now James doubted that he would ever go fishing again.

Taking the day off was a very smart idea. James thought, as he finally ranked up to diamond. *If I had gone to school today, I would have been unbelievably lonely.* Immediately after thinking this, James realised he would be lonely the next day, and on the following Monday, as nothing would have changed. He wouldn't have changed.

Loneliness engulfed him in that moment, like a cloud of poison giving him the feeling that he couldn't breathe. Burning a hole into his heart. It simply was not possible to go through the rest of high school with no friends. There had to be some kind of change, something to fix this pain he was experiencing.

Now that he had exactly what he wanted, nobody interrupting him or being involved in his life, he realised how little good it did him. That if he walked the halls of the school with nobody paying him any kind of attention like a ghost, how lonely and sad he would become.

Instantly James wanted more than anything to reconcile with Tom. They had been friends for such a long time. It had been less than twenty-four hours since the argument and James was turning into a mess. Thinking over their fight again, James realised that Tom had brought up some very valid points, points that James couldn't see before, being blinded by his own misery. Now it was obvious how right Tom had been.

Regret and shame weighed on James as he recollected the past few months and how poorly he had been acting. It was as though he had finally snapped out of his despaired trance.

Reaching diamond rank felt like such an unimportant accomplishment in comparison to what he could be achieving. As the fear of loneliness continued to burn through his heart, James became intent on making sure that how he felt now would be as bad as it ever got.

To be able to fix his relationship, which was now all James could think about, he would have to show Tom that he had changed. For this to happen, he would have to leave his house, he couldn't hide away in fear from everything anymore, but he had to face it head-on.

It was time to try again, he had lost almost everything he cared about acting how he was, and nothing positive had been gained from it. James had tried the route of ignoring people and locking himself away for several months, to deal with his father's death, but it was clear to him that it didn't make him happy.

Excitement and nervousness pulsed through James's body. Tomorrow was another day. He would try to be a different person, try to make an effort. He would try to be a kind, decent, reliable person, and importantly a good friend. Someone who doesn't infect other people with their anguish, but instead spreads warmth and happiness. That sounded like a person James wanted to be, a friend who you were happy to see no matter what.

On Friday James would have an excellent opportunity to be a new person with the people from EE. He had already forgotten who he was paired with but James was sure that he could work it out. If those people didn't like him, what did it matter, they were from EE.

Confidence filled James in a way that made him sure everything would be fine. That his entire life could be more than a crap job in Echoway. He was starting to have real hope again.

For the rest of the day, James spent his time thinking about how he would fix all of his past self's mistakes. Soon he would have his life back on track.

That night James had the first dream that didn't terrify him in some way since his father had died. He didn't have a nightmare, and he didn't see his father lying on the floor of the school.

4. Journey for a Better Me

James didn't have a chance to speak with Kara on Thursday. She spent it either with her head in the toilet or lying on her deathbed, asleep. Because of that tight schedule Kara was keeping to, James couldn't find the time to ask how she was doing and if he could help in any way.

She didn't come down for dinner, which meant that James had to have dinner alone with his mum. It was always awkward when it was just the two of them in a room, but James was desperate to do better. He made an effort to respond to her questions as best as he could. He wasn't giving full monologues spoken so beautifully it made her cry, but it was more than just yes and no.

In an extra attempt to signify his change in attitude, James set a different tune for his alarm, one that was a happy melody. Different from his old tune that had sounded like metal scratching metal. He had cleaned up his bedroom, which had been in a complete mess for a long time, and got ahead on all the homework he had been putting off.

These were a lot of small mundane things that probably made a very little difference, but it was more of a difference than if he had done nothing. Therefore, it was 100 percent worth doing.

Friday rolled around and the sun rose high and mighty in the sky as it always did. It crept through into James's bedroom to see something truly special. The light from the sun had travelled hundreds and thousands of miles through space, past other planets, floating debris, and moons just so that it could reach earth. Then it had to dodge past planes and trees, hitting the gap in James's curtains at the perfect angle, just so that it could see him already awake, reading a book.

Waking up that morning was easier than just about every other day since his father's death. Going to sleep earlier than normal meant that he had slept peacefully with dreams of hope and happiness. The calm tune that woke him made him think of a brighter future.

Today, James went through his daily routine as normal but with a slight difference, he was smiling. It couldn't be helped. The thought of being better brought happiness to him; it acted as a natural high and he never wanted to come down. It was insane to him that he hadn't tried to be like this sooner. Granted, he hadn't really done anything yet, but he was aiming to.

Leaving his house at the normal time alone again, James gave a much more enthusiastic goodbye than his normal miserable self would ever think of doing. Walking down the street, he plugged in his headphones with almost a skip in his step.

The plan was to show Tom he had changed by finding Jodie and apologizing for how he had spoken to her, even though she was clearly manipulating their friendship to get what she wanted by pretending James had been cruel to her. But he wouldn't be apologizing for her sake. In a way, he would be the one manipulating her.

James also wanted to make an effort to talk to the people who smiled at him when he walked the corridors, or at the very minimum, smile back at them. Tom had been right in saying that the town had been nothing but kind to him, and he really wanted to start appreciating it more.

As he arrived at the front of Ramwall, he took out his headphones and put them deep into his bag. He had no intention of using them until he left to go home. Standing with his hand on the front glass door, James took a deep breath. *You can do this.*

He never took much notice of Mrs Pogue, the receptionist, just like everyone else. It had only just dawned on James that she was one of the last people to properly speak to his father, and one of the people who saw everything take place on that dreadful day. Seeing something like that unravel at such an old age could never be good. Perhaps it was why she became so much crueller to people, where she was normally just unhelpful.

Most people hated her. James had no idea why she was at a job that she so clearly hated. Nevertheless, when he marched past her desk, he smiled at her and ventured a 'Good morning.'

Not too loudly, he didn't want the other students thinking he was mad for talking to the mean old woman, but loud enough for her to hear him clearly. Enough to put a small twitch of a smile on her wrinkled face.

Turning right to the cafeteria where he knew Jodie and her friends would be, James wondered how his father would have spoken to Mrs Pogue. Was he kind when asking her to collect his son? Did he give her a smile when speaking? Recalling the worst day of his life, James remembered that Mrs Pogue seemed a smidge happier on the intercom, calling him to the reception.

Unwarranted flashes of his father on the floor covered in blood screamed into his mind. These images made it a lot easier to keep heading towards the cafeteria, only because it was away from the reception area. Those moments burned in his mind, rent-free, until he saw Jodie sitting with all her friends.

By this point, his courage was wavering. He was now scared and anxious, almost to the point of having a panic attack. His breathing was ragged, the beating of his heart seemed to be as loud as gunshots. But he kept moving. One step after another.

There was a large crowd around Jodie. It would have been a lot easier if she was by herself so that they could talk in private, but for some reason, it felt like the apology should be made to all of them. It wasn't just her that James had been rude to over the past months.

Everyone was now staring at him. Andy stopped whatever story he had been telling that had people on the edge of their seat, to see what James had to say. It was the time to speak. But as he stood there with his heavy backpack and a smile on his face that was quickly fading, he realised that this was a lot harder than expected.

His mouth was moving but it didn't seem like any words were coming out. He was very aware of all the eyes on him and couldn't work out how to blink properly. A noise came from the distance, which James hoped was coming from his mouth, until he realised that it was Daphne talking instead.

'Can we help you?' she said, in a snarky tone that made James question the point of apologizing.

Then out of the corner of his eye, he saw it, his extra heart, the saviour of a lost soul, his friend. Taking a deep breath, James turned to face Jodie properly and finally spoke.

'I was wrong to speak to you like that, it wasn't right of me. You were just being kind, and for what it's worth, I'm sorry and I want to make up for it.' James now turned to Tom, 'I was being a bad friend and I want to do better.'

Tom was on the cusp of accepting the apology, but it seemed like James needed to do some more grovelling before he felt satisfied, and so he turned back to Jodie.

'I would also really appreciate it if you would let me come to your party next weekend.'

James wanted to improve himself, and eventually, he would have to go to parties to hang out in Tom's environment more, but the idea of leaving his comfort zone so much this quickly felt a bit much.

Jodie was staring at him with piercing eyes and a lot of intensity. James wasn't sure if she was trying to work out if she could get away with telling him to piss off.

After a few moments of quiet, Tom spoke for her.

'We would all love for you to come, it's about time you came to hang out with us outside of school.'

Nobody objected, and so while rolling her eyes so far back into her head James could see only white, Jodie uttered an exasperated, 'Fine.'

Nothing felt better than looking over and seeing that Tom was smiling at him, that he had already forgiven him. He truly was a decent friend. Relief filled James. This was one of the hard parts and now that Tom was smiling James' did to. The hard part was done and it was time to relish in his victory.

As he was walking away Andy called out, asking if he wanted to sit with them. James turned back around towards the table with so many people at it. With a sinking feeling in his stomach, he knew that he couldn't turn Hercules down.

However, before he could respond the bell came to the rescue for the first time in his life. The group of people dispersed around him as they went their separate ways. As luck would have it, the first lesson of the day was science and so James awkwardly joined the group with Jodie, Daphne, and Andy.

Daphne and Andy had been dating for a long time, but it was blatant to everyone that they didn't really like each other. Andy was easily the most popular person in school but grew up poor; his family were practically homeless for most of his life. Daphne was from a wealthy family and was one of the cruellest people James had ever seen. She was the kind of person who enjoyed seeing others in pain.

They were only together because Daphne's parents helped Hercules with equipment and put him in contact with the right people. In return, Daphne received school fame and the ability to get away with anything. Nobody would ever say no to the star athlete's girlfriend, because she could and would make their lives hell.

James still didn't particularly like Jodie. It felt like she was the chain of events that led him to being so miserable on Wednesday and Thursday. Wanting to be part of the conversation James asked, 'Are you feeling any better Daphne, you weren't at school on Wednesday?'

God, I sounded like someone's grandmother, he realised. But it was too late, he had already asked the question. In that moment James questioned every life choice he had ever made. Daphne gave a kind of you-are-so-lame-I-don't-want-to-be-near-you look at James, that did nothing to help with his spiralling.

'Yeah man, she's fine. Just went a little overboard at the last party.' Andy said as he high fived a group of kids in the year above.

'You can say that much, babe, although I wasn't as overboard as your sister, James. She really can't handle anything, can she?' The words were venom, made to sting, and they were doing their job well.

James wanted to retort, to show that Daphne couldn't get away with being cruel towards his sister. But, like everyone else, he was too scared to fight back.

'There's no need for that Daphne. She's a nice person,' Andy said. 'Hey, how's she doing, James? She hasn't been in school these last few days.'

Why is it that when he asks the same kind of question it sounds cool? James mumbled a half-hearted answer to Andy about why his sister was ill, as they lined up outside the classroom. He decided to separate from the group heading to the front of the line as the cool kids lagged behind, chatting away. Without anyone to talk to, all James could think about was that he would have to go to a party in a week.

An image popped into his mind of a mound of cocaine on a table that he was being forced to try. Daphne, to the side, made vile comments about him while Andy poured alcohol on his head as some kind of prank.

Freaking out, James noticed Michael standing at the front talking to Emma, and remembered that he was also going to EE with him in a couple of hours. Now was an opportunity to have an easy short conversation with someone.

'Hey Michael, how are you doing? We have that EE program today, don't we?'

What a gorgeous sentence, plenty of room for a nice long reply and a choice of questions for him to choose where the conversation would go to suit him. James was confident that he had just said the best sentence anyone had ever concocted.

'Yes,' Michael replied, not bothering to turn away from Emma.

Fury overcame him. *I might not be a conversation pro but I deserved a better answer than that, I trekked all the way over to you so that we could have a delightful conversation, and you have the nerve to say 'yes'. You didn't even look at me properly!*

This all took place in James's head. In the real world, James spoke back through gritted teeth.

'Cool.'

James no longer liked Michael. In fact, he hated him. That image with the mound of cocaine at a party surfaced again but with Michael in James's place, and James pouring vodka on his head and setting it alight. His magnificent smile reappeared at the thought of this.

It then occurred to James that two days ago, he would have answered that question exactly the same way, with even less enthusiasm. Was that how everyone felt after trying to talk to him? Perhaps Michael deserved a second chance.

Science was spent learning about different types of body organs, and James tried his very best to pay attention and show interest in the topic. But with the increasing volume of chatting and the fact that it was a PowerPoint presentation with only text on it, after twenty-five minutes, he was chatting to two other kids in the class about who would win in a fight, a Jedi or a wizard.

The hard part for James was simply getting into the conversation in the first place. After that, he had one of the best science lessons all year. James spoke about all his favourite films and games at length, knowing the other people also enjoyed them, having listened to their conversations all year. The lesson finished with James giving his player ID to them so that they could play online at some point.

Again, James had done something that he was always too scared and anxious to do, and again it came out so much better than he could ever have dreamed. Now on his way to maths, he paid attention when people in the corridor smiled at him, and he made an effort to smile back.

It was insane to him how many people were willing to talk to him. Most of them wouldn't have spoken or even looked at him if it weren't for his dad, but now instead of being resentful of this, he took it as an absolute honour.

His day was going exceptionally well. One of the best days he'd had all year. Naturally, it wouldn't matter how he acted in maths, it was still going to be dreadful. James could have every single superpower imaginable and there would still be nothing he could do to defeat that monster.

Because he'd been busy talking during science, James hadn't noticed but now in the silent classroom, he heard a distinct lack of scribbling and papers moving behind him. James remembered that Freddie had been having a pretty rough time for a while now and it seemed like it was only getting worse. He made a note to himself to check in on him on Monday.

Freddie had no friends and nobody else would ask how he was feeling so James would. It would be another way to be a good person, and considering how well it was going, James couldn't see a reason to stop.

After maths James spoke with Tom and gave him another apology. Tom seemed so happy with James he acted as though they never fought in the first place. Tom said how excited he was for the party, saying how he would make sure to stick by his side. It stung when Tom said this as James realised he wasn't by Tom's side when he went to his first party.

At 12.58 p.m., James was allowed to leave his history lesson early. He headed down to the reception area, where Mrs Pogue told him to take a seat, more kindly than usual, as they waited for Mr Kennedy to meet them. James always had a sickly feeling here, and he wanted more than anything for the PE teacher to come and meet them so that they could leave.

As James waited, trying to take his mind off of his father, he scanned the area to see Michael, as far from everyone as possible, reading a book and pushing his glasses back up when they would drop. On the other side of the area, Sarah and Andy were talking to each other. James thought about joining them, but it looked like a pretty serious conversation. Andy didn't seem happy with what Sarah was saying, as though it genuinely hurt to listen to her.

Before James could dwell too much on what they might be talking about, Mr Kennedy appeared behind him. He was sporting his dirty tracksuit, along with his black and yellow Ramwall varsity jacket, and a blue baseball cap to cover his bald spot.

Nobody cared about Mr Kennedy. His job wasn't that important. All he did was tell kids when to run, when to tackle, and when to jump. Some students, like Andy, pretended to respect him as there were some possible connections he had to scouters, but other than that, he wasn't a person anyone would remember in five years.

Mr Kennedy always stood with a straight back and good posture, even though it didn't make much of an impact since he was the same height as Tom.

The teacher spoke in the most authoritative tone he could muster.

'OK, guys and gals, let's get a move on. We don't want to be late.'

Very few people paid any attention to him. Only after James and Andy, who was just trying to get away from Sarah, stood up and started to walk out of the school, did the rest of the students unenthusiastically follow them out into the big wide world.

Joshua Stevens-Shachar

5. Meeting with the Enemy

The walk to EE was a strange one. James had experienced plenty of trips before, but none of them had such a unique set of students, ones that would never normally breathe the same air.

James was going to speak with Andy whilst walking, but he was already chatting with Mr Kennedy. Although, it was a wonder how Mr Kennedy could hear him, what with Andy's head being so far up his ass.

For some reason, Sarah kept on trying to talk to Andy, a wicked look on her face. Whenever she would start to come close to him, Andy would make sure to have something to do so that they couldn't speak. It was as if he was scared to talk to her.

As they entered Echoway East, Mr Kennedy power walked up to the reception. From first glance, you could tell it was the better-funded school. The receptionist was using a new clean computer, placed on a dark oak desk that seemed to shine as if brand new, whilst maintaining an ancient aesthetic. The entire area had a dark look to it. This wasn't like the time the lights stopped working at Ramwall. It was done on purpose and made the whole reception area look more sophisticated and elegant. However, what set the schools apart the most was that the receptionist had a genuine smile on her face.

Setting himself down into a chair, which, unlike Ramwall's, had no holes in it and wasn't the same colour as sick, James moved his head around in an arc staring up at the unnecessarily high ceiling. On the wall behind James, the school had hung pictures of students who had gone to respectable universities, showing what grades they received and what they had chosen to study.

Appreciating the high-quality pieces of laminated paper, James saw that some students were studying some truly incredible things. Dylan Kujo went to study English at Yale, Gareth Whitebread went to study Advance Aerodynamics, and Jimmy Woll had been offered a position to study at NASA. The wall did an exquisite job of showing off their students in a way that made James very envious. These students were some of the only people in town that would go on to possibly accomplish great things. They had a shot at being someone.

EE was twice as large as Ramwall, yet the top of the range receptionist managed to find out they needed to be in exercise room 3, spending half of the time it would take Mrs Pogue to tell you where the nearest toilet was. As they were herded through the clean halls, James noticed the incredible artwork and awards hung on the walls.

Entering the unnecessarily large room, the group instinctively moved closer together to protect one another in enemy territory. Andy had a furious look that made shadows appear on his face. The people from EE had fractured his leg, stopped him from competing for several months and interrupted what was probably one of the best moments of his life.

Across the room a group of students who wouldn't appear out of place in a TV show were talking happily like they didn't have a single problem in the world. All students at EE had to wear a uniform to school, unlike Ramwall which allowed you to come dressed in whatever you wanted.

Their uniform was a classic private school black trousers or skirts with a blazer over a shirt with the school crest. The blazer was black with a dark purple lining the edges, giving them a posh look. The colours didn't look all too different from what Sarah normally wore. Pure black. Except her clothes were a lot more informal and revealing.

Andy was the first person to head over towards the group of EE kids, and James was worried he was about to start a fight with them. However, he walked over to the group, his face filled with charisma and enthusiasm, without a single dark shadow.

The EE group had been taken aback by how Andy was talking to them. They had probably been thinking the same thing as James, that Ramwall's star player would want some kind of revenge. Strangely, Andy was talking to them as if they were long-time friends who hadn't done anything wrong to him, and not like they were mortal enemies.

Andy was chatting away with the group as best as he could. People from the two schools would always be careful around the other out of fear that it was some kind of trap. One of the students in the group had the same kind of physique all the football players had, along with an exceptionally straight back. More rigid than Mr Hemans, as if he had grown up with wooden planks attached to his spine.

It wasn't all that surprising to see someone like him on the program. The whole reason the two schools were doing this, was so that they could start competitions again. Remembering that he needed to be better, James walked over and started to join in on the conversation.

The other two students from EE didn't show as much initiative. Sarah had chosen to start defacing the room by drawing inside drawers, and messing up the neat stationery inside one of the cabinets. Michael was doing his best to exclude himself from any social interactions, sitting down at a table and reading his book, attracting the attention of one of the EE girls, who was covered in freckles and had red hair kept in a ponytail by a pencil.

It was curious how polite the EE students were being, considering they always made the first move attacking Ramwall students. They must have been hand-picked knowing that they wouldn't start a fight. Even if they were the best people from EE to help make changes, James was doubtful that this was going to do anything to fix the rivalry. Eight students couldn't change the views of two entire schools.

James had noticed that some of the EE students stared at Sarah with hatred until they focused back on the conversation. At first, James thought that it was because of how she dressed and that she was from Ramwall. Then he remembered that Sarah used to go to EE, and was disliked by just about everyone in the town.

Just then, a teacher from EE walked into the classroom, Mr Kennedy following behind. It felt a little pathetic seeing the small teacher wearing a dirty wrinkled tracksuit, standing next to a well-groomed man with a clean suit and shiny black shoes, showing off an expensive watch on his wrist.

The better teacher explained that they all had to find their new partners and sit with them at any table they wanted. Andy seated himself next to the well-built guy James had assumed was on the football team, someone who on the surface seemed a lot like Hercules. They had presumably spent most of their lives training to be the best at what they did so that they could make it professionally. The kind of person who would do anything to make it as a star athlete.

Michael awkwardly sat next to the girl who had been eyeing him from behind her round glasses. It was obvious Michael found this girl attractive, as the second she spoke to him he turned bright red, maybe it was his way of copying her freckles and hair, like some kind of chameleon.

Michael was best friends with Emma. So, it seemed a little strange as to how shy he was around another female, but then again Emma was very different to this girl who, by most standards was rather pretty, in a geeky kind of way.

Sarah had no obvious intention of sitting down any time soon, so James was now left with a decision. He had completely forgotten who he was meant to be with, leaving him to choose between the last two EE students. His decision making over the last few months had managed to be consistently wrong. But with his new outlook on life, perhaps somehow his luck would turn.

There was one guy at a table and a girl at the other. Fortunately for James, the guy seemed to be staring at Sarah with disappointment and dread, which meant that unless she had offended him or made his life worse in some way back at EE, which was very possible, he was partnered with her. Therefore, James needed to sit next to the girl. Which he then did in the coolest way he could muster.

Now that James had a chance to properly look at the girl he was partnered with, time stood still. She was simply beautiful. It was almost like she had a heavenly aura around her, making everything in life seem so much better. Her common brown eyes were like gateways into a better life, sparkling with the hope of a million fairies. Black bushy hair made it look like she had been in a lab explosion, trying to create a solution for a better world. It was easy to smile when sitting next to something so similar to an angel.

James tried to create an interesting sentence that would spark a conversation with the new eighth wonder of the world, something which would be the backbone of their everlasting connection that they would tell people had stuck with them their entire life. The main problem James kept on running into when constructing such a masterpiece in his head was that he couldn't remember her name.

It had now been some time since James sat down and he still had not said a word to her. All he needed to do was say anything at this point. He would settle for any kind of conversation, but every time he looked at her, he choked up and felt dizzy.

Something was better than nothing and so with a very deep breath, a word left James's mouth. 'Hey.'

Immediately, James thought it would have been better to have said nothing at all. As soon as he reached the 'e' in 'hey', his voice broke, due to him still going through puberty and because his body hated him.

No no no. She's going to get up and leave now. Why would she speak to someone that can't even speak properly? At this point, James was confident the girl would choose a new partner like Sarah, who with all her black clothes standing in the corner of the room looked like a massive crow, ready to swoop in and scavenge from his defeated body.

Evidently, there had been an error in the world, as this did not happen. For some reason, the mystery girl stayed in her seat and even turned to face James with those starry eyes and an awkward look on her face.

'Hello, I'm going to be completely honest with you, I don't remember what your name was for the life of me, as hard as I try. I sat down at this desk hoping that someone would sit next to me, which thankfully you did but I'm really sorry, I still cannot remember your name.'

She said all of this exceptionally fast, stumbling over the words pouring out of her mouth. James found this incredibly cute. Her face became redder and redder and now she couldn't meet his eyes at all.

Somehow, instead of her running away, she was apologising to him, and by some miracle, she was the one getting embarrassed. He was smitten by the way she felt it was a massive deal about forgetting his name and felt the need to apologise.

Without hesitation, James replied. 'Well, that is great news because I was trying to work out how to ask for your name.'

At this, the girl finally glanced back at James, her cheeks red as a rose. Her eyes fluttered as she extended her hand.

'Ella.'

'James.'

He grasped her soft hand; they shook, then laughed. The air around them became warmer and more comfortable. James was able to relax, he had tensed up without noticing.

'So… What's your favourite band?' Ella asked.

This time when speaking, she was slower and calmer, breathing in-between her words. James thought a lot about this question. He knew his favourite band straight away, Destiny Calling, but they weren't the most mainstream or popular. James would have to edit his answer so that Ella could relate to him more. Eventually, he thought of an answer that seemed adequate.

'I would have to say Travis Swift is pretty decent at the moment.'

'Why are you lying?' Ella said, furrowing her brow. 'There is one thing that I really can't stand about people, and that's when they try to be someone they're not. People spend all their lives being someone they aren't, building friendships, relationships, and their life around this fake version of themselves. Just because they're too afraid that if they ever, even for a second, show who they truly are, people won't like them. If someone doesn't like their fake version, what does it matter to them? It's not who they are.'

James didn't know what to do, Ella was gathering speed with her words as she became more passionate about what she was saying, moving her hands as she went.

'The issue I have with this is blindingly obvious, let's say I didn't call you out. There are two ways the conversation goes. Either I love Travis Swift and want to spend more time with you listening to him when you hate him. So, you regret every second you spend with me, listening to something you don't like. Or, I hate him like you do, which I do, and we don't spend much time together because I am led to believe you like different music to me. Imagine that situation happened every time I asked you something, slowly we would either build a fake relationship or grow further apart. Both seem like horrible ideas to me. Life is too short for that.'

It felt like James was sitting in front of a leader giving a speech about a dream they had, one that could move nations and sway people into acting differently, filled with compassion and energy in a way that made it impossible to stop listening.

'If all you have are friends and relationships who like you for the person you aren't, then eventually, when you care less about what people think, when you start to become yourself, there's going to be a wave of realisation that there hasn't been a single chance for anything memorable to happen, because when you boil it down, you don't have anything in common with these people. The things they liked about your personality, goals, attitude, and sometimes even beliefs aren't who you are. It's just some fictional character you made so that you can feel safe behind a wall. And that's something that needs to stop. I want friends who are true to themselves.'

Ella finally caught her breath. She realised suddenly that she had just given a monologue to someone she had met less than a minute ago, and was now back to being red in the face, eyes staring at the ground, wishing it to swallow her away.

It was always a bad feeling when someone gets called out on something, which was one of the reasons why James was so quiet all the time. But at the end of Ella's heartfelt speech, he couldn't have agreed more. James didn't feel embarrassed like he would have imagined in his head. It felt good that Ella cared enough to want a proper relationship with him.

'Destiny Calling. That's my all-time favourite band. Travis Swift is nothing compared to them.'

Ella's face lit up with excitement and happiness like a child on Christmas morning.

'See I was right. That's easily my favourite band as well. Have you heard their new album?'

The pair spent a long-time ravishing over the band going through all their songs and their new album. James was pleased to boast that he had a poster of the album on his wall. It was annoying when they had to stop their interesting conversation to listen to the smartly dressed EE teacher.

'Now that most of you have gotten to know each other a little bit better-' he had said most as Sarah and her partner hadn't spoken a word to one another, '-it's time to get on with some of the activities we have created to help strengthen the bond between our two important schools.'

When he spoke, it was loud and clear, his arms moving around with precision and clear intent. Making it seem like he was a professional speaker. Combined with his deep authoritative tone it was easy to focus and understand what he was saying.

The teacher went on to explain some of the activities. It was like being a toddler. All the activities were exceptionally basic and did nothing to remedy the rivalry. It seemed like they had done a good job of picking almost eight students that wouldn't rip each other to shreds, but their end goal of fixing an entire school rivalry wasn't going to work. In any case, James didn't care much for the school war, he was happy to do the tasks because it meant that he could spend more time with Ella.

James noticed that Ella was wearing a variety of different bracelets and bands. He decided that if their conversation ever became dry, he could ask about them. Kara also had different bracelets, each one meaning something special to her, like a friendship bracelet James had made for her as a kid, and a piece of fishing string from their dad's fishing rod.

However, after spending a good couple of hours talking to Ella, there was no sign of their conversation becoming dry. They both had a lot in common, from games to films to music. It was such a breath of fresh air talking to someone about things that he found genuinely interesting. This was something that would never normally happen, to truly enjoy a conversation.

Reality set in as James started to understand even more why Tom was so angry with him. Whenever Tom had tried to speak to him, or anyone for that matter, he was so uninvested that they would have been better off talking to a fish.

Focusing back on Ella's face but not her voice, James continued to spare a few moments from heaven to reassure himself that he was doing this for Tom. That the only real reason he had come to school today was so that he could show Tom he had changed.

Before he could focus properly on what Ella was saying, Mr Kennedy, trying to be helpful, blew his whistle telling everyone that the timer set by the EE teacher had gone off. The task that they were meant to be doing was talking about what school meant to them. Instead, Ella and James had taken the time to play rock, paper, scissors, whilst talking about a new game that was coming out.

Looking around the room, James could see that most of the groups were having a decent time with each other. James found out that Andy's partner was called Grayson, from a task where they went around and spoke about their partner. Grayson, as expected, was on the football team, and his parents were both in the military, which explained why his posture was so remarkably straight.

James wasn't sure if Andy and Grayson were pretending to be friendly again so that they could get back out onto the field, or if they genuinely liked each other. Either way, the teachers were happy to see them talking away about fitness. James overheard Mr Kennedy giddily say to the other teacher that they would be able to get everything back on track in no time, proving James's theory that this whole program was set up solely to restart football matches and other tournaments, not to help fix the rivalry.

When Ella spoke about James there was an odd chill that seemed to go down the back of the EE students, and an awkward blanket spread over the group after she said his name. Evidently, they had all heard of James Fuss.

There had been multiple reports done about his family. They had made national news after his father died. James had to deal with reporters waiting outside his house trying to question him about his views on his father's brutal death. That was one of the reasons why James became so miserable, he had hated those reporters who were trying to gain from his father's death. It made it seem like that's all anyone wanted.

For the last part of the session, the groups came together. They did some of the most tedious exercises James had ever seen, such as a bingo game where they had to find different things about the people in the group, like speaks another language, has a dog, is left-handed. Nobody could be bothered to do any of these because they weren't children, and were able to speak to other people normally.

In the end, everyone cheated on the tasks and spent the remaining time talking like grown-ups. Ella introduced James to Sarah's partner, Ludwig. He wore thin circular glasses and had black messy hair. He also spoke with a foreign accent that James couldn't place. Now James wasn't gay but he was aware that Ludwig was a decent-looking guy. There was a noticeable tattoo on his wrist that presumably got him into tons of trouble at such a high standards school. He also had a lip piercing that seemed completely out of place with his clothing.

After speaking with Ludwig for a few minutes, James discovered that he was Swedish. Making him the son of the Swedish family that had moved to town around a year ago. This was big news in the town when it happened. There had never been any residents from Sweden before. Ludwig seemed like a decent enough person, although he kept on interrupting people and cutting them off in the middle of their sentences to tell his own stories.

Michael was one of the smartest students in their year, and his partner seemed like she was the same kind of person, only because she was able to make Michael speak, which James knew from experience wasn't easy. James didn't speak to either of them much at all. They seemed to act like possums when approached, acting dead or as if they were busy with something else.

Unfortunately, by the point in the exercise where it was Michael's turn to say her name and a bit about her, Ella was playing noughts and crosses on some paper with James. At the time, this felt far more important than listening to what someone else was saying as they had both won two games apiece and that was the deciding game.

Eventually, the teachers announced that they were done for the day and that the Ramwall students could all head home ten-minutes early. James realised that the only reason they decided to let them go early was so that they weren't seen by any of the less peaceful students at EE.

After the teachers said they could go, Sarah, who had spent the entire time sitting in her chair picking at her painted black nails, left immediately, practically running as she left the school.

The remaining seven stayed around in the room for a little longer. Michael was speaking to his partner at length about something to do with numbers. James thought that they wouldn't look out of place as a couple.

Thinking about relationships he turned back round to Ella.

Grayson had come over to speak with her and Ludwig, Andy hovering around listening in to what people were saying, but thinking hard about something at the same time.

'That entire thing was absolute trash. If we wanted to get to know someone better just hang out with them not play some shit bingo game,' Grayson said.

'Well-'

Ella was interrupted by Ludwig.

'I have an idea, but it's a bit ... So, my dad used to own the Silver Chariot bar since we moved here, but he ... Well, it's now permanently closed because he didn't pay the bills. But it means there's still all the alcohol there and everything but it's just boarded up until it gets sold. We could all meet up there tomorrow and have tons of free alcohol and get to know each other better. That is the whole point of the program. And I hate this stupid war between our schools, I don't feel safe walking home because of it. But we can't tell anyone else about the Silver

Chariot because we can't be there, and there would be a lot of trouble if the wrong person found out.'

For someone who lived in Sweden most of his life, his English was perfect. The majority of the group had sceptical looks on their faces. It did seem strange for them all to hang out after only meeting for a few hours, at a party that they couldn't speak to people about. It felt a little too much like a trap.

Andy, on the other hand, was more than willing to go, having just had a lightbulb moment that had nothing to do with the party.

'I think that's a great idea mate, I'm down to come. I think we should all go. Come on, it'll be a bit of fun.'

Andy was great at coaxing groups into doing what he wanted having spent so much time as captain of the football team. Although, people were still unsure and Ella was the one to say what people were thinking.

'I mean it sounds like a great idea and I'm really happy you thought to invite us, Lud, but isn't it a little sketchy that we can't tell anyone?'

The tension in the room was building.

'Yeah, I see what you mean.' Ludwig started to scratch and ruffle his already messy hair. 'It's a good point. I just thought it would be fun to hang out, and there is a lot of alcohol to drink for free. It's just that it would technically be trespassing as it isn't my dad's bar anymore.'

This did nothing to ease people's tension. He was asking people who he didn't know to come and break the law with him. Andy was far too interested in the idea. Especially, for someone who had parties lined up for the rest of his life, and how breaking the law could screw up his plans at a scholarship.

'Look, guys, I know it doesn't sound great that it's technically illegal, but nobody will know. Plus, it would be awesome to get to know you all more.'

James didn't speak to Andy much, but he was never this keen to have a party. From what James knew, all Andy ever wanted to do was train and work out.

'How are we going to get in? We can't break a window. Right?' Ella asked this hoping more than anything they wouldn't be destroying a bar.

'No, nothing like that, my dad still has a key to the place. I can just get that and open the door, I could also turn on the power so that we can play on the machines, and because of the boards covering up the building, nobody will notice us.'

The fact that James could play on the machines did appeal to him but then there was that fear of going to a party with real people.

'All right, Lud, I'm in, but can we not tell any of our mates about this? They'll freak knowing that we are hanging with these Ramwall dudes.' Grayson said, putting his arm around his friend.

As James suspected, the rest of EE wouldn't have been so nice to them, and there were only a few minutes left until the bell would ring for them. Now that some of them had agreed to come, it wasn't hard for the rest of them to be convinced. The only people who hadn't said they were going were James and Michael, the two people who hadn't gone to a party in their lives. After some persuasion by Michael's blatant crush, he said that he would come along but might have to leave early for a family thing.

That was the classic excuse that James would always use and the one that had been taking over all his thoughts for what to do next. He was already meant to be going to a party in a week, which was bad enough, but now he was expected to go to a party in one day. It just didn't seem possible.

Just as James was going to open his mouth to say the old reliable excuse to a party invitation, Ella started to speak with her angelic voice that instantly grabbed his attention.

'So that settles it we are meeting there at 8:30ish.'

What a brilliant idea. Soon the EE students would fill the halls like a pack of hyenas looking for prey, not knowing there were some hiding in their den. James half-ran back to his desk where he picked up his bag so he could leave. On his way to the door, Ella intercepted him.

'Do you live close by, maybe we can walk to the bar together? I'm not keen on walking in the dark by myself.'

James was yet again shocked, a girl wanted to walk with him?

'Sure ... Wait sorry I mean, I can't ...' This was going to be his opportunity to say he couldn't make it to the party but the words wouldn't form properly. '...can't pick you up from your house, I have to do some family stuff but I can meet you at my house, it's on Foster Lane next to the burrito take-out place.'

This wasn't the exact answer she wanted but she went with it all the same.

'Ok, that works with me, I think I know where that is. Can I come a little after 8?'

Now there was no way of getting out of the party. James was thinking about just not showing up but now Ella would be going straight to his house, and he knew there was no way he could turn her away.

'Yeah, sure thing that's fine with me. I'll see you tomorrow then.'

Again, he tried to leave the classroom. James just wanted to get home and have a panic attack. Unfortunately, perfect people don't have that kind of problem and Ella wouldn't let him leave.

'Wait before you go, what's your number so I can say when I'm close by?'

Faster than the falling feeling James kept on experiencing, he scribbled down those magic numbers on a piece of card and shoved it into Ella's hand. The realisation that he would be going to a party in under twenty-four hours was hitting him, making him sweat profusely. Something that Ella didn't need to see.

Finally, James was able to leave the room. Just as he reached the door, he braved one last glance at Ella, who gave him a fleeting wave, which he tried his best to return as he bolted out of EE.

6. Swarm of Butterflies

There was not a single wearable outfit in James's wardrobe. Everything was horrible. He was amazed it took him this long to realise how ugly his clothes were. The colours didn't match, they were too small, or they could have been used as a Halloween costume. He had one suit that was used for his father's funeral, and he would rather be in a slutty nurse's outfit over that suit. This was meant to be a party, an enjoyable celebration. He didn't want any reminders of him crying his eyes out.

The rest of Friday was spent panicking about what he was going to do for the party. All he managed to achieve was making time fly so quickly he might as well have time-travelled. Before he knew it Saturday had rolled around and there were only a few hours until Ella would be on his street waiting for him.

He didn't have any clothes that he could borrow and James had left it far too late to go clothes shopping. James wished he had Tom to help him choose what to wear. Another cold sinking feeling of realisation went through his body. James hadn't even gotten to the party yet and was wanting his best friend by his side. It would be so much worse when he got there and didn't see a friendly face, someone he could trust.

The thought of just not going to the party at all entered his mind but very quickly left. *This is right. This is what Tom had to go through by himself and he grew from it, became a better person.*

After a lot of rummaging and indecisions, James found an outfit that was passable for what a normal person would wear. The outfit included dark blue jeans, a white T-shirt, and a black bomber jacket. It was different to his normal style of wearing whatever was closest to hand when he reached into the wardrobe, like some kind of pick-and-mix where the combination to choose from were snot, toilet water and mouldy bread.

Now that he had his outfit sorted there was the matter of putting on cologne. James wasn't the kind of person to normally use any sort of fragrance, but he wanted to smell good for Ella.

Going into the bathroom, James searched around in the cabinets for a bottle that had nice smelling liquid in it. After a close call where he almost sprayed on women's perfume, he settled on an unopened bottle of cologne that was given to him by his auntie many years ago. He sprayed it a couple of times, on his neck and then on his clothes. Whilst James was checking himself in the mirror, it dawned on him that he needed to shave.

Since he had turned sixteen, hair had been growing on his chin, not a lot but a noticeable amount. His dad had taught him how to shave a couple of weeks before he died. It was probably the last thing he had ever taught him. James didn't need to shave a lot, once or twice a month, which meant that he was still new to the whole experience.

With that nervous excited feeling that James had been having all day, he reached into the cabinet below the sink and grabbed out his box that contained his razors. As an extra safety precaution, James removed his jacket and shirt, in case he stained them with blood. After a thirty-minute shaving session, he had managed to do his first shave without cutting himself at all.

Sitting on his bed, he started to get even more anxious, a sickly feeling in his stomach. He would be leaving in around two hours so that they could get there for 8.30 p.m., although James didn't know if that was when he should arrive.

From what he knew about parties, which came predominantly from movies, turning up on time was never a cool thing to do. But this wasn't exactly a normal house party. Again, wanting help from Tom, he realised he had no idea what to do once he arrived. Then it hit him that the person in the room next to him was an expert at it. For all her useless qualities, she was going to be helpful now, parties were Kara's element.

Before making his way to Kara's room, James first made a detour to the loft where he moved a broken floorboard and picked up a box with a toy cuddly monkey in it. This would guarantee her help.

Awkwardly, he knocked on his sister's door. As Kara opened it, James noticed that she was regaining some of the colour in her face and was hopefully feeling better. He was thinking about asking her how she was doing but by the look of it, she was doing fine.

'I need your help,' he said.

Kara's face went from annoyed to complete confusion. James never asked for anything let alone assistance. 'You must be desperate to ask me for help.'

'Please.'

After a pause, where Kara seemed to weigh her options like James was asking for some massive favour and was seeing if it would be worth her time, she asked,

'What's in it for me?'

James knew that Kara didn't want anything for her help. She had said this to make James suffer a little before helping. That was her reward in a way, but he was going to do better.

'I'll give you back Mr Winston.'

Mr Winston was Kara's favourite cuddly toy. She used to take it everywhere when they were younger. Then one day after Kara was being annoying, James threw Mr Winston away. Kara had a meltdown and their parents went ballistic at him. After getting shouted at more than he had been for anything else in his life, he was sent to his room where he saw from his window that, by some miracle, Mr Winston was on the road. The toy must have fallen from the garbage truck right onto the concrete floor.

James had rescued the monkey but there was no need to give it back to Kara, he had already been told off for it and nothing was gained by giving it back. They couldn't un-shout at him. Kara had stopped crying about it by that point anyway, so she clearly didn't care that much.

Kara glanced at his hands to see if the toy was there, but they had been behind his back since the door opened.

'What do you mean? He's gone. You threw him away, remember.'

James couldn't help but smirk.

'I lied.' He brought his arms round to show her the toy.

Kara, as if holding ancient treasure, carefully took the monkey, and headed back into her bedroom without saying a word to James. The door was left open so he took it to mean that he was allowed in.

Before James could ask about his problems, he would have to explain himself to Kara, who was now cross-legged on her bed, cuddling Mr Winston. For some odd reason, she found the story exceptionally funny and by the time he had finished, she had laughed more than he had heard in a long time.

'So, what is it that you need help with then?' Kara asked, placing her old friend down on her side table.

Where should he start? There was so much about parties he had no idea about. James decided it would be best to start with the basics.

'I'm going to a party tonight, you know I've never been to a proper one before, what do I do?' He tried to keep the desperation at bay but his voice, as usual, failed him.

As expected, Kara was exceptionally helpful, telling him all about the parties she had gone to and what he could expect to happen. For the first time in far too long, James listened intently to his sister as she spoke about the stories she had to share.

Eventually, they reached the topic of alcohol. James had been pretty nervous about this part of the night. He would be drinking, there was no way to escape it. But as with most things, he hadn't tried alcohol before.

It came as a surprise when Kara showed off her secret alcohol supply. The surprise wasn't that she had one, that much was obvious. What shook James was that Kara decided to show him. Inside a large box that would have normally held a science experiment kit was a wide selection of 'grown-up drinks', as their grandma would say when she reached for her seventh helping at any special event.

They worked through each type of alcohol, having small portions as they went, trying to work out what kind of drink James enjoyed. As Kara started to prepare their fifth drink on the menu, James started to think that the world was spinning an awful lot. They had only tried a couple of different drinks but after one small tequila shot, some fruit cider, some beer, and some vodka lemonade, James was confident he was at least a little drunk.

Thinking about being sick started to make him feel even worse, but it was Kara passing him the new quarter filled cup of Jack Daniels and Coke that made him forget about the sickly feeling in his stomach. It wasn't the drink that helped, but Kara who was smiling back at him, in a way that was so similar to their dad.

It occurred to James that this was the first time they had done something together, other than eating food, since the funeral. They had both gone very different routes to stop the pain but now James could see in her eyes that they were in it together. That there was light at the end of the tunnel, and they would reach it together. As a family.

It wasn't hard to down the drink. It was probably the best tasting one so far. The real challenge was finishing the drink before Kara, who had been pouring herself full cups every time and was still finishing them well before James could finish his quarter-filled drinks.

'How are you doing?' James asked. He had been putting it off for too long and it was about time he said something. He wanted to know what the real answer was, and he wanted to help.

'I'm getting through it. One day at a time,' Kara said, draining the last of her cup.

James could tell there was pain in her voice, that she was struggling just as much as him. This was the first time James had made an effort to help his sister. It made him feel like a bad person that it had taken him so long when everyone else had been so kind to him.

James opened his mouth to speak without really knowing what he was going to say when Kara dropped her empty cup on the floor and gave her brother a tight hug. A phone was ringing and it made the pair let go of the other. James waited for Kara to answer her phone until he realised that it was him who was being called. Staring at his phone a little too long, waiting for it to come into focus, he noticed that it was Ella was calling.

There was no need to pick up, James knew exactly why she was phoning. He slowly stood up, using the doorframe as support and gave another glance to Kara who was smirking at him.

'You're ready, but next time I'm coming with.'

Moving away from the bedroom and carefully down the stairs, James thought about how decent his sister was, and at that moment it baffled him as to why he had been giving her the cold shoulder for so long. There was no way of denying it, Tom had been right, now was a time for a change.

Opening the door to the inviting darkness of the outside world, James flew over to Ella who was stunning in a lilac dress.

'You ready?' she asked, putting her phone away in a black handbag.

'I am now.'

No matter what happened tonight, James was glad that he had done this, not just for Tom but for himself. Many things took place in his head, but a week ago there wouldn't have been anything close to what was happening now. A tipsy James walking in the dark velvety night with a stunning girl next to him on the way to a secret party. *Now, this has to be a good life.*

Strolling towards their destination, James was filled with a kind of euphoria that was more than just the alcohol. It felt like so much of his life had been spent trying to avoid the present and worrying about the past and future that he had ended up missing everything. All those incredible moments he could have been having were wasted because he was too busy in his head. At this moment, instead of continually thinking about those things he missed, James made an effort to just enjoy the simply incredible walk.

The temperature was just right. Slightly warmer than normal, but with a brilliant breeze that cooled him down. If he closed his eyes, it wouldn't have been hard to imagine being on a ship, standing up at the highest point with the calm open seas around him. The wind, that in the real world was hitting against leaves, sounded like low mellow waves crashing into one another.

Opening his eyes, James thought that the long walk through the thick arched trees, so stunningly magical they could have been woven by elves, was better than the fake world he was imagining. The real world for once was more appealing than any imaginary reality he could think of. One foot placed itself in front of the counterpart as another gust of wind tingled his skin and sent mesmerizing rippling waves through his clothes.

What made the walk so much more incredible was that he could do it with such a pure, perfect person. The glow around her was still present, illuminating her stunning features. The few freckles scattered across her face were like the stars above them, giving even more beauty to the sky and to the face of a saint.

Time had given James a gift and allowed that one moment of a few steps and a long blink to be stretched into what seemed like an eternity, like a brief glimpse of heaven.

'Ella, I am going to be honest with you like you were with me. I've never really been to a party before or had much alcohol, and I got a small bit nervous about it. Now I am a little part tipsy as I was a small bit nervous.' James said, wanting Ella to know the truth about him.

There was the notion forming in his mind that Ella was going to be angry with him for being a total wreck before the party had even started. Instead of scrutinizing over the situation, James chose to look up past the dense rustling of trees crashing above him, to the sky which hosted great waves of clouds, bringing more darkness from above that would soon drown the pair of them. Not a bad type of drowning, like gagging for air desperately, but a warm cleansing kind like getting baptised or reborn. This oncoming storm was good.

Out of the corner of James's eye, he noticed that Ella was also looking up at the stars and the pair had reached a speed so slow they had might as well stop walking entirely.

'That's good to hear. That you're honest with me. It means a lot. Can I tell you something?'

There was no reason to say no and so the pair walked over to a bench that was off to the side of the path. James had no idea what she was going to say or what was going to happen but there was no point in worrying about it. So, he sat there patiently.

'I remember the first party I went to. It was horrible. Some cruel person went around giving drugs to people; some were pressured into taking whatever it was, and three kids ended up in the hospital. What I'm trying to say is that you don't have to do anything you aren't comfortable with. You can say no and I'll make sure people don't force things onto you.'

There it was again, that smile that made it so easy to trust and believe her. How could something so beautiful ever do bad? They sat on the bench with nothing being said and then out of the blue, Ella spoke once more.

'You were honest with me so it's only fair I return the favour.' She took a deep breath before she spoke. 'I had cancer.' The words were brutal and unforgiving. 'When I was eleven years old, they diagnosed me with it. After two of the most gruelling years I have ever had to experience, I was lying in the hospital bed getting prepped for my final surgery. There was a high chance that it would go well and that I would be cancer-free after, but there was also a chance I wouldn't pull through. Lying there in the ward with other patients just like me, I made a promise to myself. I had spent so much of my life like everyone else, following the herd, changing my personality to fit with other peoples and for what? I hadn't been myself long before the cancer. I had wasted so much of my life and only at that moment where it could be ending, I thought about how I should have just lived it the way I wanted to. I promised that if I were to survive, I wouldn't change who I was for anybody, I would be myself. Thankfully, the operation was successful and from that day, I made sure to keep my promise. That's why I pushed you to be truthful with me; life is too short to be someone else.'

There were now small diamond pearls coming from her eyes, dropping onto her dress. This was the kind of situation that James avoided as much as possible, but now he couldn't think of anything worse to do. He tried as hard as he could to say everything with a warm loving hug. His words always failed him.

James wasn't sure how much it worked, but soon Ella had regained her composure and was hugging him back. Her hair smelled like coconuts.

Wiping the few remaining tears from her eyes, she stood back up.

'We should get going. I'd hate to be late.'

Picking up her bag and handing it to her, James gave a look of understanding as they both wandered back onto the path, heading towards the moon like characters in a fairy-tale chasing after a happily-ever-after.

Joshua Stevens-Shachar

7. The Highs in Life

It didn't take them long to arrive at the Silver Chariot and as Ella and James reached the corner where the bar was, they could see that everyone else was waiting outside for them. Ludwig had mentioned that it would be better if they all went in at once so that he didn't have to keep on opening the door for arrivals, which could attract unwanted attention.

The Silver Chariot was a decently large bar on the corner of Hamlet Way and Church Street. All the bricks that made up the outside walls had been placed unevenly, making the building feel somewhat alive. Above the wooden memorial bench that was placed at the start of Church Street was a square sign that could be seen from the other end of the street. This sign had the Silver Chariot logo on it, a single Roman chariot entirely in silver on a dark midnight blue background.

Due to it being permanently closed, wooden boards had been placed on all the windows, hammered in with nails. Some of these boards had already been vandalised with spray paint, saying things like 'You got what you deserve' and other hurtful comments, feeding into that constant cycle of hatred that fuelled the evil in Echoway.

On the other side of Hamlet Way opposite the bar was a decently sized park surrounded by climbable trees that made it feel like you were the tallest person in town. Opposite Church Street stood a handful of shops a butchers, a small grocery store, and a local ice-cream store called Scooped. By this time in the evening, only the grocery store was open. It didn't appear as though they had any customers and it was far enough from the Silver Chariot that if anyone went out of the shop, they wouldn't hear or see anything.

There was no light coming from the Silver Chariot as everything had been shut off. The problem with this is that the bar's lights would normally illuminate the entire area. Without it, the T-junction felt awfully lonely and made the park appear much scarier in the darkness, lacking the lighthouse-like beacon to help show the way out.

James noticed that Michael was looking uncomfortable standing on the concrete pavement. It dawned on James that they were feeling a lot of the same things and were in the same boat, with one of the major differences that James had someone to help him.

Having gone to church at the same place as Michael's family, he knew that Michael didn't have any siblings to help him out. He also had just as many friends as James, but dissimilar to Tom, Emma Rodgers never went to parties.

Due to this, his clothing choices were a lot more generic. He had clearly decided to keep it as normal and bland as possible, wearing black chinos and a buttoned-up long-sleeved shirt as though he was going to a bar-mitzvah party. A tiny amount of sympathy went through James but there was no real need for it. Michael was very interested in his new friend and it was clear that he thought his night, like James's, would be one to remember.

Something that had been bugging James was why Andy agreed to come to the party, and why he was excited to hang out with one of the strangest assortments of teens in the town. He was, by far, the most popular person in Ramwall, so he had no real need to go to such a small secret party.

They didn't wait outside for long after James and Ella reached the steps leading up to the bar. Ludwig opened the entrance door with Andy quick to enter behind, along with Grayson. All three of them were wearing casual clothing that any sane person would bring to a party.

Stepping into the bar was like going into a fancy isolation chamber. The minor noises that could be heard outside immediately disappeared, as Michael shut the door behind everyone, cutting off their connection to the world.

After a few minutes, Ludwig managed to find the power box and turned on the lights and machines. He quickly removed all the bulbs from the entrance, having forgotten to unscrew them before.

James wasn't sure how strange or unique this situation was, but by the looks of awe on everyone else's faces, he worked out that it was a pretty special moment. He was noticing that the world was spinning a little less than on the walk over. James must have started to sober up already, but as Ludwig carefully unpackaged a box to reveal heaps of alcohol, James deduced that he wouldn't be staying sober for long.

There was carpet on the floor that was the same dark blue as the background on the Silver Chariot sign and had a design similar to the bus seats James would occasionally use, with random lines scattered around, all with different colours and curves.

Sets of tables were scattered around the bar with chairs put on top, upside down so that it looked neater. Grayson and Ludwig went over to a particularly large table and started to take down the chairs for people. Soon, seven chairs around two tables had been set up, and they all took their seats as Ludwig placed several bottles of different alcoholic drinks and mixers in the centre of the tables.

Close by to where Ella and James had chosen to sit was a machine that kept on playing the same repetitive tune in a way that, for some reason, made him more comfortable. It reminded him of when his family would go to places similar to this and have lunch at the weekend after a nice day out.

It took next to no time for Ella and James to get tipsy, along with Michael's friend who seemed to know her way around a drink. She suggested different things that Michael might like to try until he couldn't say no anymore and started to sip from a glass of vodka and lemonade, which he appeared to enjoy, or at least could keep in his stomach.

On the other side of the coin, Ludwig, Andy, and Grayson were people that went out often. They were downing drinks at triple the pace of the other four. After a couple of minutes, James and Ella found themselves playing a spot-the-difference game on one of the machines as the rest of the crowd drank even more. Andy encouraged people to drink by introducing different games to play, like the ring of fire and coin flick.

For once James found a positive to playing so many video games. He was like an apex robot, finding one error after another, leaving Ella in complete amazement of his skill. Every time he cleared a level with some minor help from her, they would high five and get all excited.

Not long into their win streak, Michael and the other girl started looking in on them, cheering along as the levels became harder. Whilst Grayson and Ludwig played pool, with Andy refilling everyone's drinks.

The whole group was having a fantastic time and after around an hour and a half of non-stop drinking, everyone was dreadfully singing Wonderwall. To an outsider, the noise the group were creating would have been similar to a dying elephant, but to James, who had never sung in front of other people before, thought it was the most exquisite noise ever. The idea of all of them forming a band was becoming more and more appealing.

After they finished singing, everyone sat back down, Ella moving her chair closer to James. Total silence filled the room, not the normal awkward silence that James was so used to. Instead, it was a new kind, it was like those few seconds after an incredible performance had finished, where everyone lay silent, the booming cheering soon to follow. The silence before the applause.

Ludwig knew that nothing short of spectacular had to follow this kind of silence, and so did his best to rise, grabbing the whole audience's attention, and the back of his chair.

'I reckon we- now hear me out. We should all do what we tech-ni-ca-lly came here to do.'

His speech wasn't the best, or the most punctual, and he had to slow down saying 'technically', but James had never been so intrigued. Unfortunately, the rest of the group weren't so inspired.

'The fuck are you talking about Lud?' Grayson said.

Grayson, who was able to string words together, became much bolder under the influence. Almost rocking his chair over as he sat back down, leaning over the table to make everything more intense, Ludwig continued speaking, now directly to Grayson.

'Getting to know the others. That was the whole point of this. We thought we could do it better than thingy ... but I still don't know anything about all you Ramwall lads.'

His English was starting to fail him, but James got the point all the same. Time to share. Grayson slumped more in his chair and put his arms on the back of his head, showing off his muscles with a shrug.

'Fair enough. Andy, why don't you tell us something about yourself. Something interesting.'

The eyes of the party that had followed Grayson and Ludwig now fell onto Andy, who was thinking about something else entirely.

'Alright, let's see. Well, I was born into a pretty poor family. We had no money for anything, all my clothes were from charity shops. It was humiliating. That's the main reason why I'm so focused on football, ya know? If I get a scholarship, I can go pro and then leave poverty behind. God, I would do anything to make sure I don't stay poor.'

Inside the warm Silver Chariot, the first secret of the night had just been shared and now James started to understand why it was that Hercules came tonight. Alcohol was expensive, at this party it was all free and people wouldn't judge him for being poor. A pat on the shoulder was given by Grayson as a sign of gratitude for speaking so openly.

'I've told very few people this because it's the kind of thing that can ruin my entire career, and my so-called friends aren't exactly ... here it is. I'm gay.'

Grayson had his head down looking at the mildly sticky tables as though he had just told his military parents and they were shouting at him.

'That sucks that you think you have to hide who you are, but you know what, don't worry. We're here for you now,' Ella said, softly holding his shoulder.

Now it was clear as to why Grayson had decided to come tonight. Similar to Andy, he wanted to be with people who just maybe wanted to have a good time, where he didn't have to worry about who he was or act differently for the sake of his future.

They all smiled at one another. It was a strange situation. People who had been sworn enemies a couple of days ago were now sharing some of their deepest secrets and concerns. Magic was in the air and allowed things to be said that normally would be terrifying.

'What a beauty of a point, I think we should all do a shot to celebrate this lovely friendship we all made, although you'd done the tell me about that already, Grayson.'

Ludwig was beyond drunk at this point but nobody could refuse the poorly poured shot. Not even Michael. Ludwig was right, they were all becoming friends.

Naturally, the shot of clear liquid tasted like petrol oil that had been set alight as it passed down James's throat. Even though it hurt, he kept it inside him and rejoiced over that perfect moment.

Miraculously, Ludwig was still conscious and was again the first to speak.

'Right well I guess it's my turn for sharing time. I fucking despise my father. I hate him so very much. He's the reason I had to leave Sweden, my happy city with all my friends, even Pete with his funny hat. Dad's now the reason why my mum has to work extra shifts because he was so stupid, he did no bills!'

Furious, Ludwig picked up an empty bottle and chucked it at the wall where it shattered into many sharp pieces, dropping his head onto the table.

'I'll get that in a second my bad.'

All the drunks jumped in their seats when the bottle smashed, Grayson went to punch Ludwig in the arm in a way of telling him off but stopped at the last second as there was now light snoring coming from the Swede. The whole table sat shocked by what had just happened, knowing there wasn't anything they could do to help, except let him sleep and sober up.

Grayson, looking for a way to move the situation away from Ludwig, turned his head to James, letting his arm limp over the side of the chair.

'James, isn't it? Your turn now, tell us something about yourself, but maybe don't pass out after.'

As one would expect, James had been sitting in silence for the past couple of minutes, knowing this moment would come. Where he would have to share something that would amount to the other secrets. Now that James's time had come, his breathing was steady and the alcohol helped numb the fear.

'I guess that I sometimes worry that the only part of me, who I am, the only thing people know me for is that my dad died stopping a school shooter. For a long time now, I've been someone I'm not. It felt impossible to move on from what happened, but now I just want to have a good time again, like right now with all of you people. I'm grateful I found you all.'

A wonderful warmth filled James on the inside. A sense of relief broke down some of the infection that had been in him for so long. More bliss pulsated on the outside of his body and it took him several moments to realise that Ella was hugging him again. Not long after that, he realised that life was going to be something special from now on.

Next up to speak was Ella, who retold the story about how she almost died from cancer and the genuine fear she would experience where she didn't know if she would wake from her sleep. It was a rather depressing couple of moments that were filled only with the happy melodies of the machines, enticing people to play.

The room turned to face Michael. However, nobody would ever get to hear his story as he ran towards the toilet to presumably throw up or hide from the pressure. From there, the whole sharing section of the night seemed to come to an end as the ponytail girl went into the toilet to help, and it didn't take long for Andy and Grayson to attempt a game of darts where the real game was to just hit the board and not the wall.

It was just Ella and James at the table, at least the only conscious people at the table. James, who had been getting more and more confident with each sip of his drink, decided that it would be a good time to ask Ella about her bracelets and bands, touching each one and grazing her arms as casually as he could.

As was expected, every bracelet around Ella's wrist meant something special to her and they spent a good while speaking about each one. She mentioned that the ones she wore tonight never left her reach. One was a band she received from the hospital when she was cancer-free. Another was a Pandora's bracelet that had multiple charms on it given to her by parents and friends, an easy gift James could get her.

Lastly, she had a blue hairband a similar colour to that of the cancer band, which made it blend in. This was from another girl she had met during her treatment that had bright blue hair. Unfortunately, she didn't beat cancer, and because of that Ella chose to carry the weight of a life not fully lived with her at all times. It was a constant reminder that she had to live her best life, not just for herself but to continue the legacy of a friend that wasn't as lucky as her.

Shortly after their conversation, Andy and Grayson came back to the table, having possibly played the worst and last game of darts the bar would ever see.

'Andy and I were just wondering if you wanted to, now no pressure, if any of you wanted to try a little zoot?'

As Grayson was saying this, Andy removed a pencil-shaped paper-lined item from his pocket that looked a lot like a cigarette but smelled much less like death. Ella sat back and lightly ran her middle and index fingers over her lip.

'Hmm. Maybe, what do you think James? I won't do any if you're not comfortable. Remember nothing you don't want to do.'

Thinking it through, weed had the potential to make the night so much better than it was. Considering this was probably the best night of his life, James was curious to see what better looked like. Although was it worth possibly throwing away such a perfect night by being sick? As if Grayson was reading his mind, he sat down at the chair next to him and did some extra explaining.

'There is genuinely no pressure. If you have none, that just means more for us, but if you do want to try some or are on the fence, this joint is kinda weak. Unlike other drugs or even alcohol, you can't overdose from this, and of course, we'd keep an eye on you.'

A small grunt from Andy confirmed that they would indeed make sure he was fine. Since Andy spoke about being poor, he had become much more reclusive than normal. Barely saying anything and thinking far too much for someone who was meant to be having a good time.

After this information from Grayson, who James was growing to like a lot, there didn't appear to be a reason not to try at least a little.

'Yeah, sure, why not, I'll give it a go.'

They gave a little cheer, and the four of them left their seats and moved into a small garden area, leaving the unconscious Ludwig alone at the table.

It was again another strange experience huddled around closely with Hercules, a rival football player, and the most beautiful person James had ever seen, all staring at the joint in the centre of their square.

As it lit James became mesmerised by the embers formed at the front, and how bright it became when Andy inhaled, then with how much smoke came from his mouth afterwards. The smell was oddly appealing. It didn't smell at all like what he had built it up in his head. Instead, it was more of a medicinal smell that you wouldn't think out of place at a spa, or perhaps at a flower store next to some lavender.

James was the last person to be handed the joint and when Grayson was smoking it, he taught him how to properly inhale the smoke. Apparently, you could breathe wrong, which didn't seem possible to James. But not wanting to look stupid, he made sure to follow the instructions exactly.

The first breath he took was a strange sensation; it almost felt like he was wearing a gas mask or trying to breathe from a bottle. Ultimately, he was breathing in fire fumes so he assumed it was meant to feel strange. Once he inhaled the second time, he could visualise the smoke going through his body down into his lungs, until he started to cough. Grayson had mentioned that if that were to happen, it was good. It meant that he had done it correctly. However, he failed to mention how much he would be coughing. After Ella smacked his back a few times, James felt as good as new, maybe even better.

All the others were giving encouraging smiles and words of support which meant a lot to James, even if he felt lame for coughing when nobody else did. The idea of trying again came to his mind, but before he could move his arm towards his mouth, Grayson had extended his hand to take the joint back.

'That should get you to a nice spot for the rest of the night, don't try anymore. Might ruin it.'

Andy thought differently and kept on offering more to James, which he declined, going with Grayson's advice. It took a surprisingly short amount of time for the effects to show in the form of a fuzzy head and the world seeming to spin a little more wackily than it already had been.

All James could think about was a joke Kara had told him years ago that would fit spectacularly in this situation if only he could remember it.

All noise dispersed into nothingness as his brain zoomed around all his memories, trying to discover the one with the joke. A flashing image of a whale flickered into his mind and he knew it was something to do with that.

Another problem now presented itself as James couldn't stop laughing. It might have just been the funniest thing anyone could ever say at that moment in time. A small amount of ash dropped to the floor as Andy, Grayson, and Ella all turned to James who was bright red, putting his hand up at them, indicating to wait a second for he had something important to say.

Smiling with a slight tilt to her head Ella asked,

'How's it going?'

Being part of the conversation just made the joke funnier, now it was hard to breathe, let alone speak. In the end, there was no need to tell the joke, Grayson and Ella joined in with the contagious laughter, even though they had no idea what was so funny.

Grayson held his stomach due to the pain of laughing too hard. Once he had started to laugh, like James, he seemed unable to stop. Ecstatic happiness filled James as he took deep breaths, gazing at the bright embers of the universe.

After they had managed to cool down and stop laughing, James started to have the sensation of needing to pee desperately. Walking on the stone floor made it feel like the world was rotating around him, causing him to stumble ungracefully every time his feet collided with the ground. Grayson reached out, ready to catch James if he fell which didn't happen but James still thanked him for the gesture.

'You don't need to thank me, man, where are you heading, you all good?' Grayson asked, worried that James was feeling ill.

'Everything's dandy,' James told Grayson, his respect towards him growing greatly. 'I just have to go to the bathroom. Be right back.'

As he left James pointed a finger gun at Ella, pretending to shoot her for no reason other than thinking it would be funny, and he was glad to see Ella reacting as if she had been shot.

8. An Unexpected Guest

Finding the bathroom was a struggle. James had never been to the Silver Chariot sober. Ideas continued to pour into his head, each one more interesting and important than the last. Thinking of how he could become rich by following a rainbow, the colourful lines on the carpet seemed to invite him into a game of tic-tac-toe.

The narrow corridor watched as James hopped and jumped around like a baby kangaroo chasing a laser. A door appeared in the hallway with a drawing of a male stickman, which James greeted with a fist bump as he waltzed into the toilet.

This bathroom stank more than anything James's nose had inhaled before. A mixture of dry sick and cheap soap filled the small area and into the many cracks displayed along the filthy walls.

A couple of minutes later, he found himself back outside, gulping the fresh air like a fish put back into the water after being hooked. Nobody was outside anymore, but a faint noise from within told James that the party had resumed by their table and so taking one last look at the starry sky, he strolled towards his new friends.

Grayson and Ella had sat down back at the table with a still unconscious Ludwig, and they waved James over, inviting him to sit with them.

'Does the purple frog dance in the waxy sky or perhaps it eats onion tacos during the day?' exclaimed Grayson, turning to Ella who seemed to be in deep thought at this.

'Maybe if the skeleton wore a neon sticky note on his arm instead of his gun, the clocks would make pencil pizza?'

James was only half listening to these sentences and was more interested in how odd the word moist was as he stared at his wet hands, which he realised hadn't been dried. He only started to fully focus on the group when Ella spoke directly to him.

'If I were to see snow in a monk's temple as a yellow car driven by a drum swims by, would it be the correct pattern?' she asked.

There was now one question going through James's head, and that was if he was having some kind of stroke. A small tinge of panic rippled through his bones at the thought of being rushed to hospital, but after staring into Ella's face, he realised that he was fine. If something was wrong with him, he wouldn't be able to see something so perfect.

During this time where James must have been staring into Ella's eyes in complete disbelief and concentration, everyone seemed to be laughing.

'We're just fucking with you mate, don't worry about it.' Grayson giggled as he proceeded to drink even more alcohol, given to him by Andy, who had found another unopened box filled with beer.

A bang from the entrance door made everyone jump. Had someone overheard them? Or maybe Ludwig's dad had noticed his keys were missing and had come to investigate? The door continued to bang, and Ludwig was still out cold, with everyone else staying completely still in absolute silence.

The rusty doorknob wiggled and the door slowly creaked open. Apparently, no one had locked the door. A streak of moonlight started to ease into the room as a figure slipped into the place of solitude.

At first, James thought that the shadow of the person had entered. He stared at the door to see who it belonged to.

'How the fuck did you get here?' Andy said, crushing his can of beer spilling the liquid onto the carpet.

At that moment it dawned on him that the black figure wasn't a shadow, but a person dressed in full black.

'You didn't think you could have a party without me, could you? I'm hurt. Oh well, make it up to me by pouring us a drink,' Sarah spoke as though the group had invited her, with this surprise entrance being a happy one.

'I'm not pouring you shit, who told you about this!' Grayson had gotten to his feet, which was no small feat considering how hammered he was.

At this, everyone looked at Sarah and then one another. Michael and the other girl were cowering in a corner next to the toilet but shook their heads vigorously when Andy turned to them.

'Ella, I bet it was you that invited her, you just couldn't keep quiet, could you!' Andy shouted, pointing a stern finger at her.

'Don't blame the EE kids, she goes to your dump, one of you must have invited her,' Grayson rounded on Andy, getting up close to him.

There it was. That constant idea that the EE people were better than the Ramwall students. Even Grayson, who was so kind, had it embedded in him.

'The fuck do you mean dump? You've known her longer, obviously it was one of you spoiled brats!' Andy shoved Grayson away from him.

The two showed signs that they were about to fight. Andy pulled up his sleeves, his bulging muscles flexing, and Grayson started raising his fists. Andy and Grayson who had been singing arm in arm a few hours ago, appeared to have nothing but complete disgust for the other now. The entire group was arguing, EE and Ramwall divided as usual.

'I love it when people fight over me,' Sarah said as she started concocting a drink mixed with whatever still had liquid in it.

The second Sarah arrived at the party, everyone was at each other's throats. As if she was a poison that had infected their sanctuary.

'Sarah, who invited you?' Ella said, trying to stop things from escalating.

Drinking from a pitcher she had found lying around, Sarah again grabbed the attention of the entire room. It was as though there had been a murder and she was the detective who would say who'd done it. Andy and Grayson, still close to fighting, had taken a temporary truce to see if she would respond with an answer.

'You know I could tell you who told me about tonight, but that just spoils all the fun we're having. How about we all do some shots instead?'

'Get out!' Both Andy and Grayson shouted.

Sarah shrugged and opened a new cardboard box filled with alcohol and started drinking from a can of cider.

'I mean it was probably Ludwig who invited her. He was the one who suggested this in the first place.' James had been desperate to say anything of value in his high-drunk state, just to prove that he wasn't like Michael, cowering away in a corner. Out cold slumped over the sticky table, Ludwig slept in a peaceful slumber.

'That does make the most sense, it was on him for not locking up in the first place.' Andy spoke in a triumphant tone, as if believing that Ludwig had been responsible meant the problem had fixed itself.

Most of the group nodded their heads in recognition that it was probably Ludwig. In the meantime, Sarah had almost cleared the entire box of cans by downing each and every one.

'It doesn't matter who invited her anymore. Just leave, nobody wants you here, Sarah.' Grayson said, lowering his fist as the tension started to diffuse.

She continued to drink as if it was her birthday party.

'I'm not going anywhere, not when there's so much free stuff, and if you throw me out, I'll just report you to the police. I'm pretty sure this counts as trespassing. It would be a shame if you all had to get written up in a police report. That stuff can go on your permanent record. Makes it much harder to get scholarships, you know.'

Grayson stormed out into the garden area to cool off, not saying another word, and Andy went off into a different area to play on one of the machines. A few minutes of nothingness passed where Michael and the smart girl, whose name James still couldn't work out, left to go and look around the kitchen for no real reason other than to just get away from the awkwardness. Not long after, Ella asked James to show her where the toilets were, leaving Sarah to drink alone.

Waiting outside the tic-tac-toe hallway as Ella used the girl's bathroom that hopefully didn't smell as bad as the boys, James leant against the wall and pondered over the last few hours. As to how a perfect group started to fall apart with the presence of just one bad person. Would the two schools' relationships always be this fragile? Able to shatter so easily? He hoped not. James was starting to grow happy, and he would hate for the strange group to grow apart.

Ella came out of the bathroom whirling one of her bands with one finger around her wrist, and lent next to the same wall as James. She was so close that their shoulders were touching and their arms had almost overlapped.

'Even with the surprise visit, I've had a really good night with you, James, but maybe next time we go out, it could be just the two of us?' She was speaking softly and carefully as her hand slipped into his.

'Yeah same, you're really fun to be around'

It was obvious what might be happening in a few seconds, but James had no idea how to get there or what to say. Ella was now so close that he could see her lips shining more than before.

Terror started to build up inside James as he wasn't sure if Ella could hear how loud his heart was thumping against his chest, but now she was so close, she had to tilt her head so their noses wouldn't collide. Just as she closed her eyes and started to lean in towards his lips, several thunderous bangs and crashes filled the hallway. Making both of them jump causing their heads to smack.

Pressing their hands on the wall for support as they rubbed their heads, James and Ella stared down the hall where the noises had echoed from. They started to run back to the main area to find out what had ruined such an important moment.

The entire group was huddled around something on the floor and from what James could see, it looked as though someone had dropped a box filled with red wine. The noise had woken Ludwig who had a look of complete shock and horror as the red liquid started to seep into the carpet that would surely stain.

Just as James was going to suggest to Ella that they have another wander away from everyone else, she let out a scream. Nobody else was speaking, not a single person made any indication that she shouldn't be screaming over spilt wine, especially when people weren't meant to know they were there.

It was only when James moved a little closer to the scene, that he realised the red liquid seeping into the carpet wasn't wine. It was blood. In the centre of the huddle was Sarah on the floor, unmoving. James felt a sharp grip on his arm as Ella clutched him for support.

'What happened? Someone help her.' Ella's breathing was quick and harsh.

Andy was already kneeling in the pool of blood, trying to feel for a pulse with a trembling hand that made it look like Sarah was shivering.

'She's, she's, there isn't a pulse.' Andy had his eyes shut tight as though he would open them again and it would have all been a terrible dream. 'She's dead.'

Those close to the scene staggered away from the body. Some tried desperately not to let their legs buckle, leaning on anything to support them. Grayson found a chair away from it all and dropped down into it, covering his face with open hands.

Michael and Ludwig couldn't bring themselves to blink, staring directly at Sarah, unable to look away. James tried to make sense of it all. How did this happen?

'W-What happened?' Ella asked, tears running down her face.

She started shivering uncontrollably, her body deflating as it fell into James's arms. James was still expecting Sarah to get up laughing as if she had pranked them.

Andy, still kneeling next to the body trying to find signs of life, seemed like the only person capable of speaking.

'I don't know. I saw her standing on the table, she had just downed some vodka. She just ... She just slipped. Must have lost her balance or something, but she fell. She fell and smacked her head on the table.'

There wasn't any point in Andy pointing towards the table next to him, it was obvious that was where she had fallen, because there was a massive splatter of blood that graffitied the old scratched table, now with a small corner broken off.

Explaining how it happened seemed to bring life to the rest of the group as they started to breathe heavily, break down into tears, or hyperventilate.

'No, no, no. We're so dead. I'm going to jail. We are all so screwed.' Ludwig shook his head, still refusing to look away from Sarah.

'No that's not true, we didn't do anything wrong, it was just an accident.' Michael tried his best to not freak out but there was a worrying amount of sweat coming from his face that mixed with his tears, as he started to pace up and down the room.

'Won't mean shit, we can't prove it was an accident, and people wouldn't believe it. Most of us hated her. Everyone's going to think we killed her.' Grayson brought his knees up to his head, hiding his face.

'We need to call an ambulance, we might be able to help her.' James, who had now seen a person lying in their blood twice in a year, wasn't about to let Sarah die so easily.

Andy was soaked in blood but still responded quicker than he could down a drink. 'NO! We can't call anyone. She's dead, there's nothing we can do for her. We call someone and we are all done, I lose any scholarship. We lose our entire life.'

'This is someone's life we're talking about; your scholarship isn't worth more than a life. If we can help her, we should.' Ella said with disgust.

'Obviously we would help her if we could, but there's no point. She hasn't got a pulse, go over and check yourself if you want. I'm not going to get my life destroyed trying to help someone who can't be saved.' Andy had lost the colour in his face.

By now the blood had stopped spreading from the back of Sarah's head, which was luckily not visible to anyone, although the rancid smell of fresh blood was now potent in the room, giving horrid flashbacks to James and scarring everyone else for the rest of their lives.

'Where's Lilith?' Andy asked.

James was momentarily distracted from the horrible situation to look around for someone he had never heard of.

'She left. She didn't want to be here anymore.' Michael said this with such sadness and despair that James finally knew the name of the red-haired ponytail girl.

James had no idea why Lilith was no longer in the Silver Chariot, but whatever happened to make her leave meant that she could wake up the next day without the thought of a dead body burned into her mind.

It took a long time for anyone to speak again. They were all thinking hard about what was about to happen to their lives, about how one small accident at the wrong place and time could lead to innocent people getting arrested for murder.

'So, what should we do?' Ludwig was looking at Grayson for help as though he would be able to reverse time and make it all better again.

Andy answered instead. 'I mean, the only thing we can do, the only way we all get out of this now without getting arrested, we have to hide the body. We have to pretend like nothing has happened.'

9. Pray for the Wicked

The shower in James's house was burning hot. It helped remove the small specks of Sarah's blood that had managed to stain his skin, whilst making it feel like he was burning in hell. James had destroyed his blood-covered clothes in the firepit that was part of the garden area within the Silver Chariot, just like everyone else. It had to be done so that nothing could be traced back to any of them. The walk back home wearing old mingy clothes left in the lost and found felt like a fever dream. Nothing seemed real anymore.

His mind raced faster than he thought possible. It had been racing since he saw Sarah on the floor. The image still burnt into his retinas and was the only thing he could see when he closed his eyes. James knew that when eventually he fell asleep or, more correctly, passed out, the nightmares would be so much worse than anything he had previously endured.

Most of the evening had turned into a blur, especially after he became high, which he was starting to become increasingly thankful for. Being able to remember the entire night would be a recipe for insanity.

Some moments from the evening had gripped on to his brain with razor-sharp claws. Like when Andy made him clean up all the blood with Ella, using as many supplies as they could find. Ella had been arguing with Andy a lot because she thought what they were doing was wrong. However, out of fear, she stopped complaining once Andy punched Michael in the face for trying to call an ambulance.

James could also remember Grayson and Ludwig carrying a large black bin bag, like Lumberjacks lifting wood, over to the park. The two of them had drawn the short plastic straw and were responsible for burying her.

Sarah wasn't a good person, that much everyone knew; but she didn't deserve to die. Nobody deserves to die. James had to continuously remind himself that really, he wasn't doing anything wrong, just what he had to do. There was no alternative solution that didn't give him jail time. He kept on thinking that he didn't deserve to go to prison for witnessing a completely accidental death.

Six people had contributed to covering up Sarah's death. All of them had now committed a crime. Before, if the police had arrived at the scene, it would have looked like they had committed murder. In that situation, Sarah would still be dead, and six teenagers would be sent on trial for murder, then it would be up to the jury to decide whether they were telling the truth or not.

Now, having covered up Sarah's death, if discovered they would without question go to prison for a great deal of their lives. However, it seemed impossible that anyone would work out what had happened. The only consequences they would have to deal with was the knowledge of what they had all seen and done.

Without Andy, they would have still been at the Silver Chariot freaking out. Andy worked out how they could escape the situation. How there was the park next to them with plenty of weak soil they could dig up. He even managed to find tools that had been left behind at the bar to help Ludwig and Grayson bury the body. He went around with a terrified Michael cleaning up any evidence that they were there, from fingerprints on surfaces to throwing away all the empty bottles of alcohol they had consumed. Andy made sure that they would have a chance of getting away with their horrible act.

The now cold water had caused James's fingertips to shrivel up and he had no idea how long the shower had been on. Drying himself slowly with a towel, James couldn't help but wonder if he was an evil person. If he should just turn himself over to the police and have that shower be the last mildly relaxing moment he would ever experience. The night turned into day as James sat on his bed, pondering the idea.

The birds had started to chirp. This didn't feel right. They should be screaming instead of singing. It was almost comforting that the birds hadn't discovered what had happened; perhaps if the birds didn't think anything was wrong, nobody would realise that during the night someone in Echoway had died.

It didn't seem real that by Monday all of them would have to go to school and pretend like everything was fine. As if they hadn't just seen a person die and then participated in the hiding of that body. Lilith got lucky, presumably not that lucky considering how heartbroken Michael seemed on top of everything else, but she didn't have to deal with covering up the death of another person.

As they all came up with alibis, a swollen-eyed Michael had realised it was going to be a problem with Lilith. None of them could mention what had happened to Sarah, but Lilith needed to be part of an alibi in case someone questioned her. In the end, Grayson managed to convince Ella, who was sobbing in James's arms, to tell Lilith that she went on a double date with Michael and James. It would need to be explained that Lilith needed to go with the story because nobody could know they were at the Silver Chariot, as it was trespassing. They then had to hope that Sarah's body wasn't found, or Lilith would start to wonder if they had killed her.

There was only one small spark of hope that James had when it came to getting away with what he had done. Nobody that went to the Silver Chariot party told anyone else that they were going. In theory, if one person got caught there was no way they could pin it on anyone else.

What made this even better was that nobody had any real connection to anyone else, except for the program, which was such a small link there would be no chance of it being thought of by the police. So, even though their chances of survival were pathetic, each person still had a chance.

Coming up with alibis had been tricky. It was vital everyone had one, in case they became suspects. Ella, James, and Michael's alibi would be the double date picnic in the park next to Silver Chariot. It wasn't the most realistic alibi, but it would hopefully do the job. There weren't any known cameras in the park, which was also why they buried the body there.

Unfortunately, they had to be in the same park as the body because Michael told his parents he was doing exactly what his alibi was, which is how they came up with it in the first place. Ella's parents had a 'find my friend' app which showed her location at all times, so she had to be somewhere near the Silver Chariot for it to be plausible for where she spent the night.

Grayson and Ludwig were already in the same friend group so their story would be that they hung out at Grayson's house, whose parents were away, and Ludwig never told his parents anything, so they both had their backs covered.

The real problem for an alibi was Andy, who had told Daphne and all his many friends that he needed to stay home and train, but told his parents that he was heading to a party. If he wasn't the most popular person in school, it would be much harder for people to remember if he was at a large party or not. Andy decided that he would just have to wing it, hoping that nobody would ask for an alibi since there was no real reason to do so.

 Luckily Ludwig's father had invested in lots of sprays and foams that removed things from carpet like alcohol, sick, and now blood. Ella and James cleaned up the blood with relative ease. Whilst the physical part was easy enough, the mental problem of cleaning fresh blood from a motionless body, was sure to create lasting damage to the pair of them.

By now the sun had completed its daily task of filling light into James' room and it was at this point he decided not to turn himself in. He would at the very least try and continue living a normal life. It was possible. Surely people had done something similar before. Plenty of murders had gone unsolved, this was a step much lower than intentional killing, so the solve rate would be even lower.

Nobody had declared Sarah as missing yet. The police hadn't found a body. Nobody suspected James of a single thing. That was a lot of stuff that needed to happen before he was in danger. If the police didn't find anything, Sarah would be reported as missing, and then presumably be marked up as a runaway. After that, they would be in the clear. One awful accident would not be the end of six incredible people's lives.

James recalled the heat coming from the burning clothes in the garden area. How they all stood around like homeless people desperate for warmth. Ella had said a few words about Sarah as if it was her funeral. There wasn't much she could say, having barely met her, but it was the least they could do. It didn't seem like she would ever receive a proper burial.

Today was Sunday. James's mum would be shopping for most of the day, leaving him in the house with Kara, who was undoubtedly going to ask about the party. James wasn't sure if he could talk about the night without breaking down into tears, even if he was only speaking about the fantastic parts of the night. The freezeframe of Sarah would always be at the back of his mind, haunting his every sentence.

Telling Kara about everything crossed his mind a few times. She was the only person he trusted enough to explain what had happened. The reason he wasn't going to now was because he was terrified of Andy, who had become unhinged by the end of the ordeal.

Having smashed multiple bottles when being contradicted about what they should do, and punching Michael in the face, everyone, even Grayson, became nervous and cautious around him whilst already trying to do unthinkable things for the 'sake of survival', as Andy kept on saying. Because Andy was so terrifying, nobody would have the courage to snitch about what had happened.

James wanted to believe that Andy was still a good person, the one that was adored by everyone, who would lift everyone's spirit up by simply being near them. That he was just looking out for all of them by making sure they got to live a life and had to be aggressive so that everything would be done as quickly and effectively as possible.

Grayson managed to stay as calm as he could throughout everything. Being raised in a military family came into practice, and helped him stay controlled under such a high-pressure situation. Although it pained him every second, Grayson was able to keep the rest of the group sane and anchored about what they needed to do. He calmed people down when they broke down on the floor, acting almost like a fairy godmother, doing his best to take care of everyone.

James had thought about everything five times over in as many different disjointed ways, angles, and interpretations as possible. All that was left now was to try and get some rest and wait to see what the following hours would bring.

After cowering in his bed for a little longer, he slowly managed to close his eyes long enough to pass out, where he spent many hours escaping a living nightmare to explore new ones.

As expected, James experienced many excruciating dreams about dead bodies, blood, and falling down a massive pit in a barren park filled with skeletons. Just as it would become too much, he would see Ella in the distance, and everything else would melt away, allowing for a few seconds of peace. Inevitably the next sequence of hell would continue, ending with Ella again, saving him just as he was getting overwhelmed by whatever was tormenting him. She was the angel from his nightmare.

By the time James awoke in a sweat from his dreadful sleep, it was just past 2.00 p.m. Kara had presumably stayed in her room all day, which was both good and bad. On one hand, it was worrying how ill she had become over the past few days; on the positive side, it meant that he didn't have to deal with any hard questions.

James checked his phone to see that he had a message from Ella. She wanted everyone to meet up again so that they could talk through what happened. Normally, James would have protested at having everyone together, considering how it was bound to be noticed and could raise suspicion. Nevertheless, he agreed to find Michael and Andy and bring them to the cinema, purely so that he could spend more time with Ella. The cinema felt like the best way to talk privately as they could get tickets to a movie nobody else in the town would, and then speak freely whilst the film played.

The first problem he ran into was that he had no way of contacting either Michael or Andy. James's phone only had a handful of contacts in the first place. After some thinking, James decided to focus on finding Michael first. He would be easier to talk to. As it was a Sunday morning, Michael would have been dragged to church with his family, unable to tell them about what had happened the night before as an excuse to get out of the service.

Many kids from Echoway were forced to attend church by their parents. Most of them became friendly, bonding over their hatred of a wasted Sunday. Michael and James were never really ones to talk to others when they didn't have to, even when things were perfect.

Usually, James would sit next to Kara and they would play some kind of easily hidden game to pass the time. Now none of the Fuss family went to church, not since the funeral service. There was no point in praying when it felt like God didn't care. The idea of going back there wasn't the most appealing, but it was the only place he would find Michael.

By the time he arrived, the ceremony had almost concluded. James chose to sit at the furthest bench from the front, which was empty except for one man, who looked so deep in thought he could have been asleep. The man reminded James of someone, but he couldn't quite work out who. His eyes seemed tired, and it didn't appear as though he had shaven for some time.

The last hymn was sung and the final announcements started to be read. It wouldn't be long until Michael left his row with his family. James was searching the room for him when the man started to speak.

'Are you looking for someone son?' He had a strange kind of voice that was soft and kind. James couldn't pin if he had an accent or if the man was just tired.

'Oh, I'm just looking for a friend.'

The man listened to James intently and went into deep thought after, like James had just said something profoundly interesting.

'Friends are good. Always be thankful for friends, but never forget family is more important. That is a lesson that I have perhaps forgotten, and I fear it's too late to fix the problems I've caused.'

James had no idea what to do. The man had gone back into deep thought and James had no idea if he was meant to say something back. This was a grown man talking to a random kid about his problems.

'I don't think it's ever too late to fix something. My father used to say 'anything broken can be fixed with enough time and love.''

The man looked over to James and it was concerning to see him hold back tears.

'Thank you. You're right, it's not too late to make amends.'

The mystery man rose from his seat and shook James's hand, then left to apparently fix his family. Sitting there on the hard wooden seat, James wondered if that conversation was real. It hit him that that was the first time he had spoken about his father so casually, giving out advice that he had once given to James. He was so focused on that conversation that he completely missed the announcements being finished, and only realised the service was over when people started to walk past him.

As he was at the very back, it wasn't hard to be one of the first to leave out onto the concrete steps outside. James started to worry that Michael had managed to escape church to freak out about last night, because the crowd leaving the building to enjoy their day was thinning, and there was no sign of him.

The last elderly couple exited through the grand doors and James lost faith in his plan. As a last desperate attempt, he poked his head back into the service area where, by nothing short of a miracle, he found Michael and his family speaking with the pastor. James was about to turn back and wait for him outside when a voice called after him.

'Ah, James, so good to see you again!'

James turned back around as slowly as possible. He had no intention of speaking with the pastor after failing to come to church for so many months.

'Pastor David.' James offered a weak smile. 'How have you been?'

Five minutes of guilt-tripping later, Pastor David had made James promise to attend more often. James noticed that every so often, Michael, who now had a full black eye, would make a move towards the exit, only for his mother to grab onto his shoulder, forcing him back.

Finally, the pastor finished his long-drawn-out conversation with James and turned back over to Michael's parents

'As always it has been a delight to talk with you, I look forward to seeing you next week.' Pastor David gave a smile to the family before walking off to somewhere else within the church.

'Hi, James. How are you doing?' Michael's parents tilted their heads slightly as they spoke together.

James had become used to the head tilt. Older people would use it to look more sympathetic when asking about how he was doing.

'I'm all good, thank you. I just wanted to ask Michael if he wanted to join me at the cinema?'

James was as far from good as you could get, but what would be the point of getting into it with Michael's parents? They didn't want a full story of how he had to deal with such a horrific ordeal alongside their son.

'Oh, of course, I'm sure Michael would be glad to accompany you to the cinema, although I was hoping to hear more about this double date the two of you went on.'

It took James a couple of seconds to realise they were talking about the fake date he and Michael went on the night before.

'Yeah, we had fun yesterday. It was nice, I would get into it, but I don't want to miss the film.'

Michael didn't have a choice about going to the cinema with James. His parents wouldn't let their son say no to going out with the kid whose father stopped a school shooting, possibly saving their child's life. So, after some desperate muffled arguing between Michael and his parents, James found himself walking alongside him on their way to the cinema.

It didn't seem like Michael had slept at all. He was walking much slower than normal and his eyes had dark bags under them. It was hard to differentiate between the punching injury and the lack of sleep. James had no idea what kind of excuse Michael had to give his parents for the black eye, but he couldn't imagine it was any fun.

James spent some time speaking to what might as well have been the air. He explained why they were heading to the cinema and that they would be meeting everyone there. It was only when James spoke about having to find a way for Andy to join them did Michael finally speak up.

'No! Not Andy. I'll come with but only if he isn't there as well.'

James didn't bother to put up much of an argument for this. He didn't particularly want Andy there either. It wasn't like Andy was a bad person, he was just dealing with trauma in a way that James didn't want to be around. That was the kind way of saying it. In reality, James didn't want to get punched or attacked, for disagreeing about something.

10. Anyone for Popcorn?

Choosing not to find Andy meant that James and Michael arrived at the cinema much earlier than what was planned. Ella had messaged James saying that they should get tickets to see the 5.30 p.m. showing of *Frozen* with audio description.

It seemed like a good idea. All they needed was an empty room where they could talk without anyone else listening in. He received a strange look from the women at the counter when he paid for the tickets, and as an instinct, pointed over to Michael who was staring out the window and explained he had an eye problem and always wanted to see the movie. It didn't put Michael in an any better mood when James explained he had to act like he was blind for the next hour before the film started.

James had made sure to get seats at the back of the room just in case someone else started watching the movie. He also bought two large slushies for the pair of them. Even if they weren't there to watch the film, they could try and have a good time whilst they waited. The whole point of not turning himself in meant that he needed to continue living his life, trying to be the best person he could.

It occurred to James that he had never really spoken to Michael before and now they were at the cinema together. Unsurprisingly, Michael was struggling to deal with what had happened, and what he was forced to do. They sat in silence for a while, sipping on their cool blue drinks, only one thing on their mind, neither of them willing to speak about it.

'So, are you gonna tell me what happened with you and Lilith before she left?' James was never really one for school romance gossip, but they needed to start talking and it was the only thing he could think of.

Michael stared at James in shock for saying something so closely related to Sarah as if the FBI were listening in. Waiting for them to slip up. Michael looked down miserably at his drink.

'I don't know why you're acting as if you care. We aren't friends.' His voice was quiet as usual.

The thing was James did care. Sure, they weren't friends, and for a while, James hated him for no good reason. The reason he cared didn't even have anything to do with the fact that Michael could ruin his entire life if he chose to. He cared for Michael because he reminded him of himself. It was a sad reminder of what James was like a few weeks ago.

'Maybe I'm not your friend, but I am one of the only people you can talk to about everything. I'm also someone who knows what it's like to feel how you're feeling right about now.'

Michael looked around anxiously, trying to work out if there was anyone in earshot of them as he started to adjust his glasses.

'Nothing happened. We went off into the kitchen after Sa-, after we all split up. We started to talk and then she leaned in. I got scared, and she left. That was it. See, nothing happened.'

James sat there sympathetically, as Michael drank his slushie so fast through the straw that he had to hide a brain freeze.

'It's almost funny how similar we are Michael because while that was happening to you, I was speaking to Ella, and she was about to lean in. I would have been like you, I reckon. I've never been in a spot like that before and I was terrified. The thing is, she never leant in all the way. A massive crash stopped anything from happening, which well ... We can talk about that later.'

Michael let out a sigh. 'What does that matter, so we were in the same spot. You got lucky, I didn't. There's nothing I can do to see her again. I can't contact her, and even if I could, I doubt she would reply.'

It was strange talking about girls. Tom used to try and speak about them with James every so often, but he had never had the decency to listen.

'Look, I'm not going to pretend like I'm an expert when it comes to girls, but it definitely isn't over yet. Even with what happened you shouldn't give up on trying, and I think that's all she wants you to do.'

Michael pretended like he didn't care about what was being said, but curiosity got the better of him as he leaned in close to James.

'Do you really think I can get her back?'

James had never been less certain about anything in his entire life; his experiences with girls consisted of Kara, a few terrible conversations with Jodie, and Ella.

'Without a doubt, you can get her back.'

It didn't matter that what James had said was completely untrue. It was what Michael needed to hear. From that moment, Michael slowly started to open up, telling James all about his feelings for Lilith, which sparked the instant he saw her. They spoke about girls for a long time, recounting all their dreadful experiences and fears. It wasn't the best thing to have in common, but at least it was something.

James was grateful he could talk about Ella to someone, and Michael was glad to pick up the small morsels of advice James could give. Two more mixed slushies later, the others started to arrive. Their conversation stopped abruptly as Ella came closer to their table.

Ella looked beaten. Her eyes were red from a presumably sleepless night, and when James spoke to her, it didn't seem like she was all there.

She sat down next to James on the hard wooden chair and her body appeared to melt as she slouched, too tired to sit up straight. James gently touched her hand to try and get her attention. She was worryingly cold, as though she had been wandering around town all day.

After James held her hand, she turned to look at him and offered a very weak smile. A few seconds of staring deep into James's eyes, she collapsed into his arms, tears streaming down her face, shivering violently with each harsh breath taken. James could think of nothing to do other than embrace her tightly, and let her know that it would all be fine in the end.

Not long after Ella arrived Ludwig and Grayson showed up. Having cried a great deal, Ella managed to stand up, holding on to James as they made their way into the cinema room.

To play it extra safe, Ludwig and Grayson went into the cinema first and then a couple of minutes later, the others followed so they wouldn't seem too suspicious, although James doubted anyone who worked at a cinema on a Sunday was paying much attention to anything other than the clock.

All five of them took seats in the back corner. Grayson and Ludwig sat on the second to last row using the back of the next row as support to lean against. As expected, there wasn't anyone else in the cinema so they would be able to speak openly.

Almost everyone from the previous night was back together. It was a strange sensation. Nobody started speaking, even Ludwig who couldn't help but speak. An advertisement for a new dog food came on when James noticed that everyone else was staring at Ella, waiting for her to say something. She had, after all, asked them all to come together.

'So, I suppose you're wondering why I asked you all to come today?' She wiped her wet tired eyes on her sleeve, holding on to James's hand.

'Yeah. I've been doing just fine; I don't understand why we have to meet up. It isn't smart. We aren't meant to know each other, remember.' Grayson was right, he seemed completely fine.

It looked as though he had managed to sleep for a good amount of time. His face wasn't broken and dishevelled like everyone else's, and his posture was still as straight as ever. He was wearing another tank top that, like the other, highlighted his muscles. He acted like today was just as normal as the last.

'How are you doing so well? Don't you remember what happened?' James couldn't help but blurt out what he was thinking.

The focus turned to James as Grayson gave an unnerving stare.

'Why shouldn't I be? Some of you are too hung up on what happened. A girl nobody liked died in front of us. Sure, it was horrible, and I would never want it to happen, but it did. We dealt with it as best as we could. I did things I never want to do again. Things I never would have imagined I would have to do, but that's life. You deal with it and move on.'

'I know we need to move on, but we still saw someone die. You buried the body yourself; that stuff sticks with you.' James didn't know where the courage to say this was coming from.

'Of course, it sticks with me, but there was nothing else we could do. She was already dead, and it would be easy for someone to assume we killed her. There was no other choice, we can't throw away our lives trying to help someone who couldn't be saved.'

'I think Ella and Michael were right to try and call an ambulance. They might have been able to save her. Just because Andy couldn't find a pulse doesn't mean she couldn't be saved,' Ludwig said, leaning forward.

'You're only saying that because you feel guilty about having invited her in the first place.' Michael was sounding abnormally confident for someone who barely spoke in the Silver Chariot

'What do you mean, I never invited her. I didn't even know who she was.' Ludwig retorted.

'Wait, but if you didn't invite her, then how did she know to come to the party?' Grayson raised his eyebrow as he looked at the Ramwall students.

'It doesn't matter anymore if someone invited her, for all we know she could have followed us there or stumbled into the building herself thinking it was empty. Whatever way she found out about the party, she's still – still dead.' Ella did her best to keep back her tears but a few still fell from her face.

The movie had now started, and the opening song was being sung whilst another voice narrated everything that happened on screen, making it challenging to focus on the conversation.

'Ella, I know this really sucks, and it's going to take a long time for most of us to get over what happened, but think about the kind of person she was. Sarah would have probably spent most of her life in prison anyway, I mean she was kicked out of EE for having drugs in her locker,' James said, trying to make the situation the slightest bit better.

'About that. I don't think it's completely true,' Grayson said, shifting in his seat.

'She didn't have drugs in her locker?' Ella asked weakly.

'Oh no she did, but I'm pretty sure they were planted there.'

'What!' James, Ella, and Michael shouted over the movie.

'A little while ago when Sarah had just been expelled, I overheard someone on my team bragging in the changing locker about how he had done it. That she had refused to sleep with him and was threatening to tell someone that he had abused her, and so he planted the drugs in her locker and told a teacher.'

'Why didn't you say anything! That poor girl was expelled because she tried to stand up against a vile person. The entire town started treating her differently after what happened!' Ella was using all the energy she had to raise her voice to show the hatred she felt towards Grayson.

'It's not that easy. Say I did do something, maybe they believe me and did something, but then what. I might be on the football team, but if I snitched on Reggie, he would have the entire school against me within the hour. Then they would start getting dirt on me to try and hit back.

How long do you think it would take them to find out that I'm gay? If that gets out, then scouters won't look at me for scholarships, the same for pro teams, my parents would go ballistic at me. It would ruin my life. Some fights aren't winnable, Ella.'

'But being expelled would have changed her, that one fight that you didn't think was worth fighting has led to this poor girl going down a dark path.' Ella seemed desperate to fight Sarah's fight for her, to prove that she could have been good.

'Maybe, but Ella, even at Ramwall she was doing stuff all the time,' Michael said.

'People would always say she had done those things, Michael, but I can't think of one time where there was ever any proof of her doing these terrible things. Do you remember when Daniel had that diaper shoved into his locker? The whole school was sure it was Sarah, but there was no proof of it. What if all her life, because of that one incident, the whole town started blaming everything on her?' James couldn't believe what had been uncovered. That Sarah could have been a well-behaved student who was shunned by everyone she tried talking to.

'But even if that were true, how could we have ever helped her?' Grayson asked.

'We could have called an ambulance!' Ludwig shouted, his voice filled with pained emotion.

'If we called the ambulance and she died, how could we ever explain what happened? We all hated her whether it was justified or not, we were in a location nobody knew about, somewhere she wouldn't be found for a long time. Everyone would think we planned to kill her. Then we would all go to prison for something we didn't do. As much as I hate to say it, Andy was right.'

At that moment, the film started to play a song about the power of friendship, and how important it was to love one another. The pretty colours from the big screen lit up the wall behind them, like the Echoway equivalent of the northern lights.

'Grayson is right. Calling the ambulance would have screwed up all our lives. It was the only thing we could have done,' Michael said.

James was surprised to hear Michael speaking like this; he had after all received a black eye for trying to call for help. However, one sleepless night allowed for a great deal of thought and change of mind.

The five of them argued for a long time. Ella, James, and Ludwig thought that they should have called the police, with Grayson and Michael believing there had been no alternative but to hide the body. Eventually, they decided that nothing good would come from arguing about what the right thing to do was, no matter what they did now, there was no way to change what they had done. It would be something they would have to live with for the rest of their lives.

'I'm guessing nobody knows how Andy is doing?' Ella asked, after a few minutes of quiet, filled only by the movie.

James doubted that Andy would be able to deal with what had happened. The way he had been acting whilst dealing with Sarah made everyone think that he would crack at some point. What with how charismatic and enthusiastic he normally was, it didn't seem possible that he could pull off a convincing normal version of himself on Monday. It was concerning that, like everyone else, Andy had the power to ruin everyone's lives. If he let something slip, it could lead to his arrest which could then possibly lead to the rest of them getting caught.

Nobody had anything to say about Hercules and there wasn't much else that anyone wanted to speak about. None of them wanted to stay around and watch the children's movie with audio description, and so they all decided to leave. It didn't occur to them to go at separate times. As they were about to leave the cinema, Ella realised she had left her phone where they were sitting and went back to get it. James was just thinking about following her when a noise came from the main area.

'Yo Grayson, Ludwig what's up!' A tall mean-looking kid James didn't recognize was coming from the toilet, wiping his massive wet hands on his jeans.

Grayson and Ludwig separated from the group and awkwardly fist-bumped the kid who was now staring at James and Michael.

'Those are dirty Ramwall kids, ain't they? Fuckers think they can beat us at football. Surprised you haven't knocked em' out yet, big man.'

'Why would I? Ramwall kids aren't that bad,' Grayson said with a little chuckle to try and lighten the tense mood.

'What do you mean? You've always hated those rats since that prick spread the rumour you were gay. We've gotta make them pay.' It was strange how the kid who went to the higher-class school spoke like a caveman.

'It's not these kids' fault for that Reggie. Anyway, it's not the end of the world if people think I'm gay.' Grayson stood in front of Reggie, who had been making his way menacingly towards James and Michael.

It wasn't right that Grayson was pretending to be straight and couldn't tell his normal friends about who he was. Fortunately, this comment stopped Reggie from charging at James and Michael. Unfortunately, it made him turn towards Grayson with a sneer on his face. 'Nah queers are as bad as Ramwall scum. None of them should be allowed in this town, can't have people thinking that about you. Reckon we should still pummel these little kids, for the fun of it.'

Reggie really wanted to cause trouble and it wouldn't have surprised James if Andy had fought with him before. For all he knew, this could have been the person that broke Andy's leg.

'Come on, let's get out of here.' Ludwig said, nudging Grayson away from Reggie.

Ella had come to join them at the wrong time. She had no idea what was happening and attempted to slip her hand into James's. By the time she realised who was standing next to Ludwig, it was too late. Just as Ella tried to pull James away towards the exit of the building, he called out to them.

'You're from EE ain't you? You should be ashamed of yourself hanging out with scum like that, you fucking slag!'

James had never been in a proper fight before, but he wouldn't let that slide. However, by the time he had turned back towards Reggie, Ludwig had swung at his face. It didn't appear to do much except surprise the beast who then quickly became enraged. He slammed Ludwig into a wall where he crumpled to the floor as his glasses flew off his face.

There were then only two more noises that came from the fight. One was Grayson connecting a punch on Reggie's jaw, and the other was the big bully dropping to the floor out cold.

Grayson didn't seem surprised in the slightest that he managed to knock someone a whole head bigger than him out in one punch. Instead, he walked over to Ludwig who was red in the face and helped place his glasses back on his face. He then pulled Reggie against a wall so that he wouldn't swallow his tongue.

They decided it would be best to go their separate ways so that nobody else saw them together. Grayson spoke about now having to deal with Reggie on top of everything else, suggesting that the two would be doing more fighting in the near future.

James was exceptionally grateful for what Ludwig and Grayson had done. It allowed him to not fight the behemoth himself. Having never been in a fight before James doubted that he would have done anything to hurt Reggie, instead getting ripped to shreds in the process.

All James wanted to do now was spend more time with Ella, not only because he liked her a lot, but because she needed someone to help her get through Sarah's death. He offered to walk her back to her house.

The two of them left after saying some hurried goodbyes. They wanted to be gone before Reggie regained consciousness. James made sure to tell Michael that he was always available to help if needed, but he appeared a little too shaken up to really understand what was said. James would have to check in on him when they went back to school on Monday.

Within one day James had changed from not liking Michael at all to wanting to help him in any way he could. It was strange how quickly bonds could be made in situations that nobody had ever been in before.

With Ella holding on to his hand and with the thought of his friends who had stuck up for him, it was hard to think what his life would have been like if he had taken Friday off. He wouldn't have had to deal with seeing yet another dead body. Yet he would be friendless. There would be no girl that wanted to be with him, and the best moments of his life would have still been in his bedroom.

11. Calling 911

Four days passed. James woke up each morning, did his routine and left alone for school. He avoided Kara as much as possible so that he wouldn't have to talk about the party.

At school, Andy walked the halls as if nothing happened. If anything, he was more charismatic than normal, making an effort to always be talking, working out, or doing anything to let his mind think. James suspected that behind closed doors, he was struggling to come to terms with what he had done, unable to talk to anyone about it, having to always keep up his celebrity personality in the public eye.

Tom seemed to have completely forgiven James but there was still a strain on their relationship. Instead of sitting next to him at lunch, Tom would eat with Jodie, speaking about random gossip. James couldn't speak about the party to Tom as it wasn't his alibi.

The problem was he then didn't want to speak about a fake double-date that never happened to his friend, but he still wanted advice for Ella. He was struggling to work out how to ask Tom naturally about asking out a girl on a proper date, or possibly how to kiss a girl, or what you're meant to say to a girl. This was made harder by Jodie who clearly hated James. She refused to acknowledge his existence and would lure Tom away from him whenever he tried starting a conversation.

Andy, who was part of the popular friend group James now found himself in, pretended like he had no idea who James was, forgetting his name and excluding him from as much as he could. Along with Daphne's constant cruel behaviour towards him about his sister and anything else she could think of, James found that any time he tried to come out of his shell by attempting to join in a conversation, he would be shut down quicker than a restaurant with a rat infestation.

As a result, James barely spoke at lunch or break, spending most of his time with his own thoughts. Which was a terrible thing to do when all his mind could think about was that night in the Silver Chariot, as well as the constant fear that the police could arrest him at any moment.

People kept on asking Andy where he was during the weekend and he always gave a different answer which was the opposite point of an alibi. Whenever anyone would try and probe a little deeper, he became hostile and aggressive, just like he did at the Silver Chariot, leaving whoever he was talking to shocked and a little scared. As though it showed them that their hero had flaws and wasn't perfect.

After James gave Michael Lilith's phone number, which Ella gave him, he became more friendly and open about everything. It took next to no time for Lilith to respond to Michael after he sent his first message, which took him three hours to concoct. From that moment on, they had been speaking as much as James and Ella.

Michael was especially excited by the fact that Lilith had invited him over to her house that weekend to 'revise', as her parents were away. All throughout science the two spoke about what she meant and what Michael could expect to happen.

When they weren't speaking about girls, Michael would tutor James whenever Emma went to one of her many extra-curriculum school clubs. Whilst James was keen to improve his grades, they spent more time talking about girls and ever so slowly processing the ordeal that they had been through. Classes were still the normal hell, but James had started to ask for help when he was stuck on something as opposed to giving up.

James had started to wonder if Sarah would ever get announced as missing. He spent all day with the thought at the back of his mind, waiting for the inevitable search. Wanting to be better and live his life as best as he could, James still made an effort to speak to people in the halls.

But in those few secluded moments during the day when he was alone in the toilet or whilst brushing his teeth, the smile fell from his face and fear encircled him.

Every night, James endured new batches of fresh hell in his nightmares. Then every morning he would wake to see a message from Ella after they had been talking all through the night until one of them passed out. Both of them were getting through what had happened and for a little while it seemed like they could deal with it.

It took until Thursday for Sarah's parents to put out the inevitable missing person report to the police. The local news made a short announcement about it and an email was sent to all parents with students from Ramwall urging them to say something if they knew anything about her whereabouts.

The report came as a relief to James. The build-up of anticipation was so much worse than the actual thing. Nobody suspected foul play, not like there was any in the first place. In fact, as far as most people were concerned, Sarah had simply run away.

For the time being, the new program had been put on hold so that they could work out what happened with Sarah. Mr Glass personally delivered this news to Andy, Michael, and James, taking them out of their science lesson. On this day the headmaster had chosen to wear a tie with a raven sitting on a thin branch. Normally, his ties were bright and colourful. It made James think that he somehow knew Sarah hadn't just gone missing. Then again, he was probably overthinking, imagining things that couldn't ever be true.

Most of the school was sure that Sarah had done something so bad that the only thing she could think to do was run away; others thought she might have overdosed in some dirty dark alley. Whatever happened, nobody seemed to care that a young girl was missing. Everyone believed that she was some kind of evil monster. Only a few people knew that in reality, she had just experienced a terrible set of circumstances that left her friendless, lonely, vengeful, and now dead.

It hurt to hear all the cruel things people were saying about her, but there was nothing James could do. Few would listen to him if he started trying to explain she wasn't a bad person, and those that did would only think that he knew something they didn't. Something that could link to her disappearance.

By the time James arrived back at his house on Thursday evening, he was desperate to charge his almost dead phone so that he could continue texting Ella. James wanted to ask her out on a date, but there never seemed to be a good time. More often than not, they would end up talking about Sarah, as she was always on their minds.

James was doing fine pretending like he was fine, but he wasn't sure how healthy that was, or how long he could act like nothing was wrong. His nightmares showed no signs of slowing down, and the constant fear of being arrested loomed over him, like a black cloud following him wherever he went. James would often think about the worst places for the police to arrest him, at school, a restaurant, in the middle of a busy street.

Raiding the fridge and cupboards for food became a new way for James to comfort himself. He treated himself to sizable helpings of chocolate and crisps since the incident. Before James was able to enter his bedroom with a pack of biscuits, Kara cut him off as he reached the top of the stairs.

'What did you do! Why did you tell the headmaster that I wasn't ill, that I was just bunking school! They're saying they might put me down a year.'

'Why would I say that to him when you are ill, it doesn't make any sense.' James had no idea what she was talking about.

Kara was furious. If she wasn't ill, there would be raging red consuming her face. Instead, she was snow white, a tinge of yellow emanating from her skin as she shouted more and more. Sweat pouring off her forehead and drenched her face, a smell of alcohol on her breath.

'He said that you told him that last Wednesday in his office! He asked you about me and you agreed that I was lying about being ill!'

It all came flooding back to him now. Sitting in-between Sarah and Andy before Mr Glass explained about the program, he had zoned out and spurted out, 'Yes' to the headmaster.

'Kara listen, you've got to believe me. It wasn't my fault.'

This did nothing to help the situation, making Kara far more enraged.

'It's never your fault, is it! I'm going to have to redo an entire year and it's all because ...' At first, James had no idea why she had stopped shouting until he noticed her falling to the floor. Grabbing Kara's arm was enough to stop her from falling down the stairs as she completely lost consciousness. However, James was too late to stop her head smashing into the corner of the hard wall.

Her breathing was slow and weak, but it was still there. James could feel her trembling body against his, the gash on her head bleeding far too much, reminded him excruciatingly of Sarah. His phone was still in his pocket, so it wasn't hard to reach, but dialling for an ambulance felt like the hardest challenge he had faced. His eyesight was becoming blurry through a cloud of tears, his hands shaking violently, making it impossible to dial those three numbers.

The ambulance was there before James could spurt out his sixth apology to Kara, who was positioned exactly as the person on the phone had said to stop her from choking. Luckily, the door was already ajar, so he never had to leave his sister's side as the paramedics came up the stairs with a stretcher and carried her to safety out into an ambulance.

Enduring the ride to the hospital felt like a horror rollercoaster, each turn terrifying James, thinking that it could be Kara's last. The people next to him kept on asking him questions, but he was too focused on his sister, as if taking his eyes away from her for just a second would mean he would lose her.

Waiting in the waiting room was worse than all the other moments before that; now alone, away from her, his worry grew a million times. The doctors had informed him that Kara was suffering from alcohol poisoning. She had a torn blood vessel from vomiting so much and her sugar levels had become so low, it was a miracle she only fainted and didn't have a seizure. Thankfully, James was told that she would be able to pull through. The impact on her head did nothing to help the situation but it apparently wasn't severe enough to cause any lasting damage.

James sat rocking back and forth, contemplating how he should have asked Kara if she was alright a long time ago. If he had tried to be there for his sister from the start, she wouldn't have gotten into this situation, drinking away all of her problems and fears.

Eventually, after an eternity of worrying, praying, and begging, he was allowed to see her. There was a large drip going into her forearm, connected to a bag filled with a clear liquid, a bandage going round her head, hiding away her beautiful hair. She was still unconscious, and her skin appeared to blend in with the clean white bed, blotches of yellow staining her skin. Her eyes, which always gave James so much hope, had been locked away by a wall of despair along with her smile. Beeping and flashing lights came from another machine monitoring different things that James didn't understand. She appeared so weak that James was amazed by how she was able to stand a few hours ago.

Every so often a doctor or nurse would come in and check on her, doing things to her that made James panic, scared that something wrong had happened. The nurses would also go to the other people in the ward that James didn't have the time to look at, let alone care about. All that mattered was staying by Kara and making sure she was safe.

Their mum wouldn't be coming down to the hospital until Saturday after her business trip finished. Apparently, losing her job to tend to her helpless child was a deal she would not make.

Meaning that the last crumb of respect James had for his mother vanished in an instant without remorse or hesitation.

It wasn't until around 4 a.m. did James's family start to flicker her eyes open in the dark room, lit only by weak lightbulbs and pulsating monitors. Kara noticed the silhouette of her brother asleep on a chair next to her and tried her best not to wake him.

However, a few seconds later James was sprung to consciousness after she dropped a cup of water to the floor, too weak to hold it.

'Here, let me help you.' James tried to hand her his bottle of water, purchased from the vending machine outside.

'I don't need your help. I can do it myself.' Kara tried to push the bottle away but to James, it was the same force as a light gust of wind.

Instead of attempting to grab the empty cup on the floor, she reached for her bracelet made of fishing line on the table. Kara had never joined James and their dad on their fishing trips, but after he died, Kara took his fishing rod and made a bracelet from it, to always keep him close. It was light enough to be held but couldn't be stretched over the wire protruding from her arm. So after desperately trying to force the memento over her right wrist where she would always have her bands, Kara resorted to just holding it as tight as she dared while staring into the darkness, too tired to push it onto the other wrist.

There was nothing James could think to say that would help his sister and decided it would be best to pretend like he needed the toilet, leaving the water behind on her paper-thin blanket. By the time he cautiously returned, like a negotiator entering a deadly situation, his water bottle had become much lighter, as though the liquid had evaporated in the time he was gone.

She had also taken his momentary absence as an excuse to turn on her side with her back facing him. This wasn't a normal version of that position. Kara was forced to place her arms at awkward angles so that nothing would pull out or press against the wire and devices connected to her. Doing this led to her looking increasingly uncomfortable but she stayed that way, solely because it was harder for James to speak to her.

It seemed pointless to try and talk with her about what they were currently going through. All the drinking, the poisoning, the sadness. All James could think to do was talk about the good times they used to have.

'Do you remember that one time when we spent the entire day going around the park finding different rocks and pebbles? Collecting them until we had so many, we couldn't carry anymore?'

Kara was still motionless in her strange position and showed no signs of moving but she still took the bait. 'Of course, I do.'

'We got all the rocks we had and set up a table with two chairs outside our house trying to get passers-by to buy our special pretty rocks. We spent hours sitting in those chairs and we didn't sell a single one. It was dark when our parents came home, but we were still trying to sell them. Then dad went into the house, changed what he was wearing and came out the back. He strolled up to us with a funny accent and pretended to be an exotic rock collector saying how we had such a splendid display that he wanted to purchase all of them. You said that we would only sell one per person so that everyone could enjoy the stones and that dad would have to choose which one he wanted. After some negotiating, he left to go back inside with his new rock. Five minutes later he came back in a different outfit with another accent, and you let him buy another rock for another dollar, and I would collect the money and give him a rock. It had gone past midnight when we sold all our rocks and called it a day because you refused to go inside until all the rocks were gone. We must have sold Dad twenty identical stones. That was a good day.'

James leaned over and stretched to place his hand on his sister's shoulder. She was still laying on her side looking away from him, and he had no idea if telling the story did him any good.

'I would have stuck with you all through the night, I would have stayed there until the sun came up if it took that long to sell all the rocks. I still would. I'm going to stay with you no matter what happens.'

There was no response from Kara, and he could only assume she was trying not to cry, so he removed his hand and sat back down in the uncomfortable chair where he would remain until she was better. Until she was happy.

Friday started slowly with James not bothering to even call in and explain why he wasn't going to school. The few hours of sleep he slipped into before Kara woke up in the night was the only rest he allowed himself that day. She still wasn't speaking to him properly, refusing to respond with anything other than no, yes, or go away.

Most of the time neither of them said anything. James wasn't great at speaking to people normally, let alone when they weren't replying. Leading to lots of silent situations which James always tried to stay away from. It was much harder to keep the nightmares caged when he couldn't focus on anything.

This meant that Sarah would dominate his thinking, in ways he hadn't experienced before. How Sarah didn't have anyone to catch her when she fell. The fact that as she died, she was surrounded in an unfamiliar place filled with people who hated her. Her body wasn't even buried properly, indelicately, unkindly, and never to be found by those few who did love her.

It was revolting for James to think about, but it almost felt unfair that Kara caused so many of her own problems yet was caught from falling down the stairs, rushed to the hospital without hesitation, had someone who loved her sticking as close as possible, and most importantly managed to survive. The hospital wasn't even going to charge the family as a favour for their father's sacrifice for the town. Sarah was just a kid. James should have done better. That mistake wasn't going to be made again. He would do everything in his power to make sure Kara always had someone by her side.

Throughout the day, James probed Kara about what happened and why she was drinking so much. Kara finally broke her closed-off act when James asked for the hundredth time what had caused her to drink so much. Instead of ignoring him like the other ninety-nine times, she snapped back.

'Why do you care? You just feel guilty because it's your fault that I'm going to be held back, and the reason I passed out.'

James didn't think this was exactly true considering it was the alcohol abuse that made her pass out shivering and weak but he thought better than to challenge Kara when he had finally got her to speak to him.

'I care because you're my sister and I've got to look after you.'

The sides of her mouth twitched ever so slightly into a smile but quickly fell back to a frown as she regained her angry voice. 'Why would you need to look after me? You know I'm eleven months older than you. I don't need you to help me.'

'Sure, but we're in the same year. So, it doesn't really count. It's like we're the same age. I have just as much responsibility for you as you do for me.' It felt like such a silly conversation, yet the childish taunt worked.

Kara sat up in her bed slowly. 'That's such bull! I'm only in your year because you got lucky that I was late and born in September and you were early. I'm almost a year older than you, I should be looking after you, not the other way round!'

As Kara finished speaking, she immediately realised that she couldn't look after James anymore because of what she had done to herself. A wave of understanding forced her to lay back down on her stack of pillows; it was as though she had only just acknowledged the severity of what she had been doing.

'You haven't done a very good job of looking after me anyway,' Kara said, tears forming around her eyes.

James didn't want to fight. He never wanted to, and now was a chance to reconcile with his sister once more. 'I know and I'm sorry. I haven't been there for you. It's just been hard after Dad ...'

Kara's tears were now in full flow, and James couldn't continue. Nor could he hold back his own tears from seeping out. They hugged each other as tightly as they dared, crying onto the other sibling's shoulder until it seemed like there was no more sadness left in them to cry out.

12. Walk in the Park

After their breakthrough, Kara started to talk to James again. At different points throughout the day, doctors and nurses came in, and James had to leave the room so they could perform tests on her. During this time, he tried to find some nice food in the cafeteria, as before he hadn't gone further than the vending machines when guarding his sister.

James wasn't planning on going to Jodie's party anymore. With everything that had been happening, he had completely forgotten about it in the first place. Sure, it was important for his relationship with Tom, but when it came down to it, Kara came first. The only reason he found himself back at home getting ready for that same party was because Kara forced him to.

On Saturday morning when Tom came to visit, Kara discovered there was a party happening later that day which James had been invited to. There were several terrifying moments where Kara seemed close to mentioning the Silver Chariot party, which would be devastating for his alibi. Fortunately, she wasn't able to speak much as Tom wouldn't stop rambling about how he should have been more helpful, exactly the same way James had done when he was holding his sister in his lap waiting for the ambulance to arrive.

Tom mentioned that Jodie wasn't able to come with him to the hospital along with all of Kara's other friends because they had to set up for the party, which led to a whole argument between James and Kara about whether he would go or not. James had made an oath to stay with her until she left the hospital. In the end, the thing that pushed James to head home was when Kara mentioned that their mother would be arriving soon.

Kara was already speaking and arguing like everything was better, but James was far from ready to let her be by herself, and so made sure to stay with her until their mum arrived. He hung around for a short while with Tom, before giving his sister a warm hug and disappearing, leaving her in the hands of their joke of a parent.

As James made his way back home, Tom spoke about everything he should expect at the party, explaining what Kara had already told him, but without any prompting.

Whilst they walked, James had the idea to invite Ella along to the party as a plus-one, so that he could spend more time with her on what could be considered a date. James could see the cogs slowly turning in Tom's head when he asked about bringing another friend. He attempted to dig into who this mystery person was, but he eventually gave up trying, conceding that he would see the person in a few hours anyway. They parted ways just as Tom finished explaining about the kind of clothing James might want to wear to the party, having to head back to his own house to get ready himself.

After showering James realised that he had done a surprisingly decent job of dealing with such horrific trauma. The thought of what he had done and the nightmares that would haunt him only kept him up for a couple of hours each night, instead of the entire duration that the moon was out. He assumed it was due to having already dealt with a similar situation not that long ago, giving him the willpower to continue living each day.

Before James left his house to meet Ella, who had agreed to come with him to the party, he opened Kara's bedroom door and searched through her secret stash of alcohol. All her drinks would be taken away by their mum the moment she came home from the hospital anyway, so there was no harm taking an unopened bottle of vodka with him.

Unlike the weekend before, James was calm and relaxed getting ready for the party. He already knew that it couldn't possibly be as wild as his first. Being easily able to eat some food beforehand, without the fear of immediately throwing up.

This time James offered to walk to Ella's house and then escort her over to the party like a gentleman. He thought about buying flowers, but he didn't want to come on too strong. They had, after all, only known each other for a week.

As James had never been to either Jodie's or Ella's house, he found himself on some unfamiliar roads trying to guess the way, until he got lost and resorted to using Google maps on his phone.

The problem was that James had been focusing so much on where he was going, he became completely oblivious as to where he was. It was only after hearing the barking of a dog from the park next to him that James paid attention to the road he was on. Too afraid to look up and see the monster, he stood staring at his phone. Hamlet Way was written in front of the blue arrow on his screen, just behind that was a road turning right called Church Street, which meant that the graffitied wooden board next to him saying 'you deserve this' belonged to the Silver Chariot.

Instinctively James stepped back from the house of horrors like it was some creature that would attack him. Unfortunately, there was a curb behind him, and moving backwards caused his ankle to twist on the road, making him collapse onto the concrete, his phone free-falling from his loosened grip along with the glass bottle he was carrying.

Gravity was not kind to James. The vodka reached the hard ground first, shattering into many sharp deadly pieces. Only a few milliseconds later, James landed on the road, bringing his hand down on a piece of glass. The pain was unimaginable. The broken glass only made a few small cuts on his pinkie and ring finger, which normally wouldn't have been too painful, but immediately after getting an open wound, his hand rested in a pool of wasted vodka.

The strong stinging sensation was so intense he had to bite down on his lip to stop himself from screaming as blood started running down his hand. It felt like the bar was trying to assault James for desecrating it, for breaking in without permission and using its products without its consent.

James carefully removed the shards from his fingers, after he dared to look away from the building. It didn't seem like any major damage had been done. He wrapped his fingers up to help mitigate the bleeding with some tissue. He picked his now cracked phone up so he could see which way to go to leave the eternal punishment.

One last piece of anguish the bar would unleash onto James was through his phone, as though the devil had managed to enter it when he wasn't looking. Like some kind of deluded miracle, the two cracks on his screen formed a cross marking the park. Directly where Sarah had been buried.

It didn't seem like the best idea for Ella's parents to see James for the first time drenched in sweat with a bloodied hand looking like he had just seen a ghost. So, he decided to text Ella saying he was outside and to bring some water, as opposed to ringing the doorbell. A new feature his phone received from the fall was that the q, w, z, x, and c buttons wouldn't register on his phone, giving him an extra challenge when typing.

After a few moments where James managed to regain some composure, he noticed a light turn off in one of the windows of the large house, and not long after, the door opened to reveal Ella. Every time James saw her, all thought of evil in the world disappeared. She met James with a worried look on her face. It looked like he had just danced with the devil.

Whilst walking, Ella made the pain in his fingers die down by emptying a water bottle over his hands. This also gave James a chance to wash them so they weren't covered in bits of dirt. By the time James had finished explaining the ordeal, neither of them were in much of a partying mood.

They reached the road where the party was being held and Ella brushed away as much dirt as possible from his clothes so that James didn't look homeless. By the time they walked past the second Ferrari on the road, he appeared respectable enough to have a good time.

The pair managed to waver a smile at Jodie as she opened the door, wearing what was bound to be a stupidly expensive dress with complementary high-end jewellery. As soon as the door had opened, James became much more anxious. This wasn't like the first party he had gone to. There were well over seven people, the music was obnoxiously loud, and it felt like there was no space to crawl into a ball and cry.

James shuffled past a group of people gathered in the hallway waiting for the toilet as Jodie led them into a clean pristine kitchen with blue LED lights along the baseboard. James poured himself and Ella a drink to the best of his ability using coke and some vodka he hoped he could help himself too. The majority of people at the party had gathered outside in the unnecessarily big garden where the generic music was playing, music that Ella and James both hated.

'You're from EE aren't you?' Jodie asked coldly, as she led the pair of them outside.

It didn't occur to James that there was still a rivalry between the two schools. Something as stupid as a school rivalry didn't seem worth anyone's time, what with the other harsh things the town had to offer. Being oblivious, James had accidentally taken Ella into a Ramwall den.

'Oh um, I mean it's just the school my parents chose for me to go to.'

Jodie chose not to respond to Ella, leading them deeper into the den. Passing someone who was throwing up in a bush, James realised this was probably the worst type of party he could ever think about attending. The only thing left for it to be the party from his previous mundane nightmares would be a table filled with drugs that he was forced to take. Therefore, his grip tightened on Ella's hand significantly, when he saw the gazebo at the very back of the garden filled with kids running their noses across a glass table.

James couldn't tell if Jodie was trying to get revenge from his small outburst at her, or if she just hated him in general, but she was leading them straight over to the terror table.

The moon above seemed so much further away than when he was alone with Ella, as if the massive chunk of rock was recoiling from the sight of the abominable party. The smaller little white rocks that were now becoming apparent as they reached the gazebo were disappearing like the stars in the night sky, as Andy cleaned the table like a vacuum picking up ketamine with his nose. Tom, who had been asking people not to use Jodie's table for drugs, turned around to find a petrified James.

Tom did his best to look comfortable and casual as he greeted James and Ella, leading them away from the table as quickly as possible. If James wasn't having a panic attack, he would have noticed Tom giving a look of disgust to Jodie for putting James in such an uncomfortable position for what was believed to be his first party.

As the three of them moved away from the mini drug den, James started to loosen his tight grip on Ella. He had no intention of ever letting go, but he didn't want to stop the blood flowing to her hand. By now Tom had steered them over to a bench in a corner of the garden, that could have been confused with a park, where the music didn't sound so deafening and nobody could see or hear them.

'Sorry about that James, I know that freaked you out a bit. I told them not to do anything but, well, Andy's not really listening to anyone.'

It was clear that Andy was starting to become a real problem. If he kept acting so recklessly, he was bound to lose the scholarship that he so desperately wanted, something so important to him that he was willing to cover up someone's death in order to keep his chances alive.

'We can just stay clear of that area. They should stay there for the rest of the night. Hopefully.' Tom turned his attention to Ella, 'Anyway, I want to know more about your plus one that I've never heard of before.'

James couldn't help but go red in the face when introducing Ella to Tom, who couldn't care less that she was from EE. The three of them talked happily together. There was a moment of silence when Tom asked where they met. Ella stared at James for help, who explained that they had gone on a double date with Michael in the most convincing way he could.

Tom could easily tell that something was fishy about the alibi, but chose not to pry. Instead, he told stories about James, reminiscing about school, the terrifying lessons with Mr Hemans, and all the times James had been a delight to be around. In that short space of happiness, James thought that the party might turn out to be a success.

That was until Tom went off to go to the toilet, causing that brief moment of happiness to evaporate as Daphne and two of her spiteful friends came over to where they had been sitting.

'Apparently we've got an EE bitch at this party.' Daphne must have been drinking by the way she was stumbling and belittling those around her, more brazenly than normal.

There wasn't much James could do. In theory, he could take all three of the girls in a fight, but he decided it was more realistic to simply get in-between Daphne and Ella in the hope that it would diffuse the situation, like how Grayson was able to do with Reggie. Sadly, James wasn't the most intimidating person and even a small group of popular girls was enough to get his heart racing.

'Go away Daphne, she's not causing any problems.'

'That's not true, James. She's giving me plenty of problems. Firstly, she's making you happy and we can't have that. Secondly, I don't want to have to look at such an ugly skank, when I'm trying to have a good time.' Daphne smiled wickedly.

Ella went to get up and Daphne tried to storm over to her. James did his best to get in the way, all he was focused on doing was making sure Ella was safe. It was his fault for inviting her in the first place.

'What are you going to do? If you so much as touch me, I'll have Andy beat the shit out of you until you can't talk.' Daphne spat on Ella's shoe. 'You're not welcome here, get out.'

Tom had made his way back and was doing his best to make the girls leave. Daphne laughed with her friends as she left, and James knew that there was some kind of insult he could say to her, but by the time any kind of remark formed in his head, Daphne was long gone and he had failed to do anything to stop her torment once again.

It felt like the best thing to do was just leave the party with Ella and call it a night, but for some reason, Tom was determined to turn it around and make sure they had a good time. After wiping off the spit from her shoe, Ella decided to stay as well. James had no idea why. He could see that she was shaken up, and he didn't want her to take any more abuse, but he wasn't about to argue with her.

Gradually they came out of their corner in the garden and started to mingle with more people at the party, mostly cheerleaders and athletes that sat at James's table during lunch. Throughout all of this, Tom did not leave James's side no matter where they went. That guilty feeling came back to James from when they had their argument about how hard it was for Tom to go through this alone, without his friend.

Ella did her best to enjoy the night, but it was obvious that this wasn't the kind of party she usually went to by how quiet she was and the way she nervously drank from her cup. James felt bad about inviting her, he only wanted to spend more time with her, and had ended up making her feel anxious. Thankfully, most of the people didn't care or were too drunk to notice that Ella was from EE and so for a while, Daphne was the only bad thing they had to worry about.

Everything seemed to be going fine until a girl received a notification on her phone from a news site. As she glanced at the notification, the girl did a double-take with her eyes and let out a gasp after realising what it said, dropping her red cup on the floor and swaying on the spot until Jodie held her.

'What is it?' Jodie asked, in a sincerely worried tone.

The girl looked up from her phone and stared into the gathering crowd. 'It's Sarah. They've found her body. She's been killed.'

The music still blasted yet the world had never felt so quiet and still. How had they already found her? Had one of them snitched to the police?

What made everything so much worse was that Andy stormed away heading back inside the house, slamming the front door as he left. Doing this made him look unbelievably suspicious. It had just been announced that there was an alleged murderer in the town and nobody knew where Hercules was last weekend.

The whole group stared at the front door. Desperately wanting people to move on from what happened with Mr Unstable, James asked the girl to read the whole article. Shakily, she managed to tell the entire story.

The local news site wrote about how a man was out in the park with his dog when he noticed it was acting strange, digging up a patch of soil and barking madly. The man went to investigate and discovered what he believed to be a body. The police quickly arrived at the scene, and after carefully removing the body from the ground, they identified the body as Sarah.

The missing person case had now turned into a murder investigation and a detective would be assigned to find the killer. The article continued to explain that the police were searching for clues as to what happened, checking for fingerprints and any signs of the murderer whilst conducting an autopsy report. One of the police officers had given a statement saying how the cruel person who did this would be found and arrested.

Despair engulfed James. There was now no hope for him to ever get out of this situation. The police officer said it, the person responsible would be caught. The cruel person. That part stuck with him more than anything. He had managed to lull himself into thinking it wasn't his fault, that he was still a good person and had just been trying to continue living his life. It was now occurring to him that no type of kind person would ever help bury a body, clean up the pool of blood, and pretend like someone hadn't just died.

James may have not killed Sarah or even wanted her to go through any harm, but he was still responsible. He deserved to receive the same punishment as a killer would. He hadn't called for help, and when that happened, James turned from an innocent bystander to a killer.

James looked around the garden. As expected, everyone was talking about Sarah. All their minds were reeling with ideas for what could have happened. Why would someone kill her? Who could have done it? It was obvious that they were all concerned, even the macho athletes. Sarah was in their school and in their year, which meant that they probably knew the non-existent murderer in some way, especially considering how small the town was.

The whole party was coming up with ideas for what could have happened to Sarah. Nobody came close to saying anything that actually happened, but it concerned James that everybody would be talking about her for a very long time and as new details appeared, people were bound to get closer to the truth.

He had been in the park himself only a few hours ago. How much longer after that had the body been found? Would the police know that James had been around the area, would they want to question him because of it? James didn't think he would survive an interrogation no matter how casual.

No. That would never happen, they wouldn't bother to bring him in just because he was near the park Sarah had been found in. Most of the town passed that park. James was still in the clear, there would be no way to link back what happened to him.

The police wouldn't find anything to do with James or Ella once they searched for clues. Both of them wore yellow cleaning gloves when cleaning up the blood, and made sure to destroy their clothes as soon as they could. On the other hand, Ludwig and Grayson buried the body, and even though they were careful, someone could have seen them. Or they could have accidentally left something that led back to one of them.

Turning towards Ella to see how she was doing, James realised she was as pale-looking as Kara before she fainted. He steered her into the house, past the empty messy kitchen and onto one of the lower staircase steps facing the front door. The majority of coats and hoodies that people had brought were hanging on the rack next to them, which provided a kind of shelter for them to hide in and feel excluded from the outside world.

Ella's eyes darted around, like two flies trying to escape a prison made only of white. James grabbed her hands, which instantly made her eyes focus on the point of contact.

'I just can't deal with this.' Ella shook her head. 'It's too hard. I thought we could make it through but we can't, we just can't continue like this. I'm sorry that I'm such a let-down, but I can't do this anymore.'

She dared to look up at James with sad puppy eyes and a frown. In any normal situation, or at least any of these insane situations where Ella was not there, James would be freaking out. There was no doubt in his mind that he would have gone mad in a heartbeat with what had unravelled tonight.

Fortunately, he didn't have the luxury of losing his sanity. Ella was in such a dark place at the moment and James was the only person that could bring her back into the light. There could be a million other pieces of brutal news sent his way and James would still try to work through it as long as it gave hope to Ella.

'Ella, of all the people I have ever met in my life, you are the furthest from a let-down. Each moment that I spend with you is so much better than any other part of my life. Now look, I know it's hard, but believe me, we can work through this. One day at a time.'

For a second, Ella forgot about all the hard parts in her life, as she sat there gazing into his eyes. James could have sworn she was leaning towards him and he was about to join her. But before anything could happen, she turned her head away to look at the wall. The sense of panic engulfed her once more.

'You don't understand how hard it will be. It's a Little Red Riding Hood situation. We now have to live every day for the rest of our lives without being caught. They need to catch us once. Just once, and then we lose. That's why people don't get away with stuff like this. It's too hard to be Little Red Riding Hood, and it's so easy for the Big Bad Wolf to track us down. It only needs for us to trip over once, and then it'll rip us to shreds.'

It was hard to argue with someone who was bringing logic to the conversation.

'You're right. I know it's gonna be hard, it might just be impossible, but we have to try. You said it yourself, you won't live a boring life amounting to nothing. Look at your bands and remember the promises you made. Both of us have to do this unbelievably hard thing, but it will get better. Maybe tomorrow will be worse than yesterday, it probably will be, but eventually, we can get through it. Please believe me.'

Ella gave a strange smile like she was remembering a distant happy memory. 'I believe you. Everyone needs to have something to believe in, it gives them hope. I used to hope that I could be the one people believed in, the saviour of their broken dreams, to help all those lonely outcasts. That's who I wanted to be. Maybe if this ever ends, that can happen.'

She gazed up to the ceiling like she could see the sky. James knew that Ella had gone through many difficult times in her life, each one hurting more than the last, with this hard time being the most challenging. The only difference was that now she had James. Not just the sad version of himself that he had grown used to, but his old positive self that was needed more than anything now.

'I don't see why you have to give up on that dream. Before you found me, I was this broken mess that was nervous around his own shadow. Now look at me, out at this completely terrifying party with all my worst nightmares, and I couldn't think of anywhere better. Because I get to do it with you.'

Then, before he could say anything else, for the first time in James's life, someone was kissing him.

13. A Day with an Angel

Not long after Ella kissed James, they left the terrible party. Not wanting to waste any more time, now that their chances of survival were diminishing, James asked Ella out on a proper date for the next day. Each day was a gift. Their days were numbered. They had no idea how long it would take until the police found a lead that would lead back to them.

Outside Ella's house, she kissed James again and walked back inside, waiting for his arrival the next day, like a princess locked in a castle desperate for the prince to rescue her.

On the walk home, James was filled with euphoria. The whole world seemed so much more fantastic than he could ever have imagined. The dreadful problem that there was now a murder investigation was somehow diminished by the fact that James now had someone he could call a girlfriend.

At the front doorstep, someone had delivered a bouquet of flowers to the house. James checked the message on it to see that it was from one of his relatives for Kara. The house was completely empty. He assumed that his mother was staying the night with Kara giving him the opportunity to play his music as loudly as he desired. He sang along happily, thinking about his future with Ella, not a thought in his mind about how it would be impossible to keep a relationship if they both went to prison.

Sunday morning came around and James had never been so eager to leave his bed. He had planned to meet Ella at her house at 11 a.m. where they would spend the day together. It was only occurring to him whilst getting ready to leave the house that he hadn't planned anything for them to do. And James had no idea what a normal couple did on a date.

He thought about taking her to the cinema, but then that idea quickly faded thinking about their encounter with Reggie. Leaving the house wearing some more cologne, James grabbed the flowers that were meant for his sister. She wouldn't want them in the first place considering she was allergic to them.

On the route to Ella's house, which James was now becoming familiar with, he decided they could go to HighJump together. A place filled with trampolines which he used to go to with Tom.

James knocked on Ella's door having left her less than twelve hours ago, thrilled to spend more time with her. She opened the door with a smile on her face, greeted with a wonderful bunch of flowers. After she placed them in some water and into a vase, and gave James another kiss for his kind gift, they left to head into the depth of the town on an adventure.

Ella had calmed down a great deal since the party and the news report. It looked like for the first time since Sarah's death, she had slept throughout the night. And James was glad to hear that her voice was filled with new enthusiasm and excitement like when they first met and all was good in their lives.

'I want to go to the park before we start enjoying our day. Just so I can see that she's really gone from that place. So she can be buried by her parents. It would make me feel so much better,' Ella said as they walked through the streets, catching James by surprise.

James hated the idea of going back to the park. To be so close to the Silver Chariot again after it had put James through such a painful experience twice felt like poking a cobra with a small stick. Going back could only bring more agony. But it was something Ella needed to do to clear her conscience.

With every nerve in his body stinging him for being so stupid, he agreed to accompany his new girlfriend to the apparent murder scene, detouring from the fun activity that would be ordinary for a first date.

As they approached the park the pair of them could see police tape all around the area. Blocking all the entrances to the towns escape into nature. There was usually a violinist that would do the most beautiful street performances on a Sunday around this time at the entrance. But now, where she would normally play, there was nothing to hear except for the chirping of less talented birds.

The musician gave no sign or any form of explanation as to why she had chosen to break her routine performance. A performance that brought so many smiles to the town, like a phoenix's song giving strength to all that could hear it. But James knew it was ultimately a result of his actions that made the town a little less colourful.

Either the idea of being out in the streets unprotected with a murder loose was why she chose not to play, or out of respect for Sarah who had been so poorly buried in the park. Neither reason mattered. No matter what, it was James's fault.

Ella had that pained expression that James had seen far too often for someone he wanted only happiness for. She was staring into the park where Sarah's body had been dug up. There was a mound of dirt to the side of the hole that currently appeared to be unguarded. The entire park had become a crime scene so that the police could comb through it in an attempt to find any clues.

'She's in a better place now,' James started to say, 'Her parents will be able to say goodbye and they can get some peace at the very least. Not enough peace. But it's better than nothing.'

'You're right.' Ella nodded slowly, 'Thanks for coming with me. I don't think I could have done it alone. I needed to know that she had been moved from that god awful resting place. Let's get out of here.'

That is the best idea anyone has had all day. James thought as he glanced at the Silver Chariot, in a way of defiance. It hadn't managed to hurt him for getting too close to it. Then just as they were leaving the park boundaries, the spiteful bar called in the cavalry for some extra support.

Reggie and all of his other barbaric friends had just passed by the Silver Chariot, having presumably come from the small Grocery store, laughing about something they had unnecessarily stolen, considering they were all drowning in their parent's money.

James had managed to notice them before they did, but it made no real difference. The streets were practically empty because families were too afraid to come near the crime scene. Ella and James tried to walk away as quickly as they could, but it was no use. The gang had spotted them and were heading over with wrath in their eyes.

'Oi boys I think it's about time we pummelled another Ramwall rat, don't you?' Reggie said this loudly with the intent of scaring James, which was working exceptionally well.

'Go away, we don't want any trouble.' James was doing his best to sound tough and confident, but he was terrified knowing there was no way of escaping this inevitable beating.

The huge EE students had now started circling Ella and James so that they couldn't run away.

'It's been far too long since we've taught one of you lot a lesson, and you,' Reggie pointed at Ella maliciously, 'You should be ashamed. Hanging around with scum like this.' Reggie spat on the floor as his friends started to cheer him on. 'There's nothin' you can do, Grayson ain't here to save you anymore, and I'm going to enjoy every second of this.'

Reggie was now so close to James that he could smell his disgusting breath as he started to crack his knuckles. For no apparent reason, one person in the crowd stopped making cruel remarks at James, choosing to start sniffing the air hard, like a dog smelling some meat.

'Yo Reg do you smell that?' The student said.

James thought it was going to be some kind of insult, but the rest of the gang stopped to smell as well, with Reggie lowering his fist as he too started to sniff the air.

'Cigi smoke' Reggie said, genuine worry in his voice.

James started to smell a strong odour of rancid cigarette smoke as well. It wasn't an appealing smell, but it was no reason to be scared.

'It's got to be him. Let's get out of here Reg.' Another bully said, preparing to run away from the direction of the stench coming from the park.

There was no chance that Reggie would run away because of a nasty smell or whoever the person was that was making the smell, especially now that he had cornered James and was ready for an easy beat up.

Yet, to his great surprise, Reggie left the street, not having laid a hand on James. The entire group started to run away from the park, like a herd of deer that had been startled by the crack of a branch.

Neither James nor Ella knew why the smell was so scary but they had no intention of staying in the area waiting to find out, or for Reggie to change his mind and come back to finish what he started. Making sure to go in a different direction, Ella and James continued with their date amazed that they had escaped completely unscathed.

After the strange attack that had them shaken up, James was keen to get to HighJump so that they could enjoy themselves. James paid the entrance fee for both of them, as well as some special socks that had extra grip on the soles so that they wouldn't slip and slide on the trampolines.

Ella and James spent hours forgetting their problems and troubles, flying around the space, laughing as they went. Both of them were terrible at it, never being able to land a flip, falling over even with the special socks on, and looking like complete fools. But it didn't matter how they looked, what mattered was it gave them a chance to release all of their pent-up emotions by flinging themselves into a pit or at a wall.

After the two of them had let out all of their energy to the point where they struggled to stand up straight, they decided to call it a day. As they made their way out of the building, Ella and James found themselves running into some familiar faces. At the front desk paying for their own entry fee were Grayson and Ludwig.

'We should go over and say hi,' Ella said excited to talk to her friends.

James had to grab Ella's arm to stop her from walking towards them.

'We can't Ella. Remember we aren't meant to know them properly. You go to school with them and I've only seen them once at the program. If we go over and start talking to them, people might get suspicious.' James was whispering in Ella's ear so that nobody could overhear them.

It wasn't a nice thing that they couldn't speak to their new friends out in public, but it was necessary. It was vital that they acted exactly as needed for their alibis to be rock solid. Ella knew James was right but she wasn't happy to hear it.

They had just finished paying and were about to head into the main area when Ludwig happened to look in James's direction. He stopped dead in his tracks, causing Grayson to bump into him. There was a moment where all four of them stared at each other, wanting to speak and chat away like that night in the Silver Chariot, but they all knew it wasn't safe.

Grayson looked depressed, but still offered a small nod to James and Ella, which they returned and Ludwig gave a grin that said he was glad to see the two of them together. Then without a word exchanged, the two pairs left to go their separate ways.

Ella didn't speak much as they walked through the town. Both of them were exhausted from jumping, but James was smart enough to know that wasn't the reason why she wasn't speaking.

'Do you think we will ever be able to spend time with them again?' Ella said finally.

It was a hard question for James to answer.

'I don't know. I hope so. We had such a great time with them before, I would hate for this to be the end, but who knows what's going to happen to us.'

Ella nodded like she expected that to be the answer.

'Maybe when this is all over, we can try and mend this stupid rivalry with our schools and pretend to become friends with them all over again.' Ella said this with hope in her voice like when they first kissed and she was talking about all the good she wanted to do in the world.

'I like that idea.' James chuckled. 'But when it's all over and we invite them to something, let's just play it safe and have a normal party. We can have one so much better than Jodie's, and if something happens to someone, we won't have to hesitate, we can get them the help they need straight away.'

They both rejoiced in that idea and continued to walk together with their arms around each other, looking into the distance and imagining a time when their lives weren't so difficult. James decided to have their date come to a smooth end by walking Ella back to her house. It wasn't that he didn't want to spend more time with her, but he hadn't visited Kara since Saturday morning, and a lot had happened since then which he wanted and could tell her about.

James hadn't told Ella about Kara being in the hospital, solely because he didn't want her to worry any more than she already did. Instead, he told the old reliable white lie that he had received a text from his mum forcing him to go back home to help with something.

On the way back to his house, James had a groove in his step thinking about how well his first date ever went. He wanted to get Mr Winston from Kara's room so that she could feel more comfortable in what was bound to be an anxiety packed place.

Stuck in his own head, James almost missed the EE gang led by Reggie walking across the street in front of him, laughing away at something they had done. James hid behind a low wall until the group passed and when he was sure they wouldn't be able to see him, he sprinted in the direction they had come from, confident he would find someone in pain.

Sure enough, as James turned a corner down a thin alleyway, he saw a person on the ground, back to the wall for support, their dark blue wool sweater stained with blood and filth.

'Freddie!' James called out, concerned for his classmate.

James ran up to Freddie who had a cut lip, a swollen eye, and many more injuries from Reggie and his goons.

'I'm fine.' Freddie could barely open his eyes as he said this.

'You're not fine, Freddie. Come on, let me help you up, we can't stay here.'

James did his best to carry Freddie to a safer part of the town until he found a bench.

'Are you alright, do you need me to call anyone for you? Is anything broken? Do you need to go to the hospital?'

James felt bad, especially since he was destined to get that beating but had been saved by some foul cigarette smell.

'I don't need your help. I can handle it myself.'

'Are you sure? I can walk you home if you need. I mean you can barely walk.'

'No. I'm fine by myself.'

Freddie stood up from the bench which must have been excruciatingly painful and started to limp away. James was worried. That one moment of loneliness James experienced after Tom had shouted at him burnt a hole in his heart. And from what James knew, Freddie had been swimming in loneliness for far too long.

'Freddie!' James shouted.

Freddie turned around the smallest amount so that he could see James from the corner of his eye.

'If you need anything, ever. You only have to ask and I'll help. I promise.'

To this, Freddie simply turned his back and continued to drag himself home. And James was left to sit on the bench alone, worrying about how he could make Freddie's life better.

At home, James was surprised to find his mum sitting on the sofa watching T.V, James didn't have the time or the care to ask why she wasn't tending to her child, choosing instead to go straight into Kara's room to retrieve Mr Winston.

'Where are you going? It's getting late,' James's mum said as he opened the front door.

James was surprised she cared at all. Although, she did also believe that there was a killer on the loose.

'To see Kara,' James said in the most judgmental tone he could.

'Visiting hours are over for the day, you can see her tomorrow after school.'

'What do you mean visiting hours? I want to go and see her.'

'It doesn't matter what you want. Now that she's in a stable condition, the hospital has decided that we can only visit during the designated hours. I've left some food in the kitchen for your dinner. I'm not really hungry.'

More than anything, James wanted to ignore what his mother had said and leave for the hospital anyway. He was sure that he could get past the receptionist and into Kara's room. But knowing it would only get him into trouble, he changed his mind. Deciding to visit her the moment he finished school on Monday.

Putting Mr Winston carefully on the kitchen table, James made himself some food, which he took up to his room, where he remained for the rest of the night, talking non-stop with Ella over the phone.

14. Sarah's Revenge

On his way to Ramwall the following morning, James overheard some kids in the year below complaining about having to go the long way round to school as they couldn't cut through the park.

James hoped that that conversation was the only thing about Sarah he would have to hear that day. He was very wrong. The media had started to get involved, to the point where a few kids were bragging about having just given an interview for a news station. During their first break, students, against the will of the teachers, ran over to the school entrance, saying anything they could about Sarah, purely so that they would have the chance to be on TV.

Most students pretended like they were close friends with her. Other students spoke the truth about what they thought about her and how they didn't care that she was dead. None of them, even those that pretended to be her friend, acted like they cared about her death.

Sickened by the sight of what had been happening, James chose to spend all of his break with Michael, going over science homework to help take their mind off things. Even though it had been only a week since James decided to be a better person, his grades had already improved.

There hadn't been the results of any tests given back yet, but James could tell that he had aced the most recent science one. It would be a good couple of weeks before he received his grade back from the test, by which time he could be imprisoned. Getting that thought out of his head, James put his head down and focused on the work he was going over with Michael.

James could remember when Adam Kleiner decided to make a tally of every single student in their science lesson to work out how many times each person spoke during the lesson. As Mrs Dinkley wasn't able to control the class in the first place, she let Adam do the tally and went over it at the end of her lesson.

The chart consisted of two colours of tallies, a green tally being someone who was speaking to the teacher, and a red one when someone spoke to another student. Most of the chart was what you would expect, with the majority of lines being red, an average being around forty red lines and under five green lines over a fifty-five minute lesson per student. Emma and Michael had almost two-hundred green lines in total.

The part of that lesson that always stood out the most to James was his tally. Throughout the entire lesson, James had not spoken a single word, he hadn't asked for a pen, answered a question, or spoken aloud for fifty-five minutes. He might as well have been mute. Going over a question James had gotten wrong, Michael once again started to speak about girls.

'Lilith hasn't been responding to me at all. I think I've done something wrong.'

James had completely forgotten about how Lilith would react to the news of Sarah being reported as murdered. He had been so wrapped up with Ella, he hadn't thought about the implications of what Lilith was bound to start thinking.

'Why, what happened?' James asked as casually as possible.

'When she saw the article about Sarah, she got a little freaked out. She asked me what happened that night she left, and I told her Sarah left almost immediately after she did. I thought she believed it, but now she isn't responding to me. I couldn't go to her place this weekend because when I asked for her address, she wouldn't reply. Do you think she's gone to the police?'

This didn't bode well. Lilith was smart, she would be able to work out something was wrong and could ruin their lives with ease. James wanted to do something, but if she wasn't talking to Michael, there was no way she would talk to him.

'I'm sure it's fine. I mean everyone in the town now thinks there's a murderer about. People's parents are bound to get stricter. They probably forced her to stop talking to you. You're from a different school and they don't know who you are, they just want to play it safe for the time being, in case you're someone suspicious.'

'But James, I am someone suspicious. Anyway, that can't be it, she told me her parents were away for the weekend, remember. I don't like this, James; I think something's wrong.'

James couldn't help but agree and get worried with Michael. Their whole lives could unravel if Lilith did the wrong thing. Or perhaps it was the right thing. Either way, James sent a message to Ella asking her to check in on Lilith, so that their minds could be at ease. At least at ease with Lilith. There was still the overwhelming pressure that Sarah's missing person case had evolved into a murder investigation.

Ella had been right. It would be getting much harder before it would get better. A single mistake would be enough for the police to be onto them. Thinking about this did nothing to help James with his science work, and so he decided to give up, grabbing some food from the cafeteria before their fifteen-minute break was over.

From what students were saying in the halls, the police had been questioning people across the town. Most people were thinking that the police would eventually start questioning people at the school, and as expected during 4th-period history, Mr Glass gave an announcement over the intercom explaining that some students had been asked by the police to come in for questioning over the next few days. Mr Glass assured the school that it was just so that they could get a better idea of who Sarah was, along with her possible whereabouts. The headmaster stressed that it wasn't anything bad and that none of them were in trouble.

This was sure to relieve some students who were getting anxious about a possible interrogation, but for James and presumably Andy and Michael, it wasn't comforting in the slightest. James had been praying for his name not to be on the large piece of paper that had been pinned next to the secretary's desk, but he wasn't surprised when he went over to it at lunch to see James Fuss written down along with Andy's and Michael's.

All of them were doing the program with Sarah, days before she disappeared. There was no chance that they were suspects yet, but James wasn't sure what would be revealed tomorrow when the sheet said he needed to be at the police station.

During English, all anyone could talk about was Sarah. The teachers had done their best to keep talk about it at bay during their lessons, but now with the announcement, nobody was focusing on the work.

Towards the end of the lesson, the teacher gave up trying to teach and started to talk with the students about Sarah, about how frightening it was that there was a murderer in the town. Hearing his teacher talk about her death, made it all feel so much more real. How the very thing that nobody knew about and everyone wanted to understand, was the only thing on James's mind.

He had been doing well with moving on from the horrific accident and the terrible deeds they had done, but it was harder to heal the wound when everyone kept poking at it. Simply sitting at his desk hearing people talk about Sarah was agonizing.

It was worse when a girl said she was now scared to walk around the town by herself, and another person said he wasn't allowed to be out of the house after dark. Because James and the others had covered up what had happened to save themselves, other people were afraid of being killed, having no idea that it was a complete accident.

It only occurred to James during the final lesson of the day, food tech, that Andy hadn't been at school. Something that didn't give James any more hope in his dire situation.

The unit they were studying was bread, which included different ways to make bread, and different types of bread. Naturally, this topic didn't exactly have the students at full attention as it was so basic. It was only part of the curriculum because there were so many different bakeries in the town that were always needing new employees.

For this lesson, they were meant to make pretzels, but like English, everyone gave up almost immediately, continuing their conversations about Sarah. This time someone mentioned that their father had to be questioned by the police because they worked at the grocery store opposite the park where she was found.

Nobody but James knew how terrifying this was. He had never thought about what Sarah could have been doing before heading into the Silver Chariot. She might have even bought something from the shop before going to ruin James's life. People wanted to talk to James because he was one of the people that would be questioned, but nobody could get anything out of him.

Eventually, the lesson started to come to an end and each group presented their low effort pretzels to the teacher. After the final bell rang, James left school quickly, making sure he would have plenty of time to visit his sister in the hospital. It was uplifting to see her getting better, and it felt like his responsibility to check up on her as much as possible. And more than anything, he needed some uplifting.

Before heading to the hospital, James wanted to make a few pit-stops. The first was at the popular coffee shop close to the school called Moonlight. James wanted to get a nice hot drink for Kara who had been having some lousy meals at the hospital.

Usually, after school, Kara would have gone to the coffee shop with her friends and chatted about random gossip. Moonlight was made to look as teen-hippie friendly as possible. Some high tables were randomly scattered around the room, with an oak bench at the entrance to wait on. Most of the normal chairs at the few reasonably heightened tables were bright red and made to look like they were hand-woven, but out of plastic instead of wood. In the background, indie music created a mellow and relaxing atmosphere. Everywhere you looked were plug sockets to charge your phone, so that you never had to leave the place.

Each wall had some kind of expressionistic art on it, making the whole area vibrant. Moonlight had never really been for James, but he could easily see why people came here. For someone who enjoyed those kinds of things, it was a perfect place to talk and cool down.

As he waited in line trying to decide what kind of drink he should get Kara, someone got into the line behind him stinking of cigarettes. The smell was so overwhelming, he struggled to breathe properly let alone focus on what to get.

James assumed it was just a homeless person that had saved enough money to get a hot drink, after buying out a store for all their tobacco. There was no point in turning around, nothing good would come of it. Instead, James did his best to focus on the chalkboard showing the list of many different drinks. After James placed his order to someone in a beanie, he did his best to get a seat far from the stench while he waited for the drink.

'Do you mind if I sit?' a tall well-dressed man asked him.

'Go ahead.'

James wasn't worried about his safety. The person seemed to be waiting on a drink and he didn't seem like a bad person, even though he sat a little too close to James than what was needed.

'Did you hear about that Sarah girl? Terrible thing to have happened,' the man said. After James chose not to respond he pressed on. 'She went to your school, didn't she?'

This was a little concerning to James, that this random ordinary man knew James and Sarah went to the same school. It was then, when he placed a recording device on the table, that James started to fully understand what was happening.

'James Fuss, could you tell me a little more about Sarah before the police start interrogating you?'

He didn't know what to do. This reporter knew his name and his face along with the fact that he was going to be questioned. In the crowded coffee shop, it felt like he was alone and backed into a corner. Just as the reporter leaned in closer to press James, a nasty stench filled both of their noses.

'Jack, buddy how about you get out of here before I throw you out.'

The homeless person had come to James's rescue. His voice was harsh and rough-sounding like he had come out of the womb using the umbilical cord as a shisha. The man's clothes looked cheap and old, and the hairs on his jaw could no longer be described as stubble reaching the point of prickly fur, that was going grey.

'Yes, Mr Edict I'll be right out.' Jack the reporter spent no time arguing with this Mr Edict, as he left Moonlight hastily, forgetting about the drink he ordered.

There was one thing that the grimy man had that made James realise he wasn't living on the street. Hung around his neck was a silver chain that held in place a detective's badge. It made James think of old cop movies like *Die Hard*.

'Don't worry about that, pal, Jack is a bit of a weasel when it comes to getting a story.' Presumably, Mr Edict was trying to calm James down, but his gravelly voice kept on making James picture someone dying of thirst.

'Oh right,' said James.

Mr Edict was the embodiment of a failed detective who had been on the job for too long and had lost the will to live or solve anything other than what drink he should buy at the bar. It felt like he was playing both the bad guy and the good guy in a cop movie.

'Don't worry about him knowing stuff about you, buddy. They're careful to never get too close or trespass and he's not the kind of person to break the law.' Mr Edict spoke as if it was good news that someone who knew a lot about James wasn't going to break into his house.

'I'm assuming you're one of the people I'll be interviewing soon?'

All James could muster was, 'Yes.'

Even with the badge, James noticed multiple people staring at him, their nostrils flared with disgust at the man.

'Is there anything you wanted to tell me now before we get all official?'

James did his best to look calm but any detective, no matter how bad, would be able to tell that he was the opposite. James didn't want to spend a second more with the detective out of fear of slipping up and accidentally giving something away about Sarah.

'No sir. I just happened to be in a program with her, I don't really know much about her at all.'

It was excruciating talking to Mr Edict. Every word James said felt like it would give away everything. Trying to sound collected, James thanked the detective for helping him and attempted to leave.

'James, wasn't it? Aren't you forgetting something?'

Millions of ideas came bursting into his head about things Mr Edict had worked out that would lead to James's arrest. Had there been some kind of hole in his story that didn't pan out? Was there some simple detail he had forgotten that made everything fall apart? James's mind was reeling and he was close to just sprinting away.

'Your drink, it's that one just over there isn't it?' Mr Edict passed over the drink after collecting his own and gave it with a curious look to a broken James. 'Are you sure there's nothing you wish to tell me?'

The smell of smoke was nauseating enough without the pure crippling pressure of the detective asking about Sarah.

'No, nothing at all Mr Edict. I'll see you later.'

As James pushed his way through the crowd to the exit, he heard the detective call out to him.

'It's Jace, I'm not arresting you, buddy. Call me Jace.'

Once James left Moonlight, he started to make his way towards his house for the final pitstop. With each step, he became more and more light-headed. His vision blurred, his heart was pumping out of his chest and he could hear the thumping noise in his ears. It felt impossible to breathe, as though the air had suddenly filled with poisonous gas. James had had enough experience with anxiety to work out that he was having a panic attack.

To stop himself from falling over, he leant against a wall, and slowly slid down it. It felt like he was about to be sick, or pass out. Sweat started to pour from his body as his balance worsened, making it hard to sit upright.

The encounter with the detective and the sheer amount of fear he felt was unmatched by anything over the past week. James wanted to scream, but it was hard enough to not choke on air. Once again James started to cry, curled into a ball at the side of the road trying desperately to control his breathing.

I have to calm down. Come on, we can get through this. Remember what your therapist taught you, count your fingers and calm down. James stretched out his arms and tried to count his fingers, but his hands were shaking so violently it did nothing to help.

What else did she say to do? Think, James, think. Five red things. Find five red things around you. James started to look around. *Those walls are red, that's one. That poster is red, that's two. Three more. There, that ball over there had red on it, two to go.*

It seemed to be working. James's breathing was becoming somewhat controlled, and the tears had stopped. Only when he tried to find another red item, he made the mistake of looking directly down. In reality, there was nothing but the concrete next to his feet, but James could only see red. In his deluded state, the ground had transformed into the carpet in the Silver Chariot, only the carpet wasn't visible, all that could be seen was blood.

The sight made him gasp and choke. He knew that there couldn't be blood covering the floor, but then why could he smell it? Why did it all feel so real? James shut his eyes as tightly as possible. *It's not real, it's not real.* Saying it wasn't real didn't help, he could still feel that brutal metallic taste at the back of his throat.

All James could see through his tightly closed eyes was that night in the Silver Chariot again, when he had to mop up Sarah's blood, with Ella. Ella. The thought of her made the sickly feeling in his body stop, thinking of her smile made him feel less light-headed. Their date out together at HighJump made the rest disappear.

Slowly he opened his eyes to find that not only was there no more blood on the floor, but the world had slowed back down and nothing was spinning any more. Eventually, James worked up enough courage to stand back up, and then slowly started to walk back to his house to pick up Mr Winston.

By the time James had reached the hospital, he would only be allowed a little over an hour with her. The hot drink from Moonlight had long since gone cold and been thrown away, although he had managed to bring the cuddly toy to brighten up her day. As expected, when James turned the corner into Kara's room, she gave him a wide bright smile. She had already become stronger and a great deal of colour had come back to her face, that nasty yellow tainting her skin had mostly disappeared. Her head bandage had been removed, as she laid in bed drinking some water.

'Man am I glad to see you. I've been so bored. Oh, sweet you brought with Mr Winston.'

James passed her the monkey and she took it from his grasp with a surprising amount of strength.

'So, are you going to tell me about how the party went? It's the only piece of gossip I care about at the moment.' Kara looked eagerly at James.

He didn't know where to start. The broken glass that cut him, seeing Andy do ketamine in front of him, or the whole thing with Daphne. It then dawned on him that something much more important had happened that night.

'Well, I might have kissed someone.'

He couldn't help blushing as Kara screamed like a little girl.

'Tell me more, tell me more. I can't believe my little brother got with someone. Was this the girl you went to the other party with?'

It felt like when they used to walk to school together before everything. Back then James would be the one getting excited for Kara, with all her new friends and people that were interested in her.

Now it felt good to be on the other end. It was such a silly conversation with red faces and little squeals of happiness, but it felt good to get away from all the grown-up things he had to deal with.

Kara kept on saying how much she wanted to meet Ella. James said how he doubted she would have to stay in the hospital for much longer, considering how much better she was getting. Although, whenever James would mention this Kara gave him a sad look and changed the topic. By the time he had to leave the hospital, it was dark out and his mum shouted at him for being home so late.

Later on in the evening, James had the pleasure of being screamed at yet again by his mother, who had received an email from the police, asking him to come to the station. This conversation was a lot less calm and relaxed than the announcement Mr Glass gave, turning quickly into an argument. James's mother didn't seem to understand that he was being asked to come in for a few basic questions about Sarah and that he had done nothing wrong.

His mum kept on saying things like, 'expected better from you' and 'what with your sister's problems', which made James much angrier than he thought possible. Whenever his mum mentioned his sister now, it would not be with love and kindness but instead disgust and disappointment like she was ashamed.

They finished the argument with James giving up explaining that it wasn't a big deal and he hadn't done anything wrong. What had made everything about the fight worse was that his mother was right for all the wrong reasons, the interrogation had the potential to end his life as he knew it, and he very much had done things wrong.

At some point during the evening, his mother shouted at him, saying that dinner was ready, but James continued to stay in his room texting Ella. As it turned out she had also been asked to come into the police station along with Grayson, Ludwig, and Lilith. Whilst it was expected, hearing it didn't make the butterflies leave James's stomach. It meant that they would all be questioned and it would only take one of them to say something wrong or suspicious for them to become suspects.

What was more worrying was that Lilith hadn't been in school that day. Which meant that something was definitely wrong. Talking through the interrogation with Ella made it easier to digest. It was just some basic questions. They weren't suspects, and it would probably be the only time they would have to go to the station. They both kept on repeating these facts in their conversation to give each other hope.

Grayson and Ludwig were smart and would be able to get through it fine. James and Ella didn't have as much confidence, but they were hopeful. Michael had been texting James and was logical, saying how there was no way they could ever connect anything. The people that seemed most likely to ruin something were Lilith and Andy.

Andy was a massive red flag. James had little faith that he would be able to convince a detective that he was innocent. In theory, he was innocent, but he wasn't doing a good job of showing it. Lilith had been going along with the alibi of the double-date, but that was only because she didn't want to get in trouble for trespassing. She saw Sarah arrive and knew that nobody liked her. Now with her being completely off the radar, it only seemed like a matter of time until the police came to arrest them all.

It was only the following morning that everyone found out how much worse life was about to get. Every day James had gotten into the habit of checking the news site for updates to Sarah's investigation.

Today there was still the major headline that Sarah was murdered, along with a photo of her looking beautiful in an all-black outfit. However, scrolling down to the next article showed a new development, one that made way for a new kind of fear and sadness that James was trying so hard to build walls against.

The report was titled 'Echoway East student commits suicide'. As with Sarah's headline, the article included a photo. She had glasses and red hair that was pulled into a ponytail, held together with a pencil.

15. The Interrogation

Learning about Lilith's suicide affected everyone. It hurt all the parents in Echoway who read about someone's child that had taken their own life. It stung for everyone that went to school with her, knowing that they could have helped in some way. It cut deep for her friends as they didn't realise anything was wrong.

For the Silver Chariot group, the news haunted them, knowing that the article about Sarah being discovered could have had some influence over Lilith's actions. Whilst everyone who read the news was in some way affected by it, Michael was broken by it.

From what the news site said and with the information James already knew, it seemed like Lilith worked out what had happened the night when Sarah's body was found, and couldn't live with the fact that she was so closely involved. There was no note left for her parents. So, there was never going to be any way of finding out why she hung herself, as the news story put it.

Instead of getting ready for school, James had been on the phone with a devastated Michael. He had found out about her at the same time as everyone else. Lilith's parents had no reason to tell a random kid who was texting their now-dead daughter about what had happened.

Once again, James was put into a spot where he had to say things that he had no idea about. Sure, his father had died and it was completely debilitating, but with Lilith, everything felt different. It wasn't some heroic saviour death, but the cowards way out. James had no clue how to calm Michael down. After seeing his father dying on the school floor, anything that anyone would say to him was just irrelevant noise.

James wanted Michael to stay at home because it was reasonable to take a few days off after someone close to you dies. However, Michael had flat out refused to miss another day of school, since the only day he had ever taken off at Ramwall was when James had first been told about the program, and he had only missed that day to attend a funeral. Michael had only attended the funeral because the school didn't count it as a day off, keeping his precious one-hundred percent attendance. As Michael refused to take the day off school it meant that James would also have to go so that he could help out his friend.

As expected, there were still reporters waiting outside. This time they just wanted to speak to Andy, Michael, and James, according to what Tom had texted. Now two people had died in the space of a few weeks and both had been part of a new program. People were immediately speculating if they were linked.

Even James was unsure if the two deaths were linked or not. It was possible that Lilith had found life itself to be too much, having many other different problems weighing her down until she decided to end her life. Although considering she'd been talking with Michael non-stop and had shown no sign of having a rough time with life, James couldn't help but worry that there was a connection.

Sneaking a glance at the front of the school, James noticed the reporter that had cornered him, in a swarm of other mosquitoes desperate to extract some kind of story. Wanting more than anything to avoid speaking to him or any other reporter, James went all the way around the school to the side entrance, where people doing PE would leave the building towards the playing field.

Thankfully, even in the decimated state that Michael was in, he remembered to enter the school the same way James did. There was no telling what would happen if the reporters managed to get a hold of him. There were old and fresh tear marks on his face, his hair was sticking up at different angles and he was still wearing the same dirty sweater-vest he had on Monday.

Without a doubt, James would have been in the same state if he found out that Ella had suffered the same fate as Lilith. Probably even worse. After more consoling, Michael was able to stop shaking and his sentences were becoming somewhat coherent. It felt like a doable task to get him to science in one piece. That was, until James saw Daphne talking loudly in front of all of her rotten friends.

'Now that one's dead, we just need the rest of them to drop dead too. Or should I say hang dead?' she said loudly, the crowd around her roaring with laughter.

Daphne would never be able to revel in how much she had hurt Michael with her remark because, before she was able to notice him, he had run off into the science classroom. Wishing only the worst for her, James rushed into the classroom hoping that Michael was concocting some kind of cursed potion to destroy Daphne.

Michael had instead gone with the coping mechanism of pretending like everything in the world was fine, which would have been more believable if his face wasn't showing so much pain. His books were ready on the table, opened to the right chapter and his pencil case unzipped, a calculator to the side.

'Are you OK? Look Daphne's a bitch she had no right to say something like that.' James said, taking the seat next to Michael.

'I'm fine, can we just get on with the lesson?' Michael refused to look anywhere near James to hide the tears going down his face.

Andy came into the classroom followed by Daphne and then the rest of the class. James was pretty sure that the reason Andy wasn't at school on Monday was because what happened with

Sarah had caught up to him. The first week that Sarah died, he had acted completely normal, if not more charismatic and talkative, but now he wasn't his normal self.

He no longer looked like he was all there, a constant blank expression on his face. James could tell that it was because everything had caught up to him and he was starting to struggle to get through it all.

All his friends tried to cheer him up in different ways, but nothing worked. When someone tried to start a conversation with him, he would either ignore them or walk away from the large crowds around him. Even Daphne couldn't help him, she would try to make out with him in the hallways but he would turn his face away, making her angry, and then she would take that frustration out by bullying some innocent person.

The fact that Andy also had to go to the police station in a couple of hours was surely another thing weighing down on him, knowing his alibi was weak, and that he had never expected Sarah to get this entwined with his life. It was hard to be sad for Andy when his girlfriend was saying such cruel things about Lilith.

The lesson started normally enough, but soon the class's conversations turned to Sarah and her killer, the reporters, Lilith, the interrogations and everything else that came with an accidental death that had to be covered up.

Mrs Dinkley attempted to teach more about the human body. After James and Michael had multiple flashbacks of Sarah, from seeing pictures of blood on the big screen and having endured far too much talk about their fallen friend, they decided to take a break from the lesson.

Instead of asking to leave, they simply got up and left as the teacher told off Jodie for joking about Lilith's suicide. It was always easier to ask for forgiveness than it was for permission as Kara said.

The pair of them decided to stroll around the school to clear their minds. A couple of teachers saw them in the corridors and asked what they were up to, but the moment they realised it was

Michael who they were talking to, they immediately let them continue walking without further questions.

A ten-minute break turned into skipping an entire lesson. As Michael and James spoke about Lilith and tried to work out why she would end her own life, every idea linked back to Sarah being the main cause, which meant they had some part in Lilith's death. Guilt was so heavy on their soul it was a miracle their heads hadn't exploded.

As Michael wasn't family and didn't know Lilith for more than a few weeks, he wasn't allowed to see her. He wasn't even sure if he would be invited to the funeral as he assumed it would be only family and close friends. It was crushing Michael that he couldn't say a proper goodbye.

They did their best to get through the day until it was time for them to head to the police station to be questioned. Just as they entered, the pair of them left through the side exit. Tom had been kind and smart enough to bring in two baseball hats for them so that they could leave unseen by the press.

James and Michael arrived fifteen-minutes earlier than their allotted time, as instructed in the email. They walked up to an old receptionist that looked far too much like Mrs Pogue. The woman asked them to sign their names on a sign-in sheet and then told them to hand in their phones so that they couldn't communicate with anyone during the interrogation.

After they had been patted down by a police officer to make sure they weren't carrying any kind of weapon, James and Michael made their way into a waiting room filled with chairs that was already being occupied by Grayson.

Grayson smiled at James and Michael as he noticed them. He seemed worried about the whole situation. Unlike the cinema or HighJump, he was at a police station and was about to be interrogated about something he had been heavily involved in, where one false move would lead to everything falling apart.

'Hey, guys. I'm so sorry about Lilith, Michael. She was a good person and she told me you were dating.'

Grayson was staring at James, trying to show with his face that they had to be careful about the things they said. The police and everyone else had to be under the impression that the only time they had seen each other was during the program.

'Thank you,' Michael replied sadly as he dropped into a chair, not paying attention to Grayson.

'Do you know if anyone we know has been in there yet?' James asked, curious to see who would be integrated first.

'From what I know, we'll be the first. Ludwig and Ella are scheduled for tomorrow, and I have no clue about Andy.'

Grayson didn't look happy with James. It was clear that he wanted them to act like they had barely spoken to each other at the program and had then completely forgotten about it, like when they had seen each other at HighJump. Going with this, James sat far away from Grayson next to Michael without saying another word.

Not long after having sat down, a familiar cancerous scent consumed the area, as Detective Jace Edict came around the corner. James was pretty sure that he was wearing the same clothes from when they met at Moonlight. It was as though the detective dressed and lived at the lowest standard to mask any kind of skill he had, a way to lull someone into a feeling of hollow safety when near him.

Michael had been stuck in a trance-like state for a while. His sullen face blended with the emptiness in his eyes making him look like a corpse. Stuck in his own head thinking about things that should never be thought about, and future memories that could now never be lived. However, the potent smell of the detective swiftly brought Michael to his senses as he tucked his nose under his stretched sweater vest in an attempt to reduce the smell, like some kind of makeshift gas mask.

'Ah James. It's good to see you again, pal. I'll start with you.' Jace said as he placed some cheap lunch in the bin.

Detective Edict's polluted blue eyes studied James as he showed the way with an open hand. Their eyes met and it felt like the detective was staring directly into his soul, searching for any evil or poison. Whilst it felt like Jace was learning everything about James from a short glance, the sickening smell of smoke again distracted James from thinking about anything other than throwing up.

Grayson didn't wish James luck, pretending to be invested in a poster about underage drinking that was hanging next to him, but just as James was about to exit the room, he gave a quick glance around the area as if searching for the toilet and gave a small nod to James. Michael was so out of it that he hadn't noticed James leave his side, too busy thinking about how sad and lonely his life felt.

James was led into an interrogation room down the hall where the detective first appeared. It was exactly like the one in the movies. The classic piece of glass that was definitely a two-way mirror had been positioned so that any onlookers could see the face of the suspect sitting down on the cheap metal chair, resting their guilty hands on the piece of sticky metal they used as a table. Surprisingly, the chair James was offered was functioning and didn't wobble at all, with only a small scab of rust on it.

An empty cup had been left on the table from when the last suspect had last been in there, possibly confessing to some mundane crime that paled in comparison to murder. Jace offered to get James some fresh water, which he accepted, allowing for a few minutes to breathe unpolluted air.

Reminding himself about his alibi was the only thing James could think to do to calm him down. As long as Michael stuck to the story about them all going to the park, it would make his alibi watertight. It was a perfectly plausible story to believe and when two other people confirmed it, the detective would have to believe it.

It wasn't long until Jace was back, filling the room with his intoxicating smell. He firmly placed the clear plastic cup next to James and extended a hand. James grasped the unsurprisingly dirty hand. His grip was strong and business-like.

'So, buddy, I'm sure you know why I've asked you here today. The terrible news about Lilith meant that this has become a little more important than before. It now means that you knew two people who have died in the past month and I just want to work out if there is any kind of connection, something that could help us find Sarah's killer.'

James was listening intently to what Jace was saying, making sure to hear and understand every word as if it was gospel.

'Now we just have to do some formalities once I start this tape.' Jace took out a large old looking tape recorder and started to play it. 'This is Detective Jace Edict speaking, having the first official questioning with James Fuss. James, could you please tell me how you knew Sarah Lee and Lilith Rumack?'

This was the early part of the interrogation which James had been expecting, the basic information that leads on to the more in-depth talks, the nice calm before the onslaught.

'Yes. Sarah went to my school. I had a few classes with her and never really spoke to her. Lilith was part of a new program our schools set up that Sarah and I were also a part of. A little after our first-time meeting, myself, Michael, Ella and Lilith went on a double date in the park.' James's voice was shaking as he spoke even though he had everything rehearsed.

'Don't worry so much, pal. Have some water, this won't take long and it's just some basic questions.'

Detective Edict allowed James some time to drink the water as he pulled out a notebook from his old leather jacket. It was peculiar hearing the detective using words like buddy and pal. James was sure the only reason Jace was using those words was to make him feel off-guard and safe, which James needed to remember he was not.

'I was hoping you could tell me what you were doing last Saturday, the night we found Sarah?'

This felt completely out of the blue considering he had a real alibi on that night, and James was very aware that Sarah had died a week before.

'Well, I was at the hospital with my sister all day until I went home to get ready for a party and then shortly after went to the party.'

'Please could you give me more specifics? Timings, where the party was. That kind of jumbo,' Detective Edict responded, with a tinge of annoyance.

Apparently, this night was more important to him than any other night, which James was fine with as he could remember it well.

'I'd been at the hospital since Thursday afternoon, I left on Saturday at around 2-3 p.m. where I went straight home for a few hours getting ready, and then I went to Ella's house to pick her up and then we went straight to Jodie's party on Curtain Fall Way.'

James was about to continue with the rest of the night when the detective held up his hand to stop him from talking.

'Is this Jodie Smith's party that you were heading to?'

The questions being asked were the most mundane uninteresting things that James could speak about. The tales he had been prepared to divulge shone so much brighter with rich interest than the dry reciting of a relatively ordinary night. Instead, James was left to give pointless information that felt trivial to anything to do with Sarah's death. In fact, he knew it was trivial because James was there when Sarah died and had every bit of knowledge about that night. Information that this dunce of a detective was nowhere near to discovering.

James was sitting in his chair more relaxed than he would have ever imagined, thinking about how easy it must be to become a detective. He had spent countless nights worrying about this day, how terrible it was bound to be. James's time would have been put to better use watching a turtle die of old age over stressing about such a simple easy interview.

'Yes, I was heading to Jodie Smith's house party. We're friends.'

James felt the need to speak as simply as possible so that Jace could understand him, like when a mother talks slowly and clearly to their newborn child. Even though James was more than comfortable, he had a small break in his smile when the detective started writing in his notepad again. As though what James had just said meant anything remotely important.

'From what I hear, she is quite popular, no?'

James could see where this was going and was already getting offended.

'I suppose so, I don't really understand why that matters?'

The detective leaned back in his chair, observing James closely.

'Well, I suppose it's just, I don't peg you as a popular kid. You know one who goes to parties all the time, and from what I understand, this was a rather small party. With only the most popular kids invited.'

James struggled to hold his nerve, Jace knew how to make people angry that was for sure.

'Well, you see ... Detective. Jodie is close with Tom who is my best friend and all of the 'popular kids' as you call them, at the party, which had quite a lot of people, have been kind to me since my father passed away.'

Most people tended to get awkward when his father's death got brought up, including James, but he decided to use it as his trump card to get away from the conversation. However, Jace did not think like a normal human being.

'Ah yes of course. Your father died trying to stop a school shooter, didn't he? I remember seeing it in the news. Something like that must have made it hard to trust people, especially those at your school. Now from what I hear, Sarah was the kind of person people thought of as dangerous. Did you also think that?'

Sipping on some water was the only way James could think of to cool him down, it wouldn't have surprised him if he was going hot in the face from anger, and when he spoke back, it was through gritted teeth.

'He didn't just try. He stopped the shooter. Many people are alive today because of what he did. I barely spoke to Sarah not because I couldn't trust people or because I thought she would kill me, but because she wasn't my friend.'

James couldn't bring himself to say that Sarah was a bad person and that was the reason he refused to ever speak to her. In truth, she hadn't done much wrong, and lived a miserable life as a result of trying to stand up for herself.

'It doesn't matter if you spoke to her a lot or not, people have many assumptions about others before they've even heard them speak. No, what matters is if you thought she might shoot up Ramwall. If you did, then maybe you would try and do something about it?'

James had no idea why Jace was painting him in such a bad way, it made him feel like he was guilty of things he had never really done, creating motives to hurt Sarah when he only wanted the best for people. After giving it some thought, James started to realise that the detective would be doing this to everyone. Jace was aware that this made no sense and was only trying to get James angry, hoping that something would slip out.

'Well, you see, I have no intention of hurting anyone, I've never been in a fight, and to answer your previous question, no. I did not think of Sarah as the kind of person to shoot up a school. I thought she was someone who had a lot of hardships and a challenging life, which was something that I honestly couldn't be bothered to try and fix.'

For some reason, the detective decided that what James had just said wasn't worth writing down. As if blatantly saying he had no thoughts about harming Sarah was less important than his exact whereabouts on a day that meant nothing in any way to when she died.

James believed that after saying what he did, he would be allowed to leave. There wasn't any motive for him to hurt Sarah, which was the complete truth. Instead, the detective made no indication that James would be allowed to leave the interrogation room any time soon, proceeding to ask him even more questions.

'Very well, how about we get back to the rest of your night. We seem to have gone off track.'

It was stupid that Jace still wanted to go over the night when nothing of any importance happened.

'Yes sir. Ella and I arrived at the party at around seven, someone at the party later saw the story about what happened to Sarah, which pretty much brought the party to an end. At around midnight, I walked Ella back to her house and went home.'

This was all being written in the detective's little notebook as if it was all vital information, and when he spoke again, he was still scribbling down the last of his notes.

'Could you please tell me where Ella lives buddy?'

'She lives on Second Street,' James said, giving an audible sigh.

At this, Detective Edict chucked his pen to the table and stared at James, annoyed.

'Did you know Second Street is one of the most common road names in America? There is almost definitely more than one in Echoway. I am going to need to ask you once more to be more specific.'

Whilst James was glad the detective didn't finish the sentence by calling him buddy, it was scary seeing him hostile.

'It's the left turning just before you reach the front gates at EE, the other side of the street is where the horse stables are.'

By the time James had finished, the fire in the detective's eyes had faded and the friendly face wore a smile on it when happily reviewing the words he had written so far.

'Can I ask at what point in the night you cut yourself?' Detective Edict asked casually.

This was the first time James was caught completely off-guard by a question. At first, James had no idea what he was talking about until his mind reeled back to that night when he fell to the floor and cut his fingers. The safest option in these uncharted territories was to play it safe and get as much information as possible.

'How did you know I cut myself?'

James hoped that saying this would reveal how much he needed to lie about how it happened. Jace gave a frown as if disappointed in James for not going with the flow and answering his question straight away. The detective pointed with his pen at James's hand.

'You have a plaster on your finger, I can only assume that was from getting it cut. It looks like a relatively new plaster so I can assume it would have happened sometime near Saturday.'

This was such a stretch James thought it was almost funny. There were thousands of ways he could have cut his finger. It could have just as easily happened any day other than Saturday. If James wanted to, he could say he simply slipped when cutting up some carrots. If he wanted to piss off the detective more, James could say it happened on a completely different day.

But something so insignificant wouldn't be worth lying about when he already had so much to remember, and it wasn't like he had done anything incriminating to have the cut.

'Oh yes. I didn't think it was relevant but I fell over on the way to Ella's house, I missed the curb and happened to fall on some glass.'

James was quick to act like the glass was already there, since he wasn't legally allowed to have alcohol. It didn't seem like the smartest plan to say he was holding an entire bottle of vodka, and his minor change of the event could never be proven as wrong. Nor could anything he had just said.

Detective Edict now leaned forward just enough for their eyes to be on the same level.

'It's a little strange don't you think buddy? How the route to Ella's house, which as you've just said you went straight to from your house, doesn't include going down Hamlet Way. Yet we found traces of your blood on some glass, presumably from that fall you say happened on that exact street. And do you know who was buried on the other side of that street?'

Shit. James hadn't done anything wrong that night but this was starting to make him look very suspicious. There wasn't much he would be able to say to persuade the detective it was a coincidence, and that he had simply gotten lost.

Replying felt pointless; he would only dig himself into a deeper hole. So, James chose to just sit in his chair, allowing the detective to explain what he thought happened. Jace had been watching James carefully when saying the misleading clue and it was clear he had received the reaction he wanted.

'Now boy, this doesn't look great for you, does it? I mean it could be a complete coincidence that we found traces of your blood on some broken glass directly next to where the body was found. I would, of course, love to believe it was a case of wrong place at the wrong time, but you have to understand, I need a little more detail as to why you were there.'

James's mind was racing, it was doing hundreds of different calculations at the same time, trying to work out how he could reasonably explain why he found himself outside the Silver Chariot, next to where Ludwig and Grayson buried the body. It wouldn't be enough to say the truth of him getting lost, James would have to come up with something much more believable.

There was only one explanation that he could think of that panned out and made sense. However, the idea of using it was sickening to James, it wouldn't feel right to use something like that as an excuse, but there wasn't any other choice.

'I went to visit my father; I didn't tell you or anyone else because I don't like speaking about it. I left the house a little earlier and spent some time with him because I was nervous about the party. You were right, it was a popular person party and I'm just not like them. I wanted to talk to him so that I could calm down.'

The single tear coming from James had nothing to do with his acting or lying, it was a real tear of sadness because he had just stooped so low to get out of trouble. In reality, James hadn't visited his father since the funeral, because he was far too scared.

Detective Edict showed no real emotion, he might have sounded like he cared about James but it was all a ruse to make him feel comfortable. He didn't offer James a tissue and so James resorted to wiping his wet eyes with his sleeve. Sniffling, James looked up at the detective to see him staring at him with piercing eyes, trying to work out if he was lying or not. It made sense that he would take that route if he did visit the cemetery, and it was more than plausible for something he would do. Finally, after a lengthy silence, the detective jotted down a few words.

'I'll accept that, but be careful I will be checking if it's true. If I find out that you have just lied to me, you're going to be in more trouble than you could ever imagine. Now you mentioned that you were going to Ella's house. Tell me a bit more about her?'

James was sweating and his leg had been jittering violently. If this is how he got when Jace said something that had nothing to do with the murder, he dreaded to think how he would act if Jace managed to stumble onto the truth.

'We met through the program, and had a lot in common so we've been hanging out a bit,' James spoke as clearly as he could. The thought of Ella calmed him down a notch.

After saying this the detective frowned again as though something didn't add up, which naturally terrified James. He turned back a couple of pages in his notebook to look at something he had written beforehand.

'If I am not mistaken, there is a big rivalry between your two schools, did that not get in the way of anything? I mean, most fights that happen in this town are spawned from the school's mini-war. I'm surprised you can speak to her at all.'

The detective was blatantly beckoning James into getting angry but he wouldn't be thrown around the ring again.

'Honestly Jace, it's not much of a rivalry, the kids at EE have the nicer school and so get the better education. It's not a rivalry because we can't exactly fight back. They are simply better trained for everything. Probably even murder. I have made my peace with that a long time ago and I'm not envious of them. They have to work much harder and get fewer holidays and are required to wear that preppy uniform. Neither Ella nor I bother with the fights and arguments because we both accept neither of us had a choice in the school we went to.'

The idea to poke at this subject a little more crossed Jace's mind, but he resolved to move on to another subject, understanding that this wasn't going to get much emotion from James. Which is what Detective Edict seemed to feed on.

'Just a few more questions and you can go, James. I wanted to know why you bothered to call an ambulance for your sister and why she was rushed to the hospital?'

What a complete fucker. James had reached his highest point of anger. The nerve of him to bring in to question his innocent hospitalised sister was despicable. James very well knew that this was Jace's intent but he didn't care that he was falling straight into his trap.

'When someone faints from alcohol poisoning, it isn't the smartest thing to leave them in your lap to die.' James may have been practising a ventriloquist act with how little he was moving his mouth.

Detective Edict could tell that he had James hooked and had him right where he wanted, deciding to speak far too casually for such a serious matter.

'It would not have been the smartest thing no, but at least you wouldn't have had to pay for all the bills,' Jace said this with a sigh and started speaking again just as James was about to protest in anger, 'but that doesn't explain why she had an injury to her head, does it? Could you be so kind as to tell me how that happened?'

Blood was almost coming from James's palms because of how hard his fingernails were digging into his hands trying to suppress his fury. James was sure that after this was all over, he would find some crescent-shaped marks carved into his hand.

'Unfortunately, I was unable to catch my sister as she fainted, which meant that she hit her head as she fell to the floor.'

It was surprising that red steam wasn't coming from his ears from how enraged he was becoming. The detective wobbled his head like a tacky gift shop toy.

'Now what doesn't add up is when the Paramedics came to the house, the front door was already ajar and from what they said, you were apologizing to her for screwing everything up.'

Had this moron interviewed every single person in the town? The more the detective spoke, the more panicked James became as he was twisting genuine facts into fake stories. James wasn't happy with telling the detective why he was apologizing to Kara on that fateful night, but now as he was pushed into a corner, it seemed like he had no choice but to come clean.

'The reason I was apologizing was because-'

There was no time to finish that sentence because of something James would never expect the quiet, calm, stinky detective to do. Without any warning, the detective jumped up from his seat and slammed his hands on the table like Mr Hemans would.

'I think you kidnapped Sarah after your mom went away! I think you and your sister were in it together and kept her in your house with the intent of hurting her, so she couldn't hurt other people! I believe that on the day Kara was rushed to hospital, Sarah had managed to escape and knocked your sister out whilst running from your house! By some miracle for you, she happened to run past you on your way back from school, you chased after her and managed to catch her just outside the park! In those panicked moments where she was filled with adrenaline, Sarah managed to grab a bottle and hit you with it! Which is why we found your blood on the road! She then desperately tried to hide in the park! Sadly, you managed to find where she was hiding because if she escaped, you would already be in prison! You then finished the job, on an already weak Sarah who you had been starving and torturing! You poorly buried the body in the park hoping nobody would find it and sprinted back to your house where you called the ambulance after finding Kara!'

Everything Jace had said was utterly wrong but it didn't matter if everyone else thought this was true. He would be going to prison for much worse than what he had done and all he could think to do was explain.

'That doesn't make any sense, you're wrong! My sister has been ill for a long time, and she could never hurt anyone, I could never hurt someone. I don't even go that route from school. I told you before that blood was from when I fell on the way to the party. It doesn't make any sense that I would torture and hurt her when the only injury she had was a hit on the head and when the paramedics came, I wasn't bleeding because she never hit me with a bottle, you can ask them if they remember me apologizing, they can remember I wasn't bleeding.'

Breathing felt like such a challenging task. With the smell of smoke along with James having a panic attack, it felt very much like he was stuck in a fire. Taking strong heavy breaths did nothing to help how scared and desperate he was feeling. He couldn't go to prison for murder when he didn't do it. It took a while for James to realise that the detective was smiling at him, a look of victory on his face.

'I know that none of that made sense, I don't think you did any of that, it doesn't add up, and it isn't what I would expect you to ever do. What is interesting is how you knew the cause of Sarah's death when that information hasn't been released.'

16. Broken Glass

There had never been another moment where James had suffered such stupidity. It was so blindingly obvious that Jace had made it all up. None of it made any sense. James had already worked out the detective just wanted to make him flustered, so he would let something slip. James had fallen into a trap that he could see from miles away because he was so desperate to prove he was innocent.

James had been caught. Ella was right, all he had to do was slip up once and the big bad wolf would catch him. Now in this grimy interrogation room, everything would soon fall apart. Jace looked victorious as he took out a packet of tobacco from his jacket and started constructing a cigarette.

'Now I want to believe you just happened to hear this from someone, I mean I know how gossip spreads, but now we've got a long night ahead of us. Believe me, when I say, I'm going to find out what happened, it's only a matter of time.'

It seemed like the time to come clean was upon him. James would do his best to protect his friends and cloud as much as he could, but it didn't seem like there was another option anymore. At least, that would have been the case if someone hadn't knocked on the door.

'Come in,' Jace said as he finished creating his stick of cancer, placing it in his mouth ready to light.

The door opened showing the secretary who was acting far too giddy for someone of her age and at such a sad time in life.

'Detective, someone's just phoned in saying they think they've found the murder weapon.'

The cigarette stuck to Jace's bottom lip as his mouth dropped. 'What ... How? I'll speak to them now.' Jace rose from his chair and made for the exit. Just before the door closed behind him, he stuck his head back into the room and glared at James. 'Stay here. You're still a prime suspect pal, and I'm gonna find out how you're involved.' With that, he slammed the door shut and James was left to drown in his own despair.

James waited for hours on end, pondering his future. He would have to come clean about everything and without his phone, there was no way to update anyone else about how he had failed to keep the truth from the detective. However, in the end, there was no continuation to the interrogation, no return from the wretched smelling man to extract those details that would send James to jail. James sat there freaking out about his future until the sun had gone down and the cleaner came in to sweep the floor.

He took it as a sign to leave the room and head back into the waiting room. James wanted to find a familiar face, but by now everyone had gone home, after presumably being told that their interrogation had been postponed whilst Jace followed up on this lead that was somehow better than a confession to the crime itself.

James made his way to the front desk where the secretary explained the detective wouldn't be back to continue his questioning, which James had deduced himself after hours on end of meticulous thinking and worrying. For the moment, he was cleared to leave until further notice and was given back his phone and asked to sign out on the sheet of paper.

This new murder weapon that James very well knew couldn't exist, unless someone brought an entire table to Jace, meant that he would surely be called back at some point when it turned out to be an inevitable dead end.

It was hard to care that the lead wouldn't pan out when it allowed James to be let off the hook. Even for just a few extra days. If even that. It would be enough to make up a reasonable story for how he knew Sarah died from a hit to the head. It was such a simple detail; James had never realised that everyone else had no idea what exactly killed Sarah.

James didn't try and complain that it wasn't fair to leave an 'innocent' person for so many hours in the station. Instead, he ran as fast as he could out of the building and sprinted home before the wolf could catch up to him. There had to be some merit to this mystery caller that gave new evidence, otherwise, the Detective wouldn't have been out following up on it for so long.

Someone must have phoned in and given genuine evidence, or what they believed to be evidence. Maybe it was similar to the broken bottle that got James into so much trouble, something that was just a random accident that could be falsely linked to what happened at the Silver Chariot.

If everything went to hell, it would be the last night James would ever spend as a free person. It wouldn't matter if he was wrongly accused; there was a lot of evidence against him. People would blame it on his father's death as well. They would say, 'How could he not go mad with all the things he experienced,' and 'He was always so quiet, I'm not surprised it was him.' Daphne would be the first on TV broadcasts casting cruel ideas to the town, like a witch helping to spread a plague.

James called Ella the moment he returned home. They spent their time refreshing the local news sites, begging something to come up with a story about how they arrested the murderer. That they had caught some drug dealer who was linked to Sarah and presumed to be the killer. James could live with that, if some washed-up evil person, who was already doing bad things in the world was convicted of doing just another bad thing.

James tried to phone Michael whilst Ella had some rushed dinner with her family, but he wasn't picking up his phone. There was no way to tell if he had been interrogated whilst James was being picked to pieces by Jace. It was possible that the murder weapon led to Michael in some way, and that he wasn't responding because he was currently detained.

Now that Michael had lost Lilith, it was frightening to think about what he might do. There is nothing scarier than someone with nothing to lose who has secrets that could destroy lives.

After calling a couple more times, James had to accept that there was nothing he could do to help. He had no idea where Michael lived, nor anyone who could contact him. James had to blindly wish that Michael had simply lost his phone, and he would pull through the night and see the light of day. It didn't take long for Ella to finish her dinner and call James, who felt so sick he was struggling to swallow saliva let alone food.

Neither of them slept that night, staying up to talk to each other, reeling off different possibilities of what this murder weapon could be and who it would lead to. How somebody could have found something so late into Sarah's death. It wasn't until 7.30 a.m. that the page refreshed with a new update about the investigation.

The article stated that Ludwig Olsson was brought into custody after new information was discovered about the investigation. James couldn't believe what he was reading. In his sleep-deprived state, he needed to triple check the headline to make sure he wasn't misreading it.

Scrolling down on his phone the article continued to explain that someone had found a shard of glass in a bush outside the park with blood on it. After doing some testing, the police found the blood to be from Sarah with fingerprints from Ludwig's fingerprints. The police still couldn't confirm what happened on the night of her death, but they had been interrogating Ludwig throughout the night to find out exactly how everything unfolded.

The police were confident that they had the killer and nobody would be able to tell them any different. Before Ella or James could talk about it, James's mum came barging into his room, telling him to get ready for school so that he wouldn't be late. School was as usual one of the least important things that James had on his mind. He was about to argue with her, to tell her what had just happened, to scream about what happened in the interrogation that she hadn't bothered to ask about. In the end, all that pent up anger and fear stayed bottled up as his mum had already left and James didn't have the willpower to chase after her.

Instead of bunking the day off school to live a good last day as a free person, because Ludwig was bound to explain what had happened, James decided it would be better to see Michael. It would be his last day as someone with a future as well. And James thought he deserved to know it. They had only found out about Lilith the day before, and now Michael would have to deal with what happened to Ludwig on top of everything else. James attempted to call Michael again to no success.

He was certain that Michael would be at school. Even if he had witnessed someone die, helped cover up the body so that he wouldn't go to prison, fell in love, had the person he loved commit suicide, and then hear that he would likely be going to prison by the end of the day, James was sure he would still keep his 100 percent attendance record. Helping Michael through it all would be the last decent deed James could do before Ludwig revealed what happened. A last gift to the world for letting him get this far.

Since that moment at the Silver Chariot, James had the sinking feeling that he was living on borrowed time. That no matter what, that night would eventually catch up with him. James thought that each day he had lived after Sarah's death was like a vivid dream, as if his soul had left him for a better place, and all that was left was some broken doomed body.

After some panicked and scared goodbyes, Ella hung up the phone to also get ready for school. She needed to tell Grayson about what had happened or to support him if he already knew. James didn't bother to shower or eat breakfast; his mind was on more important matters.

After giving it some thought, he had decided there was one thing he needed to do in the short time left as a free man, one selfish errand he would allow himself.

Before leaving the house, his mother mumbled that Kara was expected to leave the hospital in a few hours. It was ironic that as Kara would be coming home, James would presumably be heading to prison. Normally, James would have been furious that his mother hadn't told him sooner, but now it felt like a cruel gift. If he had known before, his heart would have shattered knowing how close he was to seeing her.

James slammed the door shut on his way out. He hadn't thought much about how Ludwig could have been arrested for murder. He couldn't hurt Sarah by smashing her with a bottle. Not only was it something he could never do, but the weapon also made no sense. Sarah died from a head injury after hitting her head and bleeding out, which wasn't possible with a bottle.

Unless Ludwig smashed the bottle over her head and then acted like it was an accident, breaking the table some other way. He was alone with her at the time after all. Everyone assumed he was passed out, but there was a chance he was faking it, waiting for everyone to leave them alone, giving him the chance to strike.

James shook his head as he took a turn.

Even if that was the case, he had no reason to kill her. Or maybe there was. Sarah used to attend EE with Ludwig, and she certainly made a lot of enemies in her time. Could she have done something to Ludwig that made him want to kill her?

Now it felt like James was Detective Edict, putting different things together to make some kind of story fit into what he was thinking. Ludwig couldn't have killed her. James realised that not only did Ludwig join EE as Sarah was leaving, but there would have been evidence of the smashed glass around Sarah's body. Someone would have seen it. James cleaned the blood from the carpet and there wasn't any broken glass next to where Sarah fell, and it wasn't exactly a moment he struggled to remember.

James was close to his destination and decided to stop thinking about how Ludwig was possibly framed for the murder. It was a rabbit hole that didn't seem like a good idea to get lost down, and would only leave him doubting everyone. It was too late to worry about how it happened. James would surely find out soon when the police came to arrest him anyway.

By the time he arrived at the church, school would be starting in thirty-minutes. James didn't care about being late, but then he hated the idea of leaving Michael alone to panic and freak out. The doors to the church were locked. It was still several hours before morning service. This didn't bother James in the slightest. He was interested in what was next to the church.

The dark gritty sky was a similar colour to the gravestones, each one a different shade depending on its age, height, and maintenance, but without fail all looking depressing. Most of the graves had flowers on them to help bring some colour to the dead. There was one grave in particular that had an overwhelming number of bright fresh flowers on it. Sarah's brand-new patch of ground was filled with beautiful bouquets that lit up the area like the end of a rainbow, and she was the pot of gold.

Sarah had been buried almost as soon as they found the body and performed the autopsy. She had a small ceremony with her family. The reason her parents refused to tell anyone about the burial was because of how many people would come. They decided that instead of having the cameras, the reporters, and all the fake people who would only come for likes and follows, it would be nicer to have one more moment as a family.

This is at least what James hoped had happened. In truth, he had no idea what unfolded at the funeral, only that very few people showed up, and that nobody knew when it was. Not long after the service, people started to catch wind that Sarah was buried in the cemetery. Coming to pay some kind of respect with flowers they wouldn't give to Sarah when she was alive.

James never knew Sarah all that well, but he was sure that she would have hated how her patch of grass looked. She would have undoubtedly grimaced with disgust as to how generically perfect it appeared. Backtracking out of the graveyard to a bush nearby, James found the blackest flower he could find, a small velvety blade of tainted life. James stood there for far too long staring at the petals. He wondered if it was Sarah's favourite flower. It was nice to think that they were. That she would pick one up on the way home from school after a bad day to cheer her up. That if she ever went to a happy occasion like prom or her wedding, she would wear the flower in her hair dressed in a black wedding gown. Now nobody would know, and she would never get to experience all those things because James had failed to save her.

Perhaps in death, she would live in a world filled with black flowers, a place where she was happy. James broke off one of the stems and dawdled back over to Sarah's resting body, placing the small gorgeous flower on top of the headstone. Staring at her fresh slab of rock reading the inscription on it; made James feel like he was back in the Silver Chariot, watching as Sarah lay motionless on the floor. The carving read:

Sarah Smith (2001-2018)

Hate is always cruel, love was always you, and you will always be loved.

It didn't make much sense to James. Sarah was known for her hate, even though most of it wasn't real. Did her parents want to say that their child was stupid for living the life she did? Considering they thought she was murdered by a killer, it might have meant that the apparent killer was cruel and that no matter what, Sarah will always be loved. James had never met Sarah's parents, but he chose to believe they were the kind to pick the latter.

To James, there seemed like no better place to get everything off his chest and to speak to Sarah one last time.

'I want you to know that I am truly sorry for what happened to you. Not because of how it affected me, but because you shouldn't have died. I wish you were surrounded by the people who loved you instead of me and everyone else. Then maybe someone would have caught you, and you would still be alive. Sometimes I feel like you're watching over me trying to make my life miserable at every turn. I know I deserve it. I didn't try and help you. But don't worry it's almost over now. Everyone will soon know exactly what happened and you can get justice. This deserves to be over with so that you can finally have peace. So that I can have peace.'

When James allowed himself one more errand, he really meant two, just at the same place. The last thing he had on his agenda before he left for school and for his arrest was to finally visit his father. Small droplets of rain had started to fall from the grey clouds that promised much worse than what he was experiencing.

James had only seen his father's grave once when he was buried, but James knew exactly where it was. Approaching his gravestone felt worse than Sarah's. He could see the blotch of land that gave a home to his dad. Unlike Sarah's resting place, James's father didn't have a single flower.

After he had passed away, his grave had such an overwhelming number of flowers it put Sarah's to shame. Now nobody visited him, not the people of the town, or the children whose lives he saved, and not his own family. Well, that wasn't completely true. Kara often visited their father, on occasion with their mum, just never with James.

He was disgusted with how bad of a son he had been, but he was afraid. James knew that all he would think about was that moment, when he dropped to his knees as his father died next to him, blood draining from his bullet holes drenching James in blood. Hearing the screams of students and his own hideous wails of pain. Now as he was so close to his father, James realised that he had been dreaming of the same thing every night anyway. So what was the harm in living the moment once more?

The clouds were now pouring down rain. The dirt beneath James became mud as he read his father's name, tears mixing with the water on his face. Like the rain, everything inside James came pouring out as he explained what had happened to him over the heavy noise of water crashing into the ground and thunder in the distance. Once he started to talk, it became impossible to stop speaking about all of his woes and fears.

After he had recounted every terrible detail of his experiences since his father's death, James waited for something to happen. HE gasped for breath, as though he had just come out of freezing water that he had been submerged in for months. James stood there, expecting his father to place a warm hand on his shoulder and say that it would all work out in the end.

Unsurprisingly, the gravestone didn't speak back. He had spent the last moments of his freedom talking to a corpse in the ground and weeping like a baby deer being circled by lions. He had desperately hoped that by facing his greatest fear, everything would automatically fix itself. In reality, nothing had changed and the only thing that James could think to do now was go to school. His education no longer mattered but at least he would spend some time with his friends in his final moments.

James had been so involved with his father that he was completely oblivious to another man in the cemetery, a black umbrella shielding him from the downpour. Curiosity got the better of James as he started to walk over to the man who stood at Sarah's grave. The rain made it hard to distinguish who it was from afar, and the slippery surface caused James to skid as he moved. Now next to the man James could tell that it was the same strange old man from the church.

Just as in church, the man seemed to be thinking hard or possibly praying to the grave. James was thinking of walking away when the man spoke.

'I hope you are well, and that the person you came to see enjoyed your visit.'

James was starting to realise that the man had a familiar accent, one that he couldn't place the last time they met.

'My father,' James said.

'Ah, the wise man. I am sorry for your loss. I'm sure he was a much better father than I have ever been.' The man spoke with bitterness.

James realised that the man's accent was Swedish, similar to Ludwig's when he became drunk or upset. 'You're Ludwig's father, aren't you?'

Ludwig's father hung his head in shame.

'I am doubtful he wants me as his father anymore, and now with what they are saying he has done, I don't know if I can help him.'

It was hard to hear someone speak about their child when it was alleged that he had killed someone.

'I don't think Ludwig did what they are saying. He is a good person in so many ways, and I promise that soon you will find out what happened. Right now, I think he needs his family with him. If I was in his spot, all I would want is my father to be there for me.'

'You are once again right. I can't imagine my son could ever harm this girl, but what does it matter? There is all this evidence against him, there's nothing anyone could do to help him now.'

If James wanted to, he could always hand himself in, sacrifice himself so that Ludwig wouldn't be convicted as a murderer. Jace already assumed James was part of it and it wouldn't be too hard to spin a story where he was the one who killed Sarah.

'Maybe there is nothing that anyone can do to help, but you should still go to him. Make sure he is safe. Make sure he has his family close to him.'

Ludwig's father once again extended his hand and James shook it.

'Thank you. You're a good person,' said the father.

He could have no idea that in a couple of hours James would probably be taken away by the police for the murder of a girl. The rain was still falling heavily and it would have been hard to hear anything coming from either of them, so after spending a few more moments at Sarah's grave, the father walked away to spend time with Ludwig. Like how James had chosen to spend time with his father before he would be sent to prison.

James wondered what his father would do if he were in his situation. It didn't take much thinking. In a heartbeat, his father would make sure Ludwig was safe, and to help down to the bitter end. He would be willing to give up his entire life in the hope that others could continue living theirs.

If by the end of the day, the police hadn't come to find him, if Ludwig hadn't snitched on them to save his own skin, then James would aim to be like his father, and turn himself in.

17. The Desperation of Someone with Little Hope

Each breath of fresh air James took was like a cruel last meal given to him by Satan. On his walk to the school, James realised that he had never truly appreciated how beautiful the town was. How in the morning, the sunrise could be seen at such a perfect angle, it looked like an album cover. The way the birds chirped with such a sweet melody that no other place in the world could perform. His entire life, all James wanted to do was leave the town, but now that it might happen, he realised there was nothing he wanted less.

As he reached Ramwall, the rain was coming down harder than it had for a long time. James could barely see what was in front of him. His clothes were soaked and his shoes were covered in mud. Going up the front steps into the school was a challenge. Not only was it like walking on ice, but James was aware that it was the last time he would ever climb them.

He took extra care in memorising the layout of the school as best as he could from the outside. Taking in everything he saw. The walls were closing in and it would only be a matter of time until Ludwig explained what had happened, or until he turned himself in. Detective Edict would surely be close to getting everything out of Ludwig that was needed to arrest the rest of the people involved in Sarah's death.

James was just starting to memorise the entrance doors when something surprised him so much, he lost all focus. Kara was standing at the reception desk, hair soaking wet, arguing with Mrs Pogue.

'You don't understand. I need to speak with him now, there isn't any time!'

James could tell she had been shouting for a while based on the crowd that had formed around the area.

'There's nothing I can do! How am I meant to find him? School hasn't started yet.' Mrs Pogue had had enough of Kara and decided to leave her front area into the storage room, to get nothing in particular.

Kara turned around, her hair flicking water onto those near her, as she tried to find the person she so desperately needed. After standing there for a few moments in shock, James realised that he was obviously the one his sister needed to talk to and so called out to her. She locked eyes with him and made her way over, not caring about the people staring and whispering.

'Thank god I found you, I should have told you sooner. Mums sending me away.'

There had still been some part of James's mind that was focused on Ludwig but hearing this made it all go away.

'What? She's sending you away? She can't do that.'

'James, I'm not well, I need to go to a place where they can help me. It's for the best.' James thought desperately, trying to imagine ways that she could stay with him, but then it hit him that it no longer mattered, James would never be able to see her anyway.

'How long?' He couldn't care less that his voice was filled with pain and sadness, even with a large crowd staring at them.

'Around six months, I don't know if you'll be able to visit.'

James was doubtful as well, but for different reasons than Kara's. Before anything else could be said between them, someone from the crowd started speaking in a loud shrill voice.

'Who would want to visit you? You're such a disappointment, I don't know why they bothered to keep you alive.' Daphne came to the front of the crowd with an evil grin.

She was about to open her mouth again when, SMACK. Daphne received the hardest slap James had ever seen. The shock on Daphne's face was nothing compared to the red mark already flaring up like a traffic light on her cheek. Nobody was expecting Kara to have enough strength to do something like that. Even she seemed a little shocked before she turned back proudly to James.

'I've got to go Mums waiting outside. She wanted to take me straight there but I threatened to jump out of the car if we didn't go and see you first.'

'I'll miss you,' James said, trying his best not to tear up.

They hugged much tighter than what was safe, but James didn't care. It was the last time he would see his sister without a strong piece of glass between them. He was glad to have the chance to say goodbye.

Kara ran out of school, leaving James by himself. The crowd lingered to see if Daphne was brave enough to taunt James, but she thought better of it, sprinting to the bathroom with her little gremlins following right behind, calling out for Daphne.

James managed to find Michael by his locker unpacking his bag, which made James realise that he himself had forgotten to bring his. Not that it mattered. He couldn't attend detention if he was behind bars.

'What happened? You weren't responding to any of my calls,' James asked.

Michael was far too nonchalant for someone that had been off the radar for so long.

'Yeah, sorry about that. I just passed out after I got back from the station.' For someone who apparently slept well, he was void of any emotion in his voice.

'Did they question you at all, how was it?' James was struggling to sound sincere when Michael couldn't look him in the eye.

'No, they didn't question me. I sat there for a while and then the woman at the desk got a call from Andy-'

'Andy?' James couldn't believe what he had just heard. 'You mean Andy's the one who found the murder weapon. He's the one that set up Ludwig. Where is he, we need to get him to tell the truth if we-'

SLAM. James was stopped mid-sentence by Michael slamming his locker shut.

'We aren't going to do anything. Andy was right to do what he did. Now instead of all of us going down, it's just Ludwig. We can finally move on with our lives.'

People were staring at the pair of them now, and so James gestured to an empty classroom where they could speak freely.

'You're not making any sense, Michael,' James said, closing the door behind him. 'Look, we don't have much time. We won't be free to live our lives. Ludwig will tell the police what really happened and then they'll be after us.'

'Ludwig isn't going to say anything, because he knows nobody will buy it. If he did say anything and they believed him we would already be arrested. Which means we're free now. There's no more burden to carry. We can mourn the dead respectfully and I'll thank Ludwig for his sacrifice every time I go to church, but other than that we need to move on.'

'How can you say that? We can't just let Ludwig go to jail; he's innocent. We all are. Ella and I were confident this would be our last day as free people, I only came to school today to help you get through everything. If what you're saying is right and the police won't come for us, I don't care. We have to help him. They'll convict him as a murderer.'

Michael was pacing up and down the room, shaking his head as he went.

'There's nothing we can do to help him, James. Andy's cleared the rest of our names doing what he did. If we kept having to deal with that kind of pressure, we'd all end up like Lilith.'

Without another word, Michael flung open the door and walked out, acting as if he had never visited the Silver Chariot.

James was left stunned. He had thought Michael was one of the good ones. But now, with the choice between remaining quiet and trying to help a friend, he failed to choose right.

It then hit James that there really wasn't anything he could think to do to help Ludwig. Even if he tried to hand himself in, all James had to offer was the truth, which would still land Ludwig in prison along with Michael, Grayson, Andy, and Ella.

James left the classroom bewildered as to what to do, deciding to just keep on going with the day and let it see where it led him. If the police came to arrest him then he wouldn't need to make a decision, and then if nothing happened, he would speak to Ella and work out what they could do.

After sending a message to Ella telling her it was Andy who had set up Ludwig, he started to head off his first lesson, double maths. James still couldn't believe that Andy had framed Ludwig for the sake of getting the police off his trail. That he had such little care for others that he was willing to sacrifice their entire life just to make sure he kept his dreams alive. Michael might have chosen to deal with a bad situation poorly, but Andy was the reason for the horrible predicament in the first place.

On his way to Mr Heman's classroom, James found Tom who was of course speaking to Jodie. Except this time, they seemed to be arguing.

'James, did you hear, they found who killed Sarah? It was some EE freak, I told you they're all evil,' Jodie said.

Before James could say anything back, Tom answered for him, 'They aren't evil Jodie! Sure that kid may have been a murderer and that's terrible, but it doesn't mean the entire school is like him!' It was scary to see Tom this angry.

His veins were forming a large V-shape on his forehead that met in-between his eyebrows. Neither of them had any idea that Ludwig was a decent person and nothing like how they were describing him now.

'You're wrong, all of them are like that. They're trained to be bad people!' Jodie was holding onto her bag tightly as she shouted back at Tom.

James had never paid much attention to how much Jodie hated people from EE. He had always assumed it was more mob mentality on her part, as she never participated in any competitions or had any real connection to anyone there.

'Jodie, the only reason you hate them so much is because you think you deserve to be in the school. Your parents are rich and you think that entitles you to get into EE. It's about time you realise that just because your parents wanted you to go here doesn't mean you need to be such a miserable bitch about everything!'

For the second time that day, James saw someone getting slapped in the face. However, this slap from Jodie was less in the hand and more in the bag. There had been much more power in Kara's slap. Kara's had the full force of pent-up rage and pain behind it, built up as a result of years of verbal abuse.

All the same, it was enough to make the point that whatever kind of relationship they had, was over. It was also enough to cut Tom's cheek with whatever jagged book she had in her handbag.

The bell rang for the start of the day. Reminding James that if he were to get arrested, at least he wouldn't have to hear the insufferable ringing anymore. It felt surreal that so much was happening in James's life all at once, yet he was still heading into Mr Heman's classroom for double maths like he would every other Wednesday morning.

'Thank God that's over, she was a nightmare to be around. Even worse than you,' Tom said, taking a tissue from his bag as he started to dab at the small cut.

James was about to apologize for everything again when Tom cut in by nudging him with his elbow giving a smirk. 'Don't worry about it, it's all in the past. You were going through some really hard times and I'm glad you're getting past them. Let's get through maths and then we can catch up on everything. I want to know how it was at the station, I should have called to ask yesterday, I feel like I haven't properly spoken to you in ages.'

Of course, Tom had absolutely no idea about any of the things James was currently going through. But it felt good to have Tom back at his side like the old times, where all James had to worry about was getting ruthlessly bullied.

What with everything going on, with Sarah's so-called killer being caught, and a student suicide within two days, nobody had any intention to focus on work. Mr Heman's classroom was as cold as always, and he was as angry looking as ever. However, as the students entered the classroom, it wasn't with the disciplined fear as usual.

On this occasion, everyone was talking happily, gathering in groups around the room, not paying any attention to how alarmed the beast was. Apparently, people thought Mr Hemans would allow talking and mingling because of all the horrific drama that had taken place over the last few days. But Mr Hemans was a massive robot with anger issues, pity and remorse weren't in his programming.

'WHAT DO YOU THINK YOU'RE DOING! EVERYONE SHUT UP AND SIT DOWN!'

The entire class fell silent as though a bucket of ice-cold water had been chucked over their faces.

James was in a bizarre mood. It felt like he was in some kind of sleep-deprived paranoid version of Schrodinger's cat. He lived in two separate realities, one where the police were coming for him, and the other where he was free from it all. There was the weight of his actions and the fear of being caught, whilst simultaneously experiencing the relief of escape from his dire situation. He was both a doomed kid destined for prison and the luckiest person in the world who let his friend take a bullet for him.

With all of these feelings, James had no room to care about Mr Hemans. He sat at his desk, finger drumming the table, with nothing in front of him, and not a care in the world about the consequences. As Mr Hemans started to bark about what they would be reading from the book that day, James swirled around in his chair, not bothering to keep his voice down.

'Hey, Freddie, can I borrow a pen?'

Freddie sat there miserable as ever, bruises and marks all over his face. It looked like it hurt him to simply move in his desk. As much as James wanted to help, he couldn't think how, having such little time left in the first place. He hoped that when everything was over, someone would reach out to Freddie and make his life better, like how Ella had saved James.

Freddie was shaking his head at James desperately wanting him to turn back around so that Mr Hemans didn't shout at them. The whole class was looking at James from the corner of their eyes, as Mr Hemans was interrupted for what might have been the first time in history.

'Did you just say that you were unequipped for my lesson?' said Mr Hemans in that quiet tone that would always be followed by the storm.

James already knew this routine, and he didn't have the time to waste to let it play again.

'Sir, you wouldn't believe how unequipped I am for the lesson. Not only do I not have a pen, but I haven't remembered any of my books. In fact, now this bit I think you'll find funny, I don't even have my bag with me.'

Mr Hemans did not find this the least bit funny. He stared at James with a mixture of wrath and surprise, as if they were both actors in a play and for some reason, James had gone off-script.

'Right well then ... I mean ... GET OUT THEN. IF YOU CAN'T COME TO MY LESSON EQUIPPED THEN DON'T BOTHER COMING AT ALL.'

It was like Mr Hemans was malfunctioning. Never had a student cared so little about what the decimator of happiness had to say. Without realising it, James had just worked out how to get a free double period.

'So, you're saying I can just do whatever I want for the next two hours?' James said with glee.

Mr Hemans couldn't work out what to say. James could see the wires short-circuiting in his head. Instead of fighting what the teacher decided was a lost cause, he decided to continue with what he was good at and started to shout at the class for not doing their work.

James decided to share his new discovery. Now that he had managed to escape with such ease, it would pave the way for others to follow in his path.

'Anyone here who wants to know what happened at the police station yesterday, and all about what happened with Ludwig, break your pen or something so you're unequipped, get kicked out of the lesson, and I'll tell you all about it.'

Tom, being the friend that James needed, immediately threw his pen out the window, and stood to look at an enraged Mr Hemans. Most of the students in the class were desperate to talk about what had happened in the first place. Now with the added incentive of an inside scoop, it didn't take long for the majority of the class to accidentally lose their books, pour water over their papers, or break their pens.

Mr Hemans was powerless. The students were speaking so loudly that his screams could be easily ignored. James could see that he was resisting all of his urges to grab the students and force them back into their seats.

Eventually, only Freddie was left at his desk, too afraid to move. Not particularly caring about any drama going on in the world, and more focused on not failing all his classes. James could have very easily left him there. He already had the rest of the class outside. But he refused to leave a man behind, especially to deal with the full mad outrage Mr Hemans would produce once they left. And since Freddie had already been having such a rough couple of weeks, it didn't seem right to let him stay.

'Come on, Freddie, come with us. You don't have to deal with this by yourself.' James gave an encouraging gesture for Freddie to follow him.

Freddie just sat there doing the work in his book as Mr Hemans instructed, refusing to acknowledge anything that had happened or that James was speaking to him. James knew a lost cause when he saw one. No matter what he would say, it wouldn't make Freddie move.

Once they had all left the hell-hole, it occurred to James that he couldn't tell everyone about the police station. He wasn't going to speak about what happened when Ludwig was doing such a great job of keeping it a secret.

Whilst everyone was laughing about what just happened, how they had managed to take down the terror that was Mr Hemans with ease, James slipped away from the group with Tom so that he wouldn't have to deal with any of his actions.

It was mildly unfair to the students who James promised juicy gossip, but in fairness, he had convinced them into getting a free two hours during school to do whatever they wanted. James had never felt so reckless. Every single consequence that had terrified him now seemed like the most trivial thing in the world, in comparison to what consequences might await him now.

Tom found an empty classroom and the pair settled in.

'James that was wild, I've never seen you act like that before.'

After stealing some Blu-Tack that was left on the teacher's table, Tom went to sit next to James who had been contemplating something hard at a random desk in the corner of the room.

'What's up? Is everything OK?'

'I need to tell you something, Tom. I need to tell you a lot of things, but you can't, you can't tell anyone. I need you to promise you'll keep it all a secret. There's too much at stake.'

Tom agreed. He trusted his friend and knew that this was important. For the second time that day, James explained it all. From the invite to the Silver Chariot, to how it was going great, the fall from grace, how he covered it all up, and the many, many repercussions of it. James wouldn't lift his head. He spoke for a long time without any water or breaks and refused to look at Tom out of shame.

By the time James had explained what had happened at the police station, and how Andy was the one who framed Ludwig, the clock on the wall behind them showed that there were only a few minutes until the end of first period.

'I don't get it, you've known about Sarah all this time. Whilst the whole school's been shit scared about a lunatic killer in our town, you knew it was just an accident? I don't understand why you didn't tell anyone.'

James felt terrible, as if he were physically ill from talking to Tom about everything. Before, it all felt like a different world. A fantasy. With people he barely knew going on a hellish journey together. Now it was real. Telling Tom meant that he truly had to accept all the things that had been happening were genuine and not some elaborate adventure he was dreaming about.

'I wanted to. I was going to go to the police as soon as it happened, but there was so much that could go wrong, so much at stake. I thought I was doing the right thing, you know?'

It was hard to explain the reasoning of a mad man. To talk about the kind of place he was in. Where he still was. Always feeling trapped, the never-ending fear of someone being out to get him. That constant weight of pain and regret clamped to his heart.

'Honestly, I don't know. I don't think I ever could, that was just such a hard thing to deal with. That's so much pressure to deal with and try and do the right thing. And I mean with you, that's just terrible, I'm sorry I wasn't there to help,' Tom said, barely coherent, running his hand through his hair vigorously.

'There's nothing to be sorry about, it's my fault you weren't there to help. If I hadn't been so miserable, you wouldn't have had to ditch me.'

It was comforting that Tom didn't immediately flip out and sprint to the police station. James knew that it had been a risk to tell his friend, but it had reached the point where the only other option was to crawl into a ball and cry.

'Can you help me?' James asked. Now that Tom knew about everything, he was part of all the impossible choices James had to make.

'Of course.'

Ultimately, Tom brought nothing to the table when it came to Ludwig and the police, but it was a relief that he was willing to help. They decided it would be smart to take a walk around the school whilst people went to their next lessons. It would give them a chance to stretch their legs before trying to come up with a heroic plan that would save everyone.

James wondered what repercussions Mr Hemans would receive when the headmaster found out an entire class left during his lesson, and then the irrelevant punishment James would receive for initiating it.

On their way out of the classroom, James overheard two people talking.

'Would you cheer up already, Hercules? Is it because we don't have a scapegoat anymore? We can fix that easily. All we need to do is find some other reject and we can start up our pranks again. I've heard that Johnny pissed himself, I reckon we could get away with filling his bag with toilet water or summin'. Then just like with Sarah, we spread some rumours that whoever we choose did it, and they get all the blame and we don't have to deal with any of it.'

James couldn't tell who the person speaking was, but he was very aware of who Hercules was. Hearing that it was Andy who was responsible for making Sarah's life torture made James feel an overwhelming desire to get revenge for her.

'Would you keep it down? Someone is bound to hear you,' Andy said in a whisper.

'So, what if some kid hears us, what are they gonna do? We are the kings of this school. Nobody can touch us,' Andy's friend boasted.

'Don't get it twisted, nobody can touch me. You get away with everything because you are with me. And they call me Hercules, that's not the name of a king, it's the name of a god.'

At that moment something snapped in James. Some kind of primal urge overcame any sense of reason. Listening to Andy talk so arrogantly, after all the cruel things he had done, filled James with fury, unlike anything he had ever felt. Before he could take any control over his body, James flew out of the classroom and tackled Andy to the ground.

He managed to punch Andy in the face with all his power before Andy retaliated, kicking him in the stomach. It didn't take much strength for Andy to push James off of him, landing two heavy hits in James's ribs as they switched positions. People had come out from their class to see what was happening and had no idea who to help.

Hercules, the god of the school who was loved and adored by all, was pummelling the kid whose dad was a genuine hero. James had no chance against one of the strongest and most physically fit people in school. It didn't seem like anyone would be able to stop Andy, who relentlessly punched James. Tom had been trying to pull Andy away, but like James, he was too weak.

The bell started to ring for the second period. To James, it felt like the grim reaper calling for a new soul as he continued to endure more and more pain. The bell stopped ringing much earlier than normal and James was wondering if his hearing had gone. It was only when the punching stopped that James realised Tom had ripped the bell handle off the wall and smacked Andy with it directly on his bad knee, causing him to crumple to the floor.

Even then, it took three people to pull Andy off James. Both of them were unable to stand properly. Mr Glass's voice filled the halls as he yelled at Andy, dragging him away from James and towards his office. As Andy tried to escape the headmaster's grasp he grabbed onto Mr

Glass's completely black tie, but before he started to yank on it and fight harder, he seemed to realise what he was doing, and immediately stopped trying to fight.

'I saved you, James, you should be grateful!' Andy shouted as he was dragged away.

Breathing was its own challenge for James. Each intake of air made it feel like shards of glass were piercing through his lungs. Tom was trying to explain that they were going to the nurse so that they could try and heal his injuries.

'No ... Michael ... I need Michael to take me, it's important.' In his shattered state, James still believed he could convince Michael to do the right thing. That after all they had been through, he would help Ludwig.

Michael was making his way to the front to help James to his feet. After a couple of failed attempts where James fell back to the floor, with the combined effort of both Michael and Tom, James was able to stand holding onto the pair of them for support.

His eyesight wasn't great. James wasn't sure if it was from a concussion, or if there was blood in his eye or something else that impaired his vision. Either way, Tom's scratched face was nothing compared to how beaten James was.

18. One Final Get Together

As they walked past students going to their lessons, James could hear people gasp, which meant that he looked as bad as he felt. All the same, James had no regrets about what he had done.

Even though his punches were weak and did little damage, it felt good to hit Hercules and get some payback for Ludwig, even if it was in some small, ultimately insignificant way. Michael had been trying to speak to him, but James couldn't concentrate enough to hear what he was saying. He barely had enough concentration to stay conscious.

The nurse gave James some weak painkillers and cleared away the blood from his face, dabbing away at the cuts, and stuck plasters on them so that they could start to heal. He hadn't broken anything but most of his body was badly bruised and it hurt to do anything.

After fifteen-minutes of having an ice pack on his head and ribs, the pain started to numb as the pills worked their way through his body. With this reduction in pain, James was able to take in his surroundings and he noticed that the nurse was no longer there.

'Michael, I know you don't want to, but we've got to help Ludwig out, we need to come clean.' James's speech was slurred and mumbled.

At this point, he had no idea if Michael was even next to him. From the absence of any noise, James could very well have been in the room alone.

'Look James, you've been really good to me and helped me out a lot, but there is nothing we can do. They have a murder weapon and there's no way we could ever prove that a broken piece of glass isn't what was used to kill her. Even if we prove that she hit her head on the table, it's a table from the Silver Chariot which Ludwig had direct access to,' Michael responded.

There was some vibrating in James's pocket and he painfully reached in to find he had a message. Michael had to help read the message as James still couldn't see properly.

'It's from Ella. It says to meet at the Silver Chariot as soon as possible. Grayson needs our help.'

'What are we waiting for? Let's go, they need our help.'

James tried to lift himself from the tacky chair he had been slumped in, but his body gave out and made him drop back down the few inches he had risen.

'You can't go anywhere, James. You can't even lift yourself. How do you expect to get to the Silver Chariot from here?' Michael had real pain in his voice.

'I can get there with your help. What would Lilith say if she were here?' James had said what he thought was smart, what someone in a movie might say.

'Don't you dare! Lilith can't say anything because she killed herself. She's dead. All because of this. She couldn't deal with the idea of what we did. Of what I had done.' Michael's fists were clenched and his voice broke as he spoke as if each word hurt him dearly.

'I'm sorry,' James said. 'I shouldn't have said that but we need to help, you know Ludwig would help us if we were in his situation.'

James didn't have a clue what would happen if he was the one framed by Andy for murder. Would Michael still be so unwilling to help? The nurse came back and they promptly stopped talking whilst she recleaned his cuts and replaced the plasters.

Not long after, the nurse cleared James to head back to his lesson. Apparently, getting savagely beaten wasn't enough of a reason to go home and rest. James limped heavily with his arm around Michael; each step he took made his face wince in pain. However, by now, James's swollen face had started to die down and his vision had become clearer. Whilst James had been poorly treated by the nurse, Michael had been thinking hard about his life choices.

'Do you really think it's worth it, James? We tell the truth and we all go to prison; I mean Ludwig would get a much shorter sentence because of us. Of course, we wouldn't be classed with first-degree murder, and with a good lawyer, I wouldn't be in there for long at all. In fact, if we get some hard proof of Andy lying to the police, he would get more time for diverting the course of justice.'

Michael was talking himself into helping, and James was happy to assist.

'Exactly, that's why we need to go to the Silver Chariot, that's probably what they're doing, looking for a way to prove what happened.'

At this point, James had no control over where they went, if Michael carried him to class, he wouldn't be able to leave without assistance.

'Fine we can go to the Silver Chariot, but this doesn't mean we're throwing away our life. We are just going there to see if we can find anything.'

James was expecting it to be hard to convince Michael to ditch school early, considering his whole life revolved around attendance and great grades. However, after getting spooked by a noise that sounded far too much like a police siren, Michael became eager to leave school as quickly as possible.

It was still pouring down with rain as they left, which meant that none of the security guards or stray determined reporters saw Michael and James. The rain soothed the pain, acting as a natural ice pack for him.

Every few minutes, the pair of them had to stop so that Michael could catch his breath. He wasn't built for strength and endurance, and even though he hadn't been in a fight, it was taking a lot of effort to carry most of James's weight as they walked.

Police tape flapped about in the strong wind, being held tightly to the wet metal fences around the park so that they wouldn't fly away. People had placed flowers by the entrance for Sarah. Again, just like her grave, she would have hated how colourful and beautiful it was, filled with flowers that people had picked on their walk around the park or from the local florist.

By the time they made it to the bottom steps of the bar, they were soaked through. James's plasters had fallen off long ago, and they were both shivering from the cold. On a positive side, James had mostly recovered from Andy, being able to see as clearly as anyone else could in the rain. He was even able to walk without assistance, but he couldn't do it for long and it hurt greatly, but he was able to get up the stairs without any help. Or at least any physical help.

Both Michael and James stood at the bottom of the steps, staring up at the scary monster. Every time he had come this close to the bar, it had attacked back in some way. Now James hoped it would be kinder. This time they wanted to do the right thing. Instead of trying to forget about it all and run away, they were working to fix their mistakes. Before they could climb up the front steps, James's phone started to ring. He picked up the phone to hear a panicked Tom.

'The police know what happened, Ludwig told them everything and now they're looking for all of you. From what people are saying, Andy ran out of the school after attacking you; nobody knows where he is, or you and Michael.'

The news came as a relief to James more than anything. Now he could stop living two lives. He knew where his life was heading. It wasn't anywhere good, but at least everything would be resolved within the next few hours and he could finally be done with all the uncertainty.

James saw very little point going into the Silver Chariot anymore. If Ludwig had explained the truth, all they would have to do was say the same thing and Jace would know exactly what happened.

He could easily text Ella and explain it was over, and that would be all the help they could ever need. He had just started to limp away from the entrance when they heard a sickening scream from a girl inside. There was no doubt in his mind that it was Ella.

Sprinting up the stairs wasn't nearly as painful as hearing Ella in trouble. Michael was right behind James as they threw open the doors to the bar. The scene unfolding in front of James made him freeze.

Ella was on the floor with a cut lip, Grayson was up against a wall getting hit with a flurry of punches from Andy. All around the Silver Chariot were smashed bottles, splintered chairs and broken tables as if a bomb had exploded in the centre of the bar. Grayson was stopping most of the punches, but he still couldn't get Andy off him. Andy was unhinged.

The sight of Andy petrified James. He looked like a frenzied predator; his eyes wide open, spit flying from his mouth, teeth gritted. James stood there frozen in time, too afraid to do anything. It wouldn't be long before Andy broke through Grayson's defences. If that happened, the rest of them would be done for, unable to defend against Hercules themselves. Just as Andy grabbed a bottle to hit Grayson, Michael threw himself into the action with just enough force to push Andy away from Grayson.

As Grayson tried to get back some energy using the bar counter for support, an even more enraged Andy slammed his fists into Michael, immediately dropping him to the floor out cold. Ella was screaming in a corner. Not wanting Michael to get severely hurt James picked up an empty bottle and threw it at Andy.

Doing this stopped Andy from mercilessly attacking an unconscious Michael, but did nothing to slow him down. Andy ran at James like a one-animal stampede. There was no dodging it, James was too injured to move that fast. Behind him was the open door, the slippery steps a push away. Andy was getting closer and closer to him, murder on his face. Too afraid to see his downfall, James squeezed his eyes shut, awaiting the drop down the cold concrete.

In hindsight, it would have made sense for James to have opened his eyes after hearing crashing and smashing that wasn't directed at him, but the fear of opening his eyes made James hesitate for a couple more seconds. After more loud noises, James finally opened his eyes. Grayson had knocked the corrupted hero off his course into a set of tables.

Grayson's military upbringing was shining, as he dodged and weaved Andy's bombardment of attacks, but nothing he did was enough to slow down Hercules. There was a moment where Andy started to back away, slowing his relentless attacks. James thought it was a sign that he had given up until he realised how close Andy had gotten to Ella.

Before anyone could react, Andy had rounded on her, breaking a bottle on the table and holding it to her hip. James and Grayson both stopped dead in their tracks.

'What are you going to do, Andy? If you kill her now, you'll go to prison for murder; there's no way of avoiding it.' Grayson stretched his hands outwards.

Andy panted heavily as he hid behind Ella, black mascara tears running down her face.

'I'm not going to prison! I'm gonna be someone! I deserve it, nobody's gonna take that away from me, not you, not Sarah, no one!'

James decided not to explain that Ludwig had cracked and explained everything and that the police were trying to find all of them.

'What did Sarah do? How was she going to stop you from being someone?' James couldn't think of anything to do other than stall. The doors were still open to the Silver Chariot and the downpour of rain crept into the building, making the floor slippery.

'What did she do? The little rat tried to blackmail me when she found my steroids. She threatened me. Me! She said that she could destroy my entire life, I wouldn't let that happen. I've worked too hard to get here!' Andy kept Ella between himself and the others so they wouldn't be tempted to stop him.

'Sarah didn't die by accident. You were the one who invited her and you killed her, didn't you?' James said, terrified of the truth he had uncovered.

'Like I said, Sarah found my stash; she was threatening to tell the school. It would have ruined my chances of going pro. So, I played nice and pretended like I wanted to do things for her so she wouldn't say anything, but I had to get rid of her. It was the only way to make sure she would never tell anyone. When Ludwig suggested the Silver Chariot for a party, I knew it was the perfect opportunity to get rid of her.'

A horrible smile stretched across Andy's face like he was proud of his work. That he had masterminded the death of a girl and it had gone exactly as he wanted.

'I invited her after acting all desperate saying how she could have all the alcohol she wanted. I knew she couldn't refuse. I told her a later time than when we started so that I had time to get all of you as drunk and high as possible so that I could easily convince you all to help. I could never get away with killing her myself, there was too much to do. But if I used you lot to help me, nobody would find out, none of you would have the courage to tell anyone. It was perfect.'

Nobody could believe what they were hearing, they had all been manipulated into covering up a murder.

'I hoped that when she arrived, it would be enough to make you all spread around, which you did almost perfectly. I stayed behind after putting on an act that I was angry she was there. Then when you were all far enough away, I smashed her head on the table until she stopped moving.'

Ella gasped and wriggled around trying to escape his grip, more afraid than ever. 'You killed her! You're a monster.'

'You don't understand, I had to kill her! She was going to ruin everything! It's like I said that night, I'll do fucking anything not to be poor, to go pro, and nobody will ever stop me. None of you will ever be able to stop me. The whole school adores me, I am their hero, and soon the world will love me. If I have to kill a couple of people along the way to have that happen, then so be it.'

Andy was insane. Nobody could believe what had been said. That he was willing to murder people so that he could do well in life, that he had such little sympathy for others that he would end a life without another second of thought. James had never been so terrified to be in the same room as another person.

'I don't understand. How could you have known none of us would work out what you had done?' James said, trying to keep his composure.

'Well, it sure as hell wasn't easy, James. I had to be careful because that dumb idiot Ludwig passed out next to us. When I did what I needed to do, he woke up. I had to put on an act that she had fallen over and hit her head, which was the plan anyway, but I wasn't meant to be so close to her when you all found the body. Because of that snag, I had to think quickly, I dropped onto the floor next to her and pretended like I was trying to help, which meant the blood on me didn't look so suspicious. And you know what's really wild, when I bent over to check her pulse when all of you gathered around me, she was still alive.'

This hurt more than any of Andy's punches. She could have been saved. If Michael had managed to call an ambulance or they decided to help her instead of burying her, Sarah would have lived. She would have told the whole story and they would have known Andy had tried to kill her. Everything would have been right in the world. But no, they had been deceived and tricked by Andy, forced to believe they had to cover up what had happened. Lightning lit up the Silver Chariot, closely followed by the booming thunder that cracked through the sky.

'You made me bury someone who was still alive! Someone that we could have saved.' Grayson took a few steps forward, forgetting about Ella until Andy dug the glass into her just enough for blood to come out, making her whimper in pain.

'You stay right there, Grayson, one more step and I'll kill her. I have no idea when the fuck she died, maybe she bled out when you were carrying her, or maybe she was still alive after you buried her. That would mean you killed her. Suffocated the poor girl. How could you do something like that Grayson? I thought gays were meant to be gentle.'

Grayson was shaking with anger but he stayed where he was. Michael was still out cold and James couldn't think of a single thing to do that could help Ella get out of the hostage situation.

'Anyway, it wasn't like she was going to be anyone important, the freak that she was. Everything was all going fine until someone couldn't hide a body properly!' Andy glared at Grayson with fiery eyes. 'You and Ludwig can't do anything right! Because of you, it turned into a murder investigation and they had to bring in the detective, who was going to uncover everything.'

James could tell Ella was in a lot of pain. The bottle was still piercing her skin and a ring of blood was forming on her school uniform. There wasn't anything he could do to help her, he just had to hope that if they kept on talking, someone would come and save them.

'The night of Jodie's party, you ran off after the news report came out.' James exhaled as he realised where he went. 'You left to kill Lilith.'

It was a good thing that Michael was knocked out because James had no idea what he would do if he heard this.

'Lilith was unfortunate. If Michael wasn't such a loser, he could have kept the girl in the building. But no, he made her run away, which meant she knew about Sarah but wasn't part of her death. It was always risky with her around anyway, what with Sarah being reported as missing, and then when her body was found, I knew she would eventually snitch on us. It was only a matter of time. I'd overheard Michael saying how her parents were out of town and I already knew where all of you lived just in case. It was easy enough to make it look like she hung herself. I did what I had to do to keep her quiet.'

'What you had to do!' Grayson had lost his temper again. 'You killed her! You broke into her house and you killed her!'

Andy was nothing like his usual charismatic charming self, his hair was wild, and his face was contorted with terror. 'Grayson you wouldn't get it. I've had to fight for everything all my life, unlike you ivy league EE scum! I am destined for greatness!'

Ella was getting whiter from the shard of glass piercing her side and knowing that she was in the grasp of a serial killer.

'You've killed two people in cold blood, just to make sure you keep your scholarship and go pro?' James asked, in disbelief that this could be true.

'You don't get it, James. I can't be poor again. My useless family has never accomplished anything and I will be nothing like them. I'm going to be the best. I have to be rich, and I'll do anything to get there.'

James could tell that their time was running out and he didn't think there was anything he could do to help. That was until James saw the lightning reflect off of Ella's secret weapon that was hidden in her front blazer pocket. From that moment, James knew the only goal was to continue stalling for as long as possible until Ella's plan came to fruition.

'After all you've done, why did you frame Ludwig for your murder?' James asked, his heart pounding fast.

'Are you stupid?' Andy scowled. 'I saw the call sheet for the police station and knew that the damn detective was onto us. Someone was bound to slip up and reveal what happened. Luckily for me, I already had the perfect backup plan. When Michael was off crying in the corner with his black eye and I was left to hide the evidence, I found the glass shard from when Ludwig threw his bottle at the wall. By that point, it was covered in Sarah's blood. I simply wrapped it in some cloth and hid it away to use if I ever needed to put the blame on someone.'

That was it, all of Andy's diabolical plans to keep the fact that he took drugs and steroids a secret. Now James was running out of things to talk about.

'The only reason we're all in this mess now is because Michael overheard me tell the police where to find the weapon, and because you all love Ludwig so much you want to destroy everything I've worked so hard for. You could have just moved on with your lives, but no. Here we are again at this shitty bar, and if you're not exceptionally careful there's going to be another death, all because you guys can't keep your mouths shut.'

Any second now Ella's plan would work and they would all be saved from this nightmare. 'Now Ella and I are going to head out those doors and if you want her to stay alive, don't ever mention any of this to anyone. There's no proof I've done anything and if you go to the police, I'll kill you. We can all just go our separate ways now and-'

Andy was cut off by the police sirens surrounding the building. The red and blue lights shone through the open door and cracks in the boarded-up windows, reflecting off the puddles of rainwater inside the building.

'What? How, how can the police be here?' Andy had true fear in his voice.

Ella carefully pulled from her blazer pocket her phone, which showed she was on a call with the police.

'I think they know what you did.' Ella's voice held a surprising amount of victory, considering she had just told him there was no way out, and he still had a hold of her. A speaker came on from one of the cars outside.

'WE HAVE THE AREA SURROUNDED ANDY COME OUT WITH YOUR HANDS UP!'

Andy didn't know what to do, twitching his head looking for an exit.

'No! I'm not going to prison. This can't happen to me. What's going to happen is you will -'

Andy made the mistake of pointing at James with the bottle. In that moment where the weapon wasn't against Ella's skin, Grayson lunged for Andy's wrist, giving Ella the chance to run away. After some desperate struggling, Grayson managed to knock the glass out of Andy's hand.

Having no other option other than escaping, Andy started to sprint as best as he could towards the back exit by the garden. There were no flashing lights at the back of the Silver Chariot, it seemed like the police hadn't covered that exit yet. Andy was doing his best to move quickly in his damaged state, splashing through puddles of water as he reached the outside gate.

James was sure that he was about to escape, until the intoxicating smell of tobacco blew into the room with a gust of wind, bringing comfort, like a gift from the stenchiest area of hell. Just as Andy started to climb over the gate, Detective Edict appeared from out of the shadows, a gun in his hand.

'On your knees, buddy. You are under arrest for the murder of both Sarah Lee and Lilith Rumack ...'

James couldn't catch the rest of the arrest as Ella weakly threw herself at James, sobbing with relief. The police took a frantically struggling and swearing Andy away in a police car, shouting death threats at all of them as it drove away. Michael had to be carried away by some medics along with Ella who would need stitches for the gash in her side. Grayson and James were given strange-looking blankets to 'help with the shock,' as Jace said.

Both of them sat on the wet steps leading up to the pub that had created so many memories. Waiting for their fates to be decided. For all of their terrible decisions to be judged and ridiculed, their punishment to be given with the brutal hand of the law. James had wanted to go with Ella to the hospital but Jace wouldn't allow it, saying that there were still questions that needed to be answered.

The falling rain didn't bother them, neither did the fact that the world would soon know exactly what happened. All that mattered was that it was finally over, and that the dead could rest in peace knowing that they had been avenged.

'Hey. How come you went back to the Silver Chariot with Ella?' James asked Grayson, curious as to how everything had happened.

Grayson wiped his bloody nose on the sleeve of his blazer and stared off into the distance towards the pitch-black park. 'We were going to find something that proved what we had done to Sarah. Some kind of undeniable proof of that night. Something Andy had managed to overlook whilst covering up our evidence. Of course, there wasn't anything we could use, Andy had made sure of that, but before we left, Andy came bursting through the doors, and things just escalated from there.'

James was surprised to see that Grayson, the closeted gay on the football team who was so talented at hiding his emotions, had started to cry. 'I want you to know that I've cried myself to sleep ever since that night. I've been acting like what happened was something that I could get past and move on from, but to be honest with you, this has easily been the worst thing to ever happen to me. You were right, we should have called for help. I'm not just saying that because now I know it was all Andy's fault, or even that she was still conscious. I would rather a great deal of time in prison knowing that I had tried to do the right thing over this hell we've had to go through. Not that that really matters now.'

By now most of the police cars had started to clear and the flashing red and blue reflecting off the floor like some strange disco party started to fade into the darkness. Detective Edict took a seat on the wet freezing steps next to James and Grayson.

'A few hours ago, Ludwig explained what truly happened on the night Sarah died. How you all thought it was an accident and you were just trying to do what you thought was best, that you were convinced by Andy to cover up the body and manipulated into keeping it all a secret.

Boys, I won't lie to you, the things you have done will get you into some serious trouble. However, if it wasn't for Ella's and presumably all your efforts, we never would have uncovered the real truth. In fact, if you had called for an ambulance when Sarah had been murdered and she couldn't be saved, nobody would ever know the truth about what happened. It's a sticky little spot we're in. How about we call it even?'

The pair of them shook their heads in disbelief of what Jace had said.

'What do you mean, call it even?' Grayson struggled to keep the hope out of his voice.

'I mean it wouldn't be all too hard to twist the story a smidge. Let's say you go with the notion that Andy was threatening to kill you if you tried to speak up. Now considering Lilith was killed after the body was discovered it wouldn't be that challenging to make it believable. Then with all the other factors like how you helped to uncover the truth and how much you've been through already, I'm confident you will all get off scot-free. How does that sound?'

'That sounds fantastic, Jace,' James responded, looking over at Grayson and smiling.

'Then I suggest you two head home and get a good night's sleep, there's still work we have to do, but it can wait for later. For the moment, I need to head back to the station, there's a long night waiting for me.' Jace gave a grimy yellowed smile to the pair of them and stood up. As Jace started to walk away Grayson called out,

'Detective, if you're going back to the station, does that mean you're releasing Ludwig?'

'I suppose it does, and I take it you want to greet him and tell him everything that's happened yourself?' Jace said, taking out a pack of tobacco from his car.

'If that would be OK?' Grayson asked.

The detective gave a sigh as he started rolling a cigarette from inside his car. 'Very well, get in.'

With that, Grayson patted James on the back, and left to get into a police car. Leaving James to sit alone, as the team of police officers and paramedics set up the crime scene, taking photos and placing down markers. The school nurse's painkillers had started to wear off, making James ache once more. It was appealing for him to simply stay on that corner staring over the park and fall asleep from exhaustion. On the other hand, the hospital was only a ten-minute walk or thirty-minute crawl from the Silver Chariot. Just enough time to see Ella after they had healed her.

Giving one last look at the bar that had caused so much trouble, James, knowing nobody could ever see him, gave a small bow to the building. A sign of respect for all the good and bad it had to witness. Then without another thought, James started to limp towards his happily ever after.

19. In his father's footsteps

Six eventful months passed in Echoway. In that time, Andy was put on trial for the murder of Lilith and Sarah, and the attempted murder of Ella, James, Michael, and Grayson, along with a whole list of other crimes.

Andy's family didn't have enough money to afford a good lawyer, and the one given was pathetic. Stumbling over his words and failing to produce any evidence or defence that could have helped get Andy out of trouble.

The court was told a slightly different story from the truth. One where all those still alive that were part of the Silver Chariot Slaughter, as the news headlines had nicknamed it, had been forced by Andy to help him cover up the murder of Sarah Lee, being threatened with their life if they refused.

Jace Edict, who had been placed on the stand to give evidence and testimony, bent the truth slightly by explaining that Lilith had helped with the cover-up from the start. That she had tried to contact Detective Edict, unable to keep what had happened a secret anymore. Unfortunately, before Jace could speak with Lilith, Andy caught wind of what she had done, killing her for betraying him. He made it look like she had killed herself, and so the detective couldn't follow up on whatever lead she had promised them.

During this point in the trial, Andy was seen to be smiling. Almost everyone in the court became outraged, not knowing that Andy was one of the only people to know the story being spun by the detective wasn't truthful.

Still, he didn't bother to retort against the lies, beg for mercy from the judge, or show any remorse over what he had done. The only other action he was seen doing throughout the several hours' long trial was look up at James when he was put on the stand and give him a wink.

James, just like everyone else that was part of the Silver Chariot Slaughter, gave no hesitation when confirming the story that Jace had told. He recounted everything to be exactly as the detective had described it. In the end, Hercules was condemned to a life sentence in prison, with no chance of freedom.

The judge decided that nobody else that had been part of Sarah's murder deserved to be punished.

The five of them had been on the news constantly, whether it was when they arrived at Andy's trial, or when the police first made the announcement that they had taken Andy into custody, and all the reporters scrambled to find the people who knew the most about the events.

James had been busy spending time with Ella at the hospital when all the reporters swarmed around the police station as they broadcasted the moments where Ludwig was released. Only later watching the national news, James saw Ludwig's father and mother walking out of the station alongside their son, looking happy and relieved. He also missed out on seeing Grayson take the leap of showing who he was by kissing Ludwig the second they reunited, live for the world to see.

Not long after Ludwig and Grayson became a couple, which was followed by a small chain of fights that happened within EE, leading to Reggie and several other members of the football team to be expelled from the school.

After everything had been revealed, Ramwall and Echoway East held a joint memorial service for both Sarah and Lilith. It was the first time the schools were together since the fight out on the field and everyone mourned together peacefully.

With Hercules gone from Ramwall, and a good number of athletes from EE getting expelled, both schools performed terribly in their first few matches against each other. However, except for the teachers and scouters, nobody really cared about who won. All anybody wanted to do was enjoy themselves. At the end of every match someone, usually from EE, would host a massive party with everyone being invited.

Because of these parties, interschool couples started to crop up. This led to smaller parties including both schools. All in all, within three months of that first party at the Silver Chariot, the two schools had never been closer and spirits were at an all-time high.

James had been spending a lot of time with Ella going on dates and having the time of his life. They would go to parties every weekend, and James couldn't have been happier about it, living the life Tom and Kara wanted for him. Of course, he still enjoyed those secluded moments in his bedroom playing video games and living his life as he normally did, but with the addition of a social life he cared about.

When James walked the school halls, people spoke to him in a similar way as to when his father saved them all, although this time he was glad to smile and talk back to them. This time it wasn't his father that had done the saving, but him.

Nobody had to tolerate Daphne anymore. She had no power with Andy gone. Which meant she wouldn't bully others out of fear of being reprimanded or getting slapped. Without any influence, all of her follower friends stopped talking to her and, eventually, she made her parents move to a different town.

It didn't take long for Michael to recover from his injuries, but he decided to take some much-needed time off school to pursue other interests.

Now, six months later, James was sitting in the cafeteria next to Tom, Michael, and Emma. Tom had decided to stay away from all the popular people he had been trying so hard to be friends with. Saying how he preferred spending time with fewer people where they could talk about what he found interesting.

James was finishing his lunch when he looked at the time.

'Damn. I'm late, my mum is probably waiting outside.'

It had been the longest wait, but finally, Kara was coming back home. She had gone six months sober, without any hiccups, and James couldn't have been prouder.

As James picked up his bag, Tom grabbed his wrist.

'Don't forget you're meeting me at my house tomorrow, I don't want to head there alone and look like some kind of idiot. And you're sure the girl Ella's bringing is good looking?'

'Tom, she's agreed to go out with you, somethings gonna be wrong with her. Maybe she has an extra ear, or like a really long neck. I don't really remember, to be honest with you. My neck was starting to hurt because I had to look so high up to see her face.'

Michael and Emma looked up from the exercise book they had been revising out of and started to chuckle at the horrified, wide-eyed face Tom was pulling.

'What? She's tall, I thought I told you I don't like it when they are taller than me.' Tom started scratching the back of his neck. 'It makes me feel so small.'

'Tom I'm kidding, she's the same height as you, and you're going to get on fine, just trust me. Look I really need to get out of here, but I'll be there tomorrow, don't worry about it.' They bumped fists and James gave a wave to Michael and Emma as they continued to prepare for their English exam.

It had taken some convincing for James to come with to pick up Kara. Even with Michael's help, James was struggling to keep up with all the sick days he had taken. But in the end, they had agreed that he could come with as long as he did everyone's chores for a week.

James strolled up to the exit doors past Mrs Pogue, who looked much older and not at all happier. As she went into the file room behind her to retrieve something boring, James realised something was very wrong.

Freddie was standing past the glass doors by the entrance of the school. He had two guns strapped to his back and another in his hands. His face had the same kind of murderous intent that Andy had had. There was no time to run and hide, Freddie had already seen him and had just kicked open the door. Nobody else had realised what was happening and it didn't seem like there was any way to warn them.

Freddie raised his gun at James.

'You can go, I'm not going to hurt you, you've always been nice to me and did the world a favour taking down Andy.'

Freddie flicked his gun to the side to indicate that James could move out of his line of sight, but James had already decided to stay exactly where he stood. The more time he wasted, the higher the chances were for someone to see what was happening and to tell everyone to hide.

'Stop, you don't need to do this Freddie, you're a good person.'

In truth, James knew very little about Freddie. Over the last six months, James had been so caught up with everything that had been happening, he had completely forgotten to help Freddie out. However, it felt better to say positive things over calling him a terrifying maniac, especially considering how easily he could end James's life.

Mrs Pogue would retrieve whatever she needed from the back and then return to her desk where she would be able to see what was unfolding and sound the alarm. After what happened the last time, every student had been trained on what to do in a shooter situation.

'You have no idea what I need to do. You have no idea what this school has done to me. You don't understand what these people are capable of, they need to be stopped!'

Freddie was swaying his gun around when he spoke, sweat pouring from his face. James didn't have the time to panic about the gun pointed at him. The thing that could end his life in the exact same way as his father. All that was going through his head was stalling for time to save as many people as possible.

'I don't know what people in this school are capable of? I know more than you do! I saw someone die in front of me at the hands of someone else. I saw the blood coming from Sarah's head as I listened to the killer convince us it was an accident. You're the one that doesn't understand what people are capable of!' James had stupidly lost his temper, which made Freddie regain his aim onto James which had been faltering.

Whilst they had been talking, James had been taking the smallest of steps towards Freddie. He had no intention of playing the hero, but he wasn't a coward anymore. So far Freddie hadn't noticed anything, and James was almost within lunging distance. Lunch was only halfway through. Someone was bound to walk past and see what was happening.

'People need to pay for their crimes, Andy is paying for his and since the school and police won't do anything about the others, I will. Now I'm only going to give you one more chance, James. Get out of my way!'

There was no time left, he had to act now. James took one step forward, but Freddie had finally caught on to how close James was. Freddie raised the sight to his eye and 'click-click-click'.

The gun had jammed. Before he could take out one of his other guns, James had thrown himself on top of Freddie, ripping the gun from his hands and throwing it behind him.

Someone had finally noticed what was happening and started to scream, but it was already over. Freddie wasn't physically strong, and James had already pinned down his arms so that there was no way he could cause any more harm. It was a miracle that the gun had jammed; if it hadn't, there was no doubt in his mind that he would have died there and then.

Perhaps after all this time, his father was still looking after him in heaven.

THE END

Printed in Great Britain
by Amazon

64430962R00139